The Advocate's Phantom

Teresa Burrell

Silent Thunder Publishing

This book is a work of fiction. References to real people, events, establishments, organizations, or locales are intended only to provide a sense of authenticity and are used fictitiously. All other characters, and all incidents and dialogue are drawn from the author's imagination and are not to be construed as real.

Edited by L.J. Sellers

Book Cover Design By Madeline Settle

Library of Congress Number: 2024912777

ISBN: 978-1-938680-29-8

San Diego, Ca

Dedication

To Mr. John Merrifield, my transformative seventh-grade teacher:

In a world where education often follows a well-trodden path, your classroom was a sanctuary of inspiration and enlightenment, a place where the future felt within reach. You cultivated an environment where curiosity thrived, and learning became an adventure. Your unwavering belief in my potential drew me out of my shell, sparking a profound love for knowledge and the courage to question and explore. You didn't just teach me subjects; you taught me the art of thinking for myself. Your influence has been a guiding light in my journey, and for this, I am forever indebted.

Acknowledgements

A special thanks to **Lisa Boyles** for the title.
Thank you, **Crystal Kamada**, for suggesting a key element in the book.

My Loyal Beta Readers:
Beth Agejew
Siobhan Allen
Karen Anderson
Suzie Ball
Vickie Barrier
Dianne Biscoe
Denise Bowman
Lisa Boyles
Melanie Cardullo
Lori Grace
Julie Howard
Crystal Kamada
Sheila Krueger
Linda Langille
Janie Livingston
MaryAnn Schaefer
Colleen Scott
Carolyn Silberman
Tracy Weber
Denise Zendel

Chapter 1

Tuesday late morning

Sabre leaned forward, her gaze fixed on the anxious face of lanky, sixteen-year-old Maverick McLaughlin. The light in Maverick's room cast a harsh glow on his disheveled hair and the dark circles under his eyes. He fidgeted with his sleeve, avoiding eye contact.

"Tell me exactly what happened, Maverick," Sabre urged, using a blend of warmth and sternness designed to coax the truth from troubled young people.

Maverick's legs bounced restlessly. "I was playing a video game, and then ..." He swallowed hard, his Adam's apple bobbing nervously. "Then my phone rang, and a voice on the other end said to look out the window. Just then I heard the sound of a muffled scream, so I ran to my window."

"Take your time."

The boy drew in a shaky breath. "I looked out the window, and there was this guy—just wailing on a woman. He had something in his hand, like a pipe or a bat, and he kept hitting the woman over the head. It was awful. I've never seen anything like that."

His voice trembled, as if reliving the violence scared him even more. Sabre reached across and placed a steadying hand atop his jittery one. The gesture seemed to anchor him back to the present, away from the grisly memory.

"Could you see him clearly?" she asked.

"Not their faces because their backs were to me." Maverick locked eyes with her for the first time. His pupils were dilated with fear—or truth. Sabre couldn't yet tell. "It was raining," the boy continued, "but I saw them. The streetlight was right there, shining down on them like some messed-up spotlight."

"Did you recognize the attacker, or the victim? Did anything about them look familiar?"

"No. They were both strangers. But I'm telling you, it really happened."

"All right, Maverick." Sabre gave his hand a reassuring squeeze before letting go and sitting back. "I believe you saw something. We're going to figure this out together."

The rhythmic tapping of rain against the window provided a stark counterpoint to the tense silence that filled the room. Sabre watched Maverick's face in an effort to read beyond his words. She had been representing him since he came into the system seven years ago. It was a classic drug case, father had been gone for years, mother a heavy drug user. When she died of an overdose, the kids were living on the streets, and Maverick and his sister were raising themselves. Maverick hopped around from one foster home to another until Sabre finally got him in this home with the Venables. That was almost three years ago and he had become part of the family.

"Tell me about the lighting again," she prompted. "How much could you really see through the downpour?"

Maverick swallowed hard, his fingers gripping the edge of the table. "It was pouring, yeah, but the streetlamp ... it was like it was there just for that moment. It lit up everything—the attacker, the weapon in his hand."

"Was there any fog? Mist from the rain that might have obscured your view?"

"No mist." A touch of impatience crept into his voice. "It was clear underneath the light. I saw it all happen, Sabre."

"Okay. But the police found no evidence at the scene. No weapon, no blood. How do you explain that?"

His voice cracked. "I don't know! But I'm not lying! I can't unsee it. The beating keeps playing in my head over and over."

Sabre watched him closely, raw emotion etched into his youthful features. The quiver in his voice cut through her with a reminder of the stakes at play—not just a case, but a boy thrust into an adult world of violence and skepticism.

"Okay, Maverick," she said softly. "We'll get to the bottom of it."

He nodded, his expression conveying gratitude and reliance on her commitment.

With meticulous care, Sabre jotted down the information on her notepad, the page soon filling with details." Was it streetlighting only, or did something else add to it?"

"Streetlight only, I think."

"Any cars passing by?"

"I don't think so."

"How far away were you from the incident?"

"Maybe thirty feet? From my window to the wall. I didn't measure it."

"You were in this room?"

"Yes."

"Show me where you were." Sabre said.

“I was sitting on my bed playing a game.” He pointed at the narrow bed. “Then my phone rang. I didn’t hear it at first, because I had the sound turned down. It was late, and I didn’t want to wake my foster parents. But I saw the screen light up, so I answered it, and the voice said, ‘Look out the window.’”

“Tell me what you did next.”

“I got up and went over there.” Maverick motioned toward the window.

“Show me exactly where you were standing.”

As the teenager walked over, Sabre followed.

“I looked out and saw them, about five feet from that streetlight.”

“On your property or the sidewalk?”

“On our lawn, against the block wall near that bush.”

“I can’t see much.”

“I know. It seemed brighter last night.”

“What exactly did you see?”

“I saw a man in a long, dark coat. I couldn't see his face." Maverick shuddered. "But the way he swung that—whatever—was deliberate, heavy."

"Could you describe the weapon?"

"It glinted, like a metal pipe or bat.”

"Good." Sabre penned *metal pipe or bat* with a question mark. No evidence had been found; no traces of violence left behind. The vividness of Maverick's testimony clashed against the clean slate of the crime scene.

"Was there anything else? Any detail you haven't mentioned that stuck with you?" she prodded.

"Nothing." Maverick let out a breath, then walked away from the window.

"All right." Sabre closed her notepad with a soft snap. She tried to give him a reassuring smile, but her mind whirred with skepticism and theories. "Picture it for me again, Maverick," Sabre prompted, her voice calm and even. "The rain—was it heavy?"

"Like sheets." Maverick fidgeted with a button on his jacket. "It was pounding on the sidewalk."

"Could you see clearly through the downpour?"

"Kinda blurry, but yeah." He squinted, as if trying to peer once more into that rainy abyss. "The street-lamp was doing this weird flickering thing, but I saw him—the guy with the weapon."

Sabre noted *streetlight flicker* alongside the previous details on her notepad.

"Other than the rain and the streetlights, was there anything else that might have affected what you saw? Or obstructed your view?"

"Nothing."

"Maverick, were you alone, or was there someone else who might have witnessed what you did?"

He paused, brow furrowing then lifted his eyes to meet hers. "No. I was here alone."

"Except for your foster parents?"

"They were asleep, I think."

"But if there was someone else, even just passing by, it's important that you tell me."

Maverick shifted, a sign that he balanced on the edge of disclosure.

"Nobody." He finally exhaled.

Sabre detected a quiver in his voice. Whether it was borne of evasion or a memory too fragile to disturb, she couldn't be sure. But she did know one thing—her pursuit of the truth had just become more enigmatic. Sabre capped her pen with a decisive click. "Look, Maverick," she said, "anything you remember, anyone you might've mentioned this to—could help us."

He chewed the inside of his cheek, a habit she'd come to recognize. "I texted Darius," he finally admitted, the name tumbling out like an afterthought.

"Darius?" Sabre echoed. Her mind was racing with the implications. She scribbled the name in her notebook, underlining it twice. "Is this a friend?"

"Yeah," Maverick mumbled. "He didn't believe me at first. Thought I was just messing around. But I swear I wasn't, I—"

"Hey," Sabre interrupted gently, reaching across the space to still his fidgeting hands. "I believe you're telling me what you saw. Now, about Darius. How did he react when you told him?"

Maverick shrugged. "He kinda freaked out and said we should keep quiet. That nobody would believe a couple of teenagers anyway."

"But you didn't, right? I mean, you called the police."

"I told Mr. Venable this morning as soon as I got up, and he called. The cops came, looked around and then left."

"And they found no evidence of a crime?"

"They said they didn't."

"I'll reach out to the police today."

"But they don't believe me. What if they say I'm making it up, like before?"

What? This was new. "What do you mean?"

"About a month ago, the same exact thing happened."

"You witnessed an earlier assault?" She sounded skeptical—because she was.

"It's the second time he was here. I'm pretty sure it was the same man, but I don't know if it was the same woman, but she looked the same. They both had red hair."

"You didn't mention that before."

He shrugged. "I guess I didn't think of it, but it was definitely reddish. I only saw it for a few seconds, but I saw the color in a flash, a light reddish-blonde."

Sabre gave him a puzzled look.

"It was raining then too, and the man hit the woman with the same kind of weapon. I know it sounds crazy, but I saw it."

"Why didn't you call me last time?"

"Because nothing came of it. The cops came out, found nothing, and left. I never heard from them again. This time, Mr. Venable told me to call you, or he was going to."

"You did the right thing."

Maverick looked at Sabre with wet eyes. "I'm not making this up."

Chapter 2

Tuesday afternoon

Sabre sat at her desk in her office, working on a difficult case. The faint scent of leather and aftershave made her look up. JP Torn entered the room, his black Stetson tilted at a jaunty angle. He closed the door with a soft click and took the chair opposite her.

"Hi darlin'." JP planted a quick kiss on her lips.

"Thanks for coming here."

"You said it was urgent. So, I moved as fast as small-town gossip."

Sabre pulled her notepad from her briefcase. "This is everything Maverick told me, the details of what he claims he saw."

"Walk me through it." JP leaned forward, his attention fixed on her.

Sabre recounted the alleged assaults with methodical precision.

"Did he see the actual assault?"

"According to Maverick, yes. He saw the blows to the head and the victim drop to the ground."

"Any chance he'd seen either of those folks before? Maybe hanging around the neighborhood?" JP's brow furrowed in concentration.

"No. Neither looked familiar to him, but he didn't see their faces at all. Maverick has never seen anyone like that in the neighborhood, but he's a teenager, so I don't know how much attention he pays to the people around him."

"I'll need to visit the property, see the lay of the land myself. Might jog something loose if we retrace the kid's steps."

"Agreed." Sabre folded her hands neatly on the desk. "We need to find something concrete, or the police will never believe him."

"Do you believe him?"

"I think he saw something. I'm just not sure what."

"But the same murder twice?"

"I've spent hours with Maverick," she said, her voice carrying the weight of conviction. "I've heard his story, seen the fear in his eyes. It's not just some tale he's spun for attention. He's scared, and I believe him. He's convinced he saw someone get killed."

JP leaned back in his chair, drumming his fingers on the armrest, unable to conceal his skepticism. "Sabre, you know as well as I do that memory can be a tricky thing. And this is the second time the kid claims to have seen a similar assault?"

"Exactly," she affirmed. "And it's that repetition that makes me think there's more to it. Maverick isn't one to seek the spotlight; he's been trying to keep a low profile. He's had some problems in the past, mostly fights with other foster kids and not getting along with foster parents. But in all fairness, he was in some homes that offered conditional love, and he tested the boundaries. He hasn't had any trouble since he came to this home. And why would he make up the same story again?"

"Let's say I'm willing to entertain the idea that Maverick stumbled onto something real—twice—which is pretty farfetched. What do you want me to do?"

"Just get me evidence that proves something—one way or the other, and go to the scene as soon as you can and have a look around."

JP stood, adjusting the brim of his black Stetson with a practiced motion. "I'll put some feelers out, talk to DuBois in homicide. He'll be straight with me." JP paused. "What kind of background does this kid have? Any history of telling tall tales? Any drug use?"

"His history sucks. He was born to a drug-addicted mother who died of an overdose when he was only five. When he was picked up, he and his sister had been living on the streets, but she took off and they only got Maverick. He bounced from foster home to foster home, not so much because of his problems, just circumstances, which made his situation worse. He never knew his father, but caseworkers later found his older half-sister in the system and placed them together when he was eight and she was twelve. They were only together a few months when she was murdered in a cheap hotel. Maverick had a bit of a breakdown then, but nothing that required institutionalization."

"That's a lousy start to life."

"Yes, it is. On the brighter side, he's been with these foster parents for about three years, and they seem to really love him. He has no history of drug abuse, or theft, or of telling lies. He's basically a good kid, with emotional baggage, of course."

"All right," JP said. "I'll see what I can find out."

~~~

JP slid behind the wheel of his pickup truck. He fished his cell phone from the pocket of his worn jeans and called his detective friend.
~~~

The connection rang only once before a gruff voice said, "What's up, McCloud?" DuBois gave JP that nickname while they were on the force together. He called him that because he wore a cowboy hat like the character on an old TV series.

"Got time for a meet?"

"Depends," DuBois replied, his tone cautious. "What's this about?"

"Something I'm working on for Sabre. Kid claims he's seen a murder. Twice." His engine roared to life as JP turned the key.

"Is that the McLaughlin kid?"

"Right."

"Might've known you'd be involved in that crazy case, McCloud."

"I don't pick 'em. I just work 'em."

"All right. Swing by the precinct. But make it quick."

"Thanks. I'll be there in twenty."

The call ended, and JP maneuvered the truck out of the parking space, glancing around with an investigator's keen observation. He knew the conversation ahead would be a tough sell. Maverick's story was far-fetched, but something in Sabre's conviction had lit a spark of curiosity in him.

After clearing security at San Diego's main police department, JP found DuBois leaning against a desk cluttered with case files and coffee cups.

The detective straightened to greet him, his face lined with years of service, eyes sharp beneath graying brows.

"DuBois." JP tipped his hat. "Appreciate you seeing me on short notice."

"Let's hear it," DuBois said, folding his arms.

"As you know, the kid's name is Maverick McLaughlin. Claims he witnessed a murder or at least an assault, not once, but twice—same perp, different days. Says no one believes him."

DuBois snorted. “Yeah, we looked into it. He’s got more imagination than sense. We didn't find squat—no body, no evidence, nothing."

"Could be," JP conceded, scratching his stubbled chin. "But Sabre's putting her neck out for this boy. He’s her client in a dependency case, and she's convinced there's truth to his claim."

DuBois sighed, rubbing his temples. "The kid probably just wants attention, cooking up stories. You know how troubled teens can be."

"Maybe so, but what if he's not just spinning yarns? What if someone's smart enough to cover their tracks? We could be dealing with a meticulous killer."

DuBois' skepticism hung heavy in the air, but the crease in his forehead deepened, a sign that JP's words were finding purchase.

"I'll give it another look, but I'm telling you, it's a wild goose chase."

"Fair enough," JP replied. "I just don't want to miss a beat if the kid's actually onto something."

"I'll see what I can find out. But don't get your hopes up."

"Wasn't planning on it." JP pushed himself up from the chair. "Thanks. Keep me posted."

"Listen here," DuBois added with a pointed finger, "if we get called out again with this story and we find squat, we’ll have to charge McLaughlin with making false accusations. We can't have the department chasing phantoms because some kid cries wolf."

"Understood." JP turned to leave. "You won't hear from us unless there's solid ground to stand on."

"Make sure of it," DuBois warned. As JP strode toward the door, a reluctant respect hung between them—the kind forged in the fires of countless cases, some won, many lost.

On JP's way home, he stopped by Maverick's house and looked around. He found no evidence that supported Maverick's claims.

Chapter 3

Wednesday morning

The heavy oak doors of Department One at the Juvenile Superior Court swung open with a sound that echoed through the hushed room. Sabre, her sharp gaze fixed on the vacant judge's bench, barely registered the sound. She was lost in thought, considering every angle of the case at hand.

"Earth to SOBs," Bob Clark chided, leaning back in his chair so it creaked under his weight. "You look like you've seen a ghost."

"There's more truth to that than you know."

"Spill it, Sabre. What's got your brain in a knot?" Bob's blue-gray eyes twinkled with a mix of concern and mischief.

She sighed, brushing a strand of brown hair from her face. She told Bob about Maverick and his claim to have seen two murders committed.

"Wow! That's cool. When did this happen?"

"The night before last."

"Did the cops find the killer?"

"No," Sabre said. "That's one of the problems. They can't find evidence that anything happened."

"So, you think Maverick made it up?"

“He sounds so sincere. I think something happened. I'm just not sure what.”

“Maybe the perpetrator is really careful and cleaned up, not leaving any evidence.”

“Maybe, but...”

“But what?”

"Maverick claims he's witnessed the same murder twice.”

“You mean once in reality and once in a vision or a dream or something?"

“No. He claims the same murder happened twice.”

Bob scrunched up his face. “With the same victim?”

“He doesn't know who the victim was, so he thinks it could be a different person, although she looked very similar.”

“That's pretty crazy.” Bob raised an eyebrow. "Sounds like the kid's got an overactive imagination. Maybe what he needs is a therapist, not a lawyer."

"Maybe." Sabre wasn't entirely convinced. "There's something about this that feels off. I can't ignore it." Her usual sense of certainty flickered with doubt. "He's a good kid, Bob. Troubled, sure, but not a liar."

"Hey, if anyone can get to the bottom of this, it's you." Bob clapped a hand on her shoulder. "You're like a dog with a bone when it comes to the truth."

"Let's hope you're right." Sabre glanced at the clock. "We should be underway any minute now."

They finished their case in Department One and stepped out of the courtroom. When she brought up Maverick again, Bob said, “You have a sixth sense about things like this. You'll figure it out.”

"Thanks, Bob. I just hope my *sixth sense* isn't on the fritz with this one."

"Your track record says otherwise." He leaned in conspiratorially. "Besides, if all else fails, you can always consult your ghost for advice."

"Very funny."

As Sabre left the courthouse, the January morning sun seemed to pierce straight through her, a big change from all the rain San Diego had received in the last month. In her BMW, she navigated to Gary and Edie Venable's house, where the red-brick veneer gave off an air of suburban tranquility.

"Ms. Brown, please come in." Edie, a short middle-aged woman with bright red hair, ushered her into the living room. Gary sat on the edge of a plush sofa, hands clasped together. He was about the same age as his wife, slightly overweight and nearly bald.

"Thank you for seeing me on such short notice." She took a seat across from them.

"Of course," Gary replied. "We're just worried about Maverick, aren't we, Edie?"

"Absolutely." Edie nodded.

“He has had such a troubled life.” Gary looked up. “But why am I telling you? You know what he has been through. You’ve represented him for years.”

"He actually had more problems when he was younger," Edie said, not taking Gary’s clue to move on. She spoke of his struggles with anger and trust issues, but also of his talent for art and his love for animals. Sabre's heart twisted as she listened to Edie recount Maverick's troubled past. “He acted out in school for a while, got into several fights. We thought having a stable home would help him, and it has for the most part, but now this.”

"It wasn't his fault," Gary added. "He never had a chance to be a normal kid."

Sabre nodded sympathetically, her mind racing with the implications of Maverick's traumatic childhood. She knew firsthand how difficult it could be for children who grew up in the foster care system, and his story was worse than many.

"He's a good kid, Ms. Brown," Gary said, pleading for Sabre to understand. "He just needs some help."

"I believe you," Sabre assured them. "And I promise to do everything in my power to get to the bottom of this." She could see the worry etched on their faces and couldn't help but feel sympathy for them.

"The thing that is so disconcerting is that he has never been a liar," Gary said. "Even when he gets in trouble for something, he's not like most kids. He doesn't try to lie his way out. He just admits it and takes his lumps."

"As long as he has lived here," Edie said, "he's never been a troublemaker, but he's ... distant, quiet, a bit of a loner. And after this whole murder claim ..."

"Which is why we've arranged for him to see a therapist," Gary interjected. "Someone who can get to the root of whatever he saw—or thinks he saw. He really believes what he is saying."

"Good move." Sabre nodded. "It'll help us understand what's really going on."

"Exactly," Edie agreed. "We just want what's best for him."

"Do you know his friend, Darius?"

"He seems like a good kid." Edie smiled. "He comes over quite often because he only lives a few blocks away."

"How much do you know about him?"

They both thought for a moment, then Edie said, "He lives with his parents and an older brother and two foster children. Young boys, about five or six."

As Sabre stood to leave, the Venables' expressions were a blend of worry and relief. "One more thing," Sabre said. "Do you believe Maverick saw what he claims?"

"We did the first time," Gary said. "We were pretty upset when the police dropped it. But after the second time ... it just doesn't make any sense, right?" Then he quickly added, "But that doesn't mean *he* doesn't believe it."

Chapter 4

Wednesday afternoon

JP approached the modest suburban house, his eyes automatically scanned the surroundings — a habit honed from years of investigation. The door swung open, and a woman in her mid-forties leaned out, her expression warily curious.

"Mrs. Hendrix?" JP asked, tipping his hat slightly.

"Yes. Can I help you?" Her voice was cautious but not unkind.

"I'm JP Torn, an investigator looking into some claims made by Maverick McLaughlin. I understand your son, Darius, is friends with him."

"Ah, yes, Maverick." She sighed, the name seemingly heavy on her tongue. "Come in, Mr. Torn. I'll get Darius for you."

"Much obliged, ma'am." JP stepped inside, his boots muffled against the carpet.

Darius appeared from the hallway, a tall, slender teenager with wary eyes who seemed to size up JP in an instant. He led JP to the living room, where they took seats across from each other, a coffee table laden with family photographs between them.

"I understand you and Maverick are good friends. Is that correct?"

"We've been tight for years now, ever since he moved into the neighborhood."

"He must confide in you then?"

"We tell each other everything."

"Did he tell you he saw something pretty disturbing—a murder?"

"Oh yeah. He called me right away."

"Before he told his foster parents?"

"Yes. I'm the one who told him to tell."

"He wasn't going to?"

"He was afraid they wouldn't believe him."

"Why do you suppose?" JP asked. "Has he lied to them before?"

"I don't think so. They're pretty cool. They don't get upset about much, except they wouldn't tolerate drugs or stealing or anything like that."

"Has Maverick been known to do any of those things?"

"No." Darius was adamant. "Maverick would never touch drugs. He knows that meth killed his mother, so he's very anti-drug. And he'd never steal anything. He's just not like that."

JP gave a slow nod, encouraging the boy to continue. He noted the earnestness in Darius' eyes.

"Tell me about the first call—the first one where Maverick said he saw a murder." JP kept his tone casual.

Darius took a deep breath, his gaze distant, as if reliving the moment. "It was late, like way past midnight. Maverick's voice was all shaky, like he couldn't get the words out fast enough." Darius' hand mimicked a trembling motion, and his voice dropped to a whisper. "He said he saw it happen—saw someone get killed."

"Did he say how?" JP prodded gently, sensing the boy's reluctance to delve into the grim details.

"A beating with a bat or something." Darius shivered. "He described it so clear, so … real. The way the weapon sounded on the skull, and the muffled screams. It scared me just hearing about it."

"And you believed him?" JP watched Darius closely, searching for any sign of doubt.

"Completely." Darius' affirmation was swift, his conviction apparent. "Maverick was genuinely freaked out. He doesn't scare easy, but that night … he was terrified."

JP leaned back, his mind churning over the information. "When Maverick talked about seeing the murder again, what changed for you?"

"Second time around, something was off." Darius paused, biting his lip. "He told me the same story, but this time, it was like he was reciting lines from a script. The fear was gone. It felt rehearsed."

"Rehearsed?" JP arched an eyebrow.

"Like he was trying too hard to convince me," Darius explained, his confidence faltering. "And I started to wonder … why? Why would he need to convince me if it were true? But at the same time, why would he tell me if it wasn't? If he just wanted attention, why wouldn't he make up a completely different story?"

JP mused it over. Darius had a point. "As far as you know, Maverick has never lied to you about anything else?"

"Not at all. He's always truthful."

"So, he's not known for making things up?"

"That's why none of it makes sense. I want to believe him, you know, but it's just so strange. But I feel bad not trusting him too. You know what I mean?"

JP leaned back and studied Darius for a moment, watching the young man's eyes shift uncomfortably... The silence stretched between them, punctuated only by the faint tick of an old wall clock and the distant hum of a refrigerator.

"Look, Darius," JP began, "skepticism ain't a crime. It's a survival tool, especially in a world that can be as crooked as a barrel of snakes."

Darius' shoulders relaxed slightly, his guarded expression easing. He met JP's gaze with a flicker of gratitude. "Thanks," he muttered, sounding relieved.

"Son," JP continued, tipping his hat back with a thumb. "I've seen many a case where the truth was more twisted than a mesquite branch. But it's folks like you, willing to speak up, that help straighten it out." He paused. "We need to know what Maverick has really seen. Not just for the law's sake, but for his own."

Darius nodded. "I want to help Maverick, I do," he said earnestly. "Just... when he told me that story the second time, it felt off, you know?"

"Trust your gut; it usually knows the score before your head has the sense to follow." JP locked eyes with Darius. "But remember, the truth has a way of rising to the top, even when lies try to drown it."

"Is that what you believe?" Darius asked, a shadow of doubt crossing his face.

"Every darn day." JP nodded. "And it's the reason I'm sittin' here with you now, trying to get to the heart of Maverick's tale."

Darius seemed to relax. "Anything else you need from me?"

"Just keep your eyes open and your ear to the ground." JP stood and offered a firm handshake. "Your friend Maverick, he's going through a rough patch, and it's hard to say what's real and what's him cryin' out for help. We're gonna find out the truth, for his sake."

"Understood."

JP tipped his hat in a gesture of parting and turned toward the door.

Chapter 5

Wednesday evening

The doorbell rang at Sabre and JP's house.

"That must be Ron," Sabre said. "I invited him to dinner."

"I'll get it." Morgan, JP's ten-year-old niece came to live with JP and Sabre when her parents went to prison, ran for the door. She peeked through the keyhole, then opened it. "Hi, Uncle Ron."

"Hi, Morgan." Ron, Sabre's brother, gave her a big hug. "You look like you've grown an inch while I was gone."

Morgan beamed. "I'm taller, for sure."

"You look fabulous."

"How was your trip to Montana?"

"It was great. Thanks for asking."

Morgan crossed her arms. "Why didn't Lana come back with you?"

"Why do you ask?"

"Because you like her, and I want to meet her. See if I approve."

Ron pulled her pigtail. "Why would you say that?"

"I hear things."

"Well, Lana is a very nice girl, and she may come here one day. I'll tell her she should, so you can decide if she meets your standards."

"Okay." Morgan darted off to her room.

Ron was the picture of relaxed determination, his strides confident as he approached Sabre, giving her a hug as well. His smile, easy and warm, cut through the room.

"Hey, Sabey," he said, using a childhood nickname. He handed her a folder, his eyes sparkling with excitement.

Sabre took the folder and mirrored his smile, an unspoken acknowledgment of the bond they shared.

"What's up?" she asked. She nudged her reading glasses atop her head, granting him her undivided attention. Her gaze flickered to the folder, recognizing its potential significance. "It's that time again, isn't it?"

Sabre walked to the sofa and sat down. Ron followed.

"I need your insight, Sis," he said. "Aunt Goldie left me this legacy, and I'm determined to do it justice."

"The Incognito Angel." Sabre traced the edge of the paper as she read over the heading. "You will."

"It's such a big responsibility." Ron leaned in, lowering his voice as though the walls might be listening. "It's not just about the money—it's about changing lives without ever claiming the credit."

"That's exactly what she wanted you to do." Sabre's eyes lifted to meet his, a silent understanding passing between them. "So, you're here to find the right person? Someone truly deserving?"

"Exactly." Ron tapped a finger against the folder. "And no one knows more about people struggling against the odds than you do."

"All right." Sabre said. "Let's think about what Aunt Goldie would have wanted. She was all about making a real difference, wasn't she?"

"Absolutely," Ron agreed. "And I intend to honor that—quietly, effectively, and with your help."

Sabre's smile returned, proud and supportive. "I know you will."

"Okay, so where do we start?" Ron asked, riffling through the folder as if it contained a treasure map. "Local charities are a good bet, but they often have so many hoops to jump through."

"True," Sabre agreed. "And that was never Aunt Goldie's intent. She wanted something more personal."

"Community centers then?" Ron perked up at the thought. "They're in the thick of it, connected to the people."

"They see the daily struggles, but..."

"Schools?"

"They have counselors." Sabre turned to face him. "And confidentiality could be an issue. We need something more discreet."

Ron's smile waned, replaced by a furrowed brow as he considered the challenge.

Sabre looked squarely at her brother. "What about the local shelter? The one that supports foster children?" Her voice was soft but certain. "They're on the front lines with families in crisis. If anyone knows who needs a helping hand, it's them."

Ron's eyes brightened. "That's perfect, Sis! Foster kids... yeah, they slip through the cracks all too often."

"And the shelter's staff deals with financial hardships every day. They could point us to a family—a child—who could truly benefit from Aunt Goldie's generosity."

"Do you think that's what Aunt Goldie had in mind?" Ron asked.

Sabre shook her head. "Not really."

"Maybe you could look into your client files." Ron suggested. "Someone in there must be in dire straits, someone we can help without it getting too complicated."

Sabre smiled. "Aunt Goldie chose you for this," she reminded him gently. "She knew you had the heart and the smarts for it. You're more than capable of finding the right person."

He sighed, running a hand through his hair. "Yeah, I know she did, but—"

"No buts." Sabre chuckled. "You've always been good at reading people, better than me sometimes. Trust your instincts."

Ron nodded slowly. "You're right. I'll do it. I'll find our recipient." His voice was now infused with determination.

"Besides," Sabre added, feeling a mix of pride and challenge, "Aunt Goldie would have wanted you to make these choices, to feel the connection with the people you're helping."

"Connection," he repeated, mulling over the word. "Okay. I'll dig into my life, see who crosses my path that might need an angel looking out for them."

"Exactly." Sabre nodded. "Look at the relationships you've built, the stories you've heard. Someone out there needs a miracle, and you're going to find them."

"Thanks, Sis," Ron said, a smile breaking through his uncertainty. "For believing in me."

"Always, Ron. And remember, this is *your* journey. Enjoy the ride as much as the destination."

"You're right." Ron smiled.

"You can't let even a whisper of this slip," Sabre reminded him. "The moment you do, the Incognito Angel might as well hang up its wings."

He nodded gravely, understanding the weight of the responsibility. "I won't risk exposing the Angel's identity. That's part of the magic, part of the gift."

Sabre stood. "Now come help me in the kitchen. JP will be home any minute, and I know the kids are getting hungry."

Ron put his arm around her as they walked into the kitchen. Sabre thought how lucky she was to have such a great older brother. Ron, who could charm anyone with his easy smile and casual demeanor, had depths that few could fathom. His journey as the Incognito Angel would test not just his resolve, but the very core of his character.

"You'll make a difference, Ron, in a lot of lives. You'll be the miracle someone's praying for."

Chapter 6

Thursday morning

JP adjusted his hat against the glare and scanned Maverick's neighborhood, enjoying the sun, which was shining for the first time in several days. JP had spent hours the night before going through property records for the neighborhood. He also checked social media and found out what he could about each home within a block radius of Maverick.

He started toward the first house immediately next door, the white paint chipping off its wooden frame like old bones. A garden gnome smirked at him from among the petunias. He rapped firmly on the door.

"Ma'am," JP said when the door opened, revealing a pair of wary eyes that took in his rugged features, then lingered on his silver belt buckle. "Name's JP Torn. I'm a private investigator."

"Is that so?" The woman's voice held a note of skepticism as she sized him up through the narrow opening.

"Yes, ma'am." JP tipped his hat. "I was hopin' you might spare a few moments to talk. Could be you've seen or heard somethin' recently that could help."

She pursed her lips. "Well, I don't know if I—"

"Every detail counts," JP said. "No matter how small."

The woman wore a cardigan buttoned to the neck and chewed on the corner of her lip before stepping aside to allow him entry. "I'm Mrs. Jenkins."

"Nice to meet you. I appreciate your help."

As JP crossed the threshold, he made a mental note of the immaculate living room, where dust was a stranger and everything had its place. It was the home of someone who paid attention to detail, and he wagered that if Mrs. Jenkins did know something, the information would be precise and potentially invaluable.

"Please, have a seat, Mr. Torn." She motioned to a floral-patterned armchair, her movements stiff.

"Thank you kindly, please call me JP." He eased himself into the chair. He placed his hat on his knee and leaned forward, elbows on the armrests. He observed Mrs. Jenkins as she settled into her own chair, a fortress of needlepoint cushions and polished wood arms that seemed to dwarf her small frame. "Mrs. Jenkins," he began, "were you in your home on Monday night around ten o'clock?"

"I was."

"It seems there was a disturbance next door at the Venables' house. Did you happen to notice anything out of the ordinary?"

Her eyes flitted to the window. "Out of the ordinary?" she echoed, tugging at the bottom of her cardigan. "I can't say that I did. I'm not one for eavesdropping on the street's comings and goings. I prefer my books and my gardening." She had a tremble in her voice, a note of apology for not being the witness he needed.

"Nothing at all? No strange noises, no arguing, or unfamiliar cars?" JP pressed gently.

"I'm afraid not."

"Do you know Gary and Edie Venable?"

"Of course. They've lived here for years. Not as long as I have, of course. But they're very nice people. And they take in those poor children who have nowhere else to go. It's very admirable. Some people in the neighborhood don't like it because they say the kids are trouble, but I've never seen that." She paused. "Except that time one of the kids broke into a home, but they took care of it right away."

"Do you know Maverick?"

"Yes. He's a nice young man. He's helped me several times when I needed something carried in from the car." She scowled. "He isn't in trouble, is he?"

"No. Maverick is fine."

"So, what's this all about?"

"There was a disturbance near their house, and I was hoping you may have seen or heard something."

"No. Sorry."

"Do you remember when we had the last rain?"

"Yeah. It rained pretty hard for just a day or two. Unusual to get so much rain here."

"Did you see or hear anything that night?"

Mrs. Jenkins shook her head, her hair, silver and set with meticulous care, barely moving. "I'm afraid I'm not much help to you, Mr. Torn. My evenings are quiet. By eight o'clock, I've usually drawn my curtains and shut out the world."

JP nodded. "I understand, ma'am. Still, if you do remember something, anything at all, here's my card."

"Of course, I'll let you know," she promised, as she took the card.

"Thank you for your time, ma'am." JP stood and headed towards the door.

"Good luck with your investigation," she called after him.

JP stepped back out into the morning light. As the door shut behind him, he couldn't shake the feeling that Mrs. Jenkins saw more than she let on, or knew something she wasn't telling. But he couldn't put his finger on it. Maybe he was just hoping for more. With a sigh, he made his way down the street, seeking a neighbor who might have more information.

At the next house, JP strode up the walkway through a neatly trimmed yard. Without hesitation, he rapped sharply on Mr. Thompson's front door.

The door swung open and there stood an older man, his posture rigid, as if he'd never quite left the parade. His hair was cropped short, peppered with gray, and his eyes held the kind of scrutiny that could only belong to a man who had spent a lifetime assessing threats.

"Can I help you?" His voice sliced through the air, every word clipped and precise.

JP introduced himself, offering a brief nod rather than a handshake, sensing that physical contact might not be welcome. "I'm working a private investigation regarding an incident that occurred recently in this neighborhood."

Mr. Thompson's eyebrows furrowed, a small line forming between them as he folded his arms across his chest. "What incident?"

"Last Monday night and about a month back, during the rainstorms, did you notice anything unusual?"

The veteran's brow unknotted as he shook his head, the sternness in his face softening into a dismissive frown. "Nothing escapes my notice during daylight hours, but after taps, it's lights out for me."

"So, you didn't hear any disturbances or see any unfamiliar vehicles those evenings?"

"I hit the rack at 2100 sharp every night. What happens after that, I wouldn't know. I don't hear much because of my sleep apnea machine. So, unless it was really loud, I wouldn't know."

"It was raining pretty hard and likely not that noisy."

"Is this something I should be concerned about?"

"I don't think so. At this point, we're just gathering information." JP gave him his card and asked for a call if anything came up. “Thank you for your time and your service to our country.”

“Of course.” Mr. Thompson gave a single nod before he shut the door with a decisive click.

JP turned away and scribbled a quick note. He walked toward the next house, hoping for a break in the silence of suburbia. The home was modest, with a freshly painted front door and a welcome mat that looked barely stepped on. The door swung open before he could knock, revealing a young couple who seemed taken aback by the sight of him.

"Good morning." JP introduced himself and explained his purpose. “Mind if I ask you a few questions?"

The couple exchanged a nervous glance before the woman, a petite brunette, stepped forward. "Of course. Please come in. I'm Anna Parker, and this is my husband, Victor. We were just on our way out, but we have a few minutes."

"Thank you, ma'am." JP crossed the threshold into a living room, where the scent of fresh paint still lingered. He took note of the sparse furnishings, a clear sign of a recent move-in.

"Can I offer you something to drink?" Victor motioned toward the kitchen.

"Just information, if you don't mind," JP replied. "Did you happen to notice anything unusual in the past few nights in the neighborhood? Any odd noises or disturbances?"

Anna wrapped her arms around herself, as if the question had ushered in a draft. "It's been so quiet here.” She turned to her husband. “Hasn't it, honey?"

"Quiet as can be," Victor confirmed, though his posture remained stiff. "We're usually in bed early and haven't noticed anything out of place."

"We did see a couple of cop cars over at the Venables' place," Anna added. "But we didn't think much of it. We're new here, so we don't really know what's normal for this street. I know they have foster kids, not that that means there is going to be trouble, but my parents took in kids too, and we saw cops more often than most of our neighbors. Don't get me wrong. I think it's admirable what they do. We may be foster parents ourselves someday."

"Did you see the police here a month ago as well?"

"I did, and I talked to Edie afterward. She didn't give much detail; she just said it turned out to be nothing. But we just bought this house a few months ago so we're still adjusting to the neighborhood."

"Understandable," JP acknowledged. "Moving can be quite the adjustment. If you remember anything, even a small detail, give me a call." He extended a business card, which Victor accepted with a polite smile.

"Will do. Thanks for stopping by," Victor said, showing JP to the door.

"Appreciate your time." JP headed to the next house on his list.

Chapter 7

Thursday early afternoon

JP approached the weathered front door of Quaid Gearhart's residence. Unlike the previous house, this one had a forlorn look, with overgrown shrubs and moss under the windowsill. But the curtains were open, letting in the sun. He knocked.

"Who is it?" A gruff voice barked from within, more an accusation than a question.

"Mr. Gearhart? Name's JP Torn. I'm a private investigator working on a case nearby."

A series of locks clattered, then the door opened just enough to reveal a sliver of Gearhart's face, marked by the passage of many stern years. His eyes were like flint, hard and unyielding.

"Whaddya want?" The old man's voice was gritty, matching the hardened lines of his visage.

"Only a moment of your time, sir." JP tipped his hat respectfully. "Wondering if you might've seen or heard anything unusual recently. There's talk of a serious incident in the neighborhood."

"Talk is cheap." Gearhart grunted, his tone laced with disdain. Nevertheless, he unbolted the door fully and stepped back, granting JP entry into a living room that smelled of tobacco and must.

"Mind if I ask a few questions?" JP noted the sparse furnishings and the layer of dust that had settled on everything like a second skin.

"Sit." Gearhart gestured to a worn armchair. He lowered himself onto a matching couch, which groaned under his weight.

"Did you see anything out of the ordinary Monday night? Or maybe heard something that struck you as odd?" JP watched the old man's reactions closely, looking for any flicker of awareness.

"Look here, son." Gearhart folded his arms over his chest. "I've lived long enough to know when to keep my nose where it belongs. This neighborhood's full of whispers and curtains twitching at shadows. I've got better things to do than pay attention to the latest round of gossip."

JP studied the man, the set of his jaw, the dismissive wave of his hand. It was clear Gearhart held a fortress of solitude around him, one not easily breached by idle chit-chat or nosy neighbors. "Have you heard some gossip about what went down on Monday night?"

"I saw the cop cars the next morning. They were hard to miss. The street was full of them. I'll tell you the same as I told them."

"Which was?"

"I couldn't sleep. The storm was keeping me awake. I went out on the front porch for a bit and saw someone dragging something around the southwest corner." He pointed in the direction of Maverick's home. "I figured they were taking trash out or something. I just saw the tail end of it and couldn't even tell you if it was a man or a woman. I didn't understand why they were out in the rain, but people do crazy things."

"Did you see a vehicle of any kind?"

"No. That's it."

JP asked a few more questions, but the more he asked, the less confident the old man seemed that he saw anything at all.

"Thank you, Mr. Gearhart. If you do recall anything else, even the smallest detail, it could be important." JP rose from the armchair and held out a card.

Gearhart took it reluctantly. "Fine. But don't expect me to come running with tales." The old man's voice grumbled like distant thunder.

"Wouldn't dream of it." JP gave a small smile and made his way out the door.

As he stepped back into the daylight, JP thought about Gearhart's stubborn seclusion. At least he'd learned something—unless the old man was mistaken. He wasn't very sure of what he saw, but he was the only one who gave some kind of credibility to Maverick's story.

JP strode down the sidewalk toward the final house on his list. The Andersons' home sat back from the street with an unwelcoming air. Several newspapers lay in the driveway indicating they were likely on vacation. He checked the mailbox. It was full of mail. He would ask around and see if any of the neighbors knew where the Andersons were. JP circled the property, noting the small, black domes of surveillance cameras perched high on each corner like watchful eyes.

He walked in a straight line from one of the cameras to the corner of the Venables' house, where Maverick had seen the crime. The device had likely captured what he needed. He'd have to check back and convince Anderson to hand over whatever footage he had from the nights in question.

With one last glance at the cameras, JP tucked the notebook into his coat pocket and headed back to his truck. The neighbors had yielded little in terms of human insight, but technology didn't have the option to stay silent.

JP decided to check with Maverick's foster parents to see if they knew when the Andersons would return. He strode up the path and knocked on the door. Gary Venable answered, his face creasing into recognition.

"Mr. Torn, isn't it? We've crossed paths before, if I recall correctly." Gary extended a hand that was rough from work.

"Yes. But please call me JP." He accepted the offered handshake. "I'm here on behalf of Sabre, Maverick's attorney."

Gary stepped aside. "Come on in."

Edie Venable emerged from the kitchen, drying her hands on a dishtowel. "Would you like something to drink?" she asked.

"Thanks, but I'm fine."

"Follow me." Gary led JP into the living room, where family photos competed for space on the mantelpiece. They settled into the well-worn furniture.

"Is Maverick at school today?" JP asked.

"Yes," Edie replied. "He's been trying to keep up with his studies, despite… everything."

"Good." JP nodded. "How's he holding up? This kind of thing can turn a kid's world upside down."

Edie bit her lip, exchanging a glance with her husband. "It's been hard on him. Teenagers can be cruel, and the whispers at school have been tough. It's a shame he told anyone about it."

"At first, his friends thought it was exciting, but now they're not so sure what to think," Gary added.

"Understandable," JP murmured. "Do you know the Andersons?"

"Yes. Natalie and Chuck. Directly across the street." Gary furrowed his brow. "Why do you ask?"

"I couldn't reach them when I tried to call, and it looks like they've been gone for a while. I noticed they had a lot of cameras around their house, and I'm hoping one picked up something that might be helpful."

"What do you need from us?" Gary asked.

"Do you know when they're expected to return? I'd like to see the camera footage, if they'll let me. How well do you know them?"

"I see Natalie around quite often when she walks her dog. Such a sweet woman. I talk to her from time to time, but I don't know them well."

"Did she mention anything about going on a trip?" JP prodded.

"Actually, yes," she replied, a flicker of recollection in her eyes. "Natalie said they were taking a cruise," Edie said. "She said they were looking forward to disconnecting for a while."

"Disconnecting?" JP's interest piqued.

"From the world, you know. No phones, no internet. A complete break."

"And when are they due back?"

"Sunday. They'll be at sea for a few more days."

"Thank you. I'll check back next week."

"Of course," Edie said, relief softening her features. "We just want to help Maverick, poor boy."

"So do I."

Chapter 8

Thursday afternoon

Ron Brown sat at a corner table in the bustling coffee shop, his stare fixed on the world outside, but his mind was elsewhere. The steam from his freshly brewed coffee curled into the air, mingling with the hum of hushed conversations and the clink of porcelain on wood. He shifted in his chair, the weight of responsibility pressing down on him as he contemplated the perfect recipient for his Incognito Angel gift.

"Got to find someone truly in need," he murmured to himself, running a hand through his hair.

He pulled out his phone and scrolled through his contacts, each name sparking a brief vignette of memories and past interactions. Lana's name flashed, bringing a smile to his lips. She was a spunky red-headed woman who was likely the best hacker in the world. She was certainly the best he knew. But his interest was more personal. He'd met her through his friend Tuper, who lived in Montana, and they'd started a long-distance relationship. He missed her and hoped they could see each other soon. Also, her skills might come in handy in one of his gift-giving situations, but first he had to find a recipient.

Come on, there's got to be someone, he thought. He paused his thumb, hovering over a contact. *No, not them, they'd just squander their chance.* On he went down the list, looking for that one friend who could use an invisible helping hand.

"Everything all right, Ron?" The forty-something barista broke through his concentration as she wiped off the empty table next to him.

"Yes, thanks, Jenna. Just got a lot on my mind."

"Anything I can help with?" she asked.

"Unless you can tell me who needs a life-changing gift, I think I'm on my own with this one," he said, half-jokingly.

"What exactly do you mean?"

"It's a family joke. When you've had a lousy day, find someone who's had a worse one, and you'll feel better."

"That's easy. We could all use a life-changing gift." She smiled.

"Are you struggling with something?"

"Not really. I'm just trying to get through life like everyone else I know. The difference is that I have two children I'm responsible for, and my daughter takes up a lot of my time."

"That must be hard."

"It is, but I wouldn't change it for the world. She's an angel." Jenna smiled and moved back behind the counter.

Ron let out a soft sigh, resuming his search. There were plenty of folks down on their luck, but he needed to find someone whose life could genuinely turn around with what he had to offer. He knew too well that money alone wasn't always the answer; it was about finding someone ready for the change, willing to embrace it.

Not finding anyone in his phone contacts, he switched to Facebook and scrolled through recent posts. He needed to make a decision, and soon. The trust's mission was clear: random acts of kindness, no strings attached, but with profound impact.

As he scrolled past name after name, he considered their circumstances, their hardships, and their potential. Finally, he paused mid-swipe, his breath hitching as the screen filled with a lengthy Facebook post that snagged his attention. The words *tough times* and *overdue bills* leaped out at him. It was a status update from Greg, a friend who had always prided himself on his resilience and independence. The candid disclosure of financial struggles felt out of character, which only amplified Ron's concern.

He reread the post, absorbing the gravity of Greg's situation. Hospital bills piling up, a job lost to unforeseen layoffs, and the strain it was putting on his wife and two children. The narrative painted a picture of a man cornered by life's harsh realities, a man whose pride might prevent him from asking for help directly.

A surge of empathy coursed through Ron.

Hey, Greg, Ron typed into the messenger app. *Just saw your post. I can't imagine how tough things must be right now. Is there anything I can do to help?*

He hit send and leaned back in his chair. Minutes ticked by, until a ping from his phone announced the arrival of a new message. Greg's reply appeared on the screen.

Appreciate you reaching out, Ron. I'm just trying to keep my head above water. Not sure what can be done, to be honest.

Ron tapped a rhythm against the side of his cup, his mind sifting through possibilities. He could easily write a trust check to cover the bills, but he knew that Greg needed more than a temporary fix. He needed a new start, a chance to regain control over his life.

Let's meet up, Ron replied. *There's no harm in talking things through. Maybe we can come up with a plan together. My treat—dinner on me.*

Ron waited for a response while the café buzzed with the usual mid-afternoon energy, patrons shuffling in and out, wrapped in their own worlds. His gaze wandered from his phone to the window.

"Can you believe it? Another layoff notice. They're chopping us down like trees." The weary voice drifted to his ears from a nearby table.

"Three years on the job, and now what? I've got mouths to feed," another voice responded full of anger and desperation.

Without meaning to, Ron found himself drawn into their conversation, a silent witness to their struggle.

"Daycare's already past due, and Sarah's meds aren't getting any cheaper," the first voice cracked.

"Hey, we'll figure something out. We always do, right?" It was an attempt at reassurance, but the doubt was palpable even to Ron.

Curiosity piqued, Ron glanced over the rim of his cup. Two men sat hunched over a small table, one gripping his coffee like a lifeline, the other with hands that couldn't seem to find a place to rest. Their faces were etched with the marks of sleepless nights and worry lines.

He considered approaching them and offering some form of solace or assistance, but what could he say? He was a stranger, an eavesdropper who had stumbled upon a private moment of vulnerability. Instead, he committed their faces to memory—just in case the Incognito Angel might aid them in the future. There was no way for him to know who they were, no contacts to scroll through, no mutual friends to bridge the gap. They were just faces, names unknown, yet their stories resonated within him. Ron felt the familiar stir of purpose, the desire to lift others from the mire of misfortune.

His phone vibrated, snapping him back. Greg had accepted his offer. A sense of relief washed over him, but the voices of the two patrons lingered, a haunting reminder of the countless others waiting for their lives to improve. Ron checked his phone, then stood and walked out. It was time to pick up Conner from school.

Chapter 9

Thursday afternoon

Ron had his radio on, and was singing along with Chris Stapleton to *Tennessee Whiskey.* As he pulled up to the school gates, teenagers spilled out onto the sidewalk like a colorful, noisy tide. He spotted Conner immediately. The young man had the same unruly hair and easy swagger his uncle JP did.

"Hey, Uncle Ron!" Conner greeted, his backpack slung over one shoulder.

"Hey, kiddo." Ron smiled. "Ready to roll?"

"Can we give Aiden a ride?" Conner gestured to the brown curly-haired boy a few inches shorter than him with a hesitant smile who stood beside him.

"Of course." Ron nodded. "Hop in, Aiden."

The short car ride was filled with chatter about a new girl in their science class. At a modest, well-worn house, Aiden thanked Ron and hopped out. But before he could pull away, the front door opened.

"Wait! You've got to meet my sister, Lily," Aiden called out, waving them over.

Ron exchanged a look with Conner, shrugged, then stepped out onto the driveway. He followed Aiden into the living room, where a small girl with bright eyes and a shock of curly hair sat on the floor surrounded by toys. She looked up, her smile bright, despite the deformation of her face.

"Hi, I'm Lily," she said cheerfully.

"Hello, Lily. I'm Ron." His heart clenched as he crouched down to her level. "It's very nice to meet you."

Lily fiddled with a brace encircling her tiny leg, her eyes filled with a weary maturity that spoke of countless doctor visits and whispered conversations she wasn't meant to overhear. "Thank you for bringing Aiden home," Lily said.

"Anytime." Ron stood and shared a meaningful glance with Aiden.

As he walked back to his car, the weight of the Incognito Angel's mantle felt heavier, yet more purposeful than ever. Lily's bright spirit amidst her challenges sparked a familiar surge of empathy, his thoughts now firmly fixated on how he might change the lives of those two children.

"Do you want to drive?" Ron held out his keys to Conner.

"Sure. I love driving your car."

"You just love driving. This car is nothing compared to Sabre's BMW or JP's truck."

Conner grinned and got behind the wheel. As they drove off, Ron asked, "What's wrong with Lily?"

"She was born with problems in her bones. I'm not sure what they call it, but she needs plastic surgery to make her look normal."

"Do they have insurance?"

"Yeah, but it doesn't cover it, and they don't have the money to get it done. Aiden's mom works extra shifts at the diner, just to make ends meet. There's no way they could ever afford the surgeries Lily needs."

Imagining the relief that an Incognito Angel gift could bring to the family, Ron felt a renewed sense of purpose. He pictured Lily without the stigma of deformity and Aiden free to be a teenager without the albatross of adult worries.

Ron retrieved his cell phone from his pocket and sent a text to Sabre.

Ron—*I need to talk to you. Can we meet?*

A few seconds later, the phone vibrated in his palm. He glanced down at Sabre's reply.

Sabre—*In court until 5. Did you pick up Conner?*

Ron—*Just about to drop him off.*

Sabre—*Stay there. I'll see you soon.*

Ron sent her a thumbs up emoji.

Perfect, Ron thought, tucking the phone back into his pocket. He'd have time to formulate his thoughts, to shape the swirl of emotions and ideas into something coherent. As an attorney, Sabre had a mind like a steel trap, able to discern motive and consequence with razor-sharp precision. She would see angles he hadn't considered, potential pitfalls, and the best way to deliver his gift without causing undue attention or embarrassment.

When they reached JP's house, Ron said, "Can you find out exactly what Lily is diagnosed with? And please don't tell Aiden that I asked."

"Sure. But why the secrecy?"

"I have a friend who might be able to help, but I don't want to get their hopes up. Just let me check it out first."

"Sure. I can do that."

Conner and Ron hung out until Sabre arrived. She shivered as she walked in. "It's starting to look like rain out there."

"We're supposed to have another storm this weekend." Conner scowled and headed off to his room.

Sabre stepped toward her desk to drop off her shoulder bag, and Ron followed.

"I need your help." Ron took a deep breath before launching into his explanation. He told her about Lily and her family's financial struggles and how he wanted to use this year's IA gift to help them. "I still need to find out Lily's diagnosis so I can figure out what kind of treatment she needs."

"That's quite a lot to take in." Sabre leaned back as she considered everything he'd said. "How are you going to find out her diagnosis?"

"Conner said he'd ask Aiden, but he won't tell him why or who's asking."

"That should work."

Ron nodded in agreement. "That's why I came to you first, Sabre. I trust your judgment and experience in these matters."

"Well then, let's start making a plan." Sabre had a determined glint in her eye. She pulled out a notepad and pen from her bag and took notes as they discussed their next steps. "First, you need to make sure what Lily has is operable. Then you need to find the best surgeon for the job."

"And I'll need to make arrangements with the surgeon to have it done with the anonymous gift." Ron smiled. "Then I need to get the information to Lily's mom and hope she accepts it."

"Do you have any reason to think she wouldn't?"

"I don't know, pride maybe?"

"Any parent, unless they have some religious conviction that won't allow it, would accept a medical gift for a disabled child."

Chapter 10

Saturday late night

Sabre's phone buzzed on her nightstand, and she sat up, startled. It was nearly midnight, and the screen flashed Maverick's name. Her heart skipped a beat as she snatched it up, knowing that Maverick wouldn't call this late unless he was desperate.

"Sabre." His voice cracked. "I saw it again, the... the murder."

She swung her feet to the floor and pressed the phone closer to her ear. "Slow down, Maverick. Tell me exactly what you saw."

"My phone rang, and then I saw a flash of light on my window, so I got up and looked out."

"Who was on the phone?"

"I don't know. They hung up before I could answer it. I was already at the window by then. Everything else was just like last time." His breaths came fast and uneven. "And there—outside against the wall by the bushes—it happened all over again."

"Put it on speaker," JP said, already getting dressed.

Sabre pressed the speaker icon. "Okay, take a deep breath for me, Maverick." Sabre found a pad of paper. "Can you describe the person you saw?"

"I'm sure it was the same guy, the same trench coat." Maverick's words tumbled out, each laced with terror. "He had something shiny in his hand, and then there was this scream."

"Did you recognize any features, anything that could help us identify him?" she prodded.

"He was a big guy, muscular—not much else I could make out." A shudder in Maverick's voice sent chills down her spine.

Sabre scribbled *flash of light, trench coat, tall & lean.* "All right, Maverick. You've done well to tell me this." Her tone was calm, but her pulse tapped with the urgency of the situation. The boy trusted her; she couldn't let him down. "Stay where you are. JP and I will be right over. You need to tell your foster parents."

"Please, Ms. Sabre," Maverick pleaded, "no one else believes me."

"We'll get to the bottom of this. Just hang tight."

JP scowled as he pulled on his boots. He wasn't one to jump at shadows or chase phantoms, but Sabre's voice held a conviction that couldn't be ignored.

"Maverick needs us to take this seriously," she added with an urgency that matched the storm brewing outside.

"All right," JP grumbled. "We'll check it out, but don't get your hopes up."

"Thank you," Sabre said as she grabbed her jeans.

The heavens opened just as they arrived at Maverick's house, a relentless deluge that soaked through their clothes. Rainwater streamed down the street, carrying away the detritus of the city, but perhaps also any evidence that might have been left behind. Thunder rumbled ominously in the distance, a low growl that seemed to warn him off, while lightning briefly illuminated the scene in stark flashes. Rare weather for San Diego.

JP squinted against the downpour, as he surveyed the side yard where Maverick claimed to have seen the assault from his bedroom window. The rain had turned the dirt to mud, the kind that sucked at your boots and tried to pull you under.

"Damned if we're gonna find anything in this mess," JP muttered, wiping rain off his face. His gaze lingered on a nearby bush, its branches swaying violently in the wind.

"Why don't you go inside and talk to Maverick? I can handle this. Let's see if the kid's got an ounce of truth in him." Despite his doubts, JP's sense of justice wouldn't allow him to dismiss the possibility outright. He owed it to Maverick—and to that flicker of belief in Sabre's voice—to look deeper.

Sabre squeezed his wet arm, then went inside.

JP took a step forward, his boots sinking into the saturated earth. If there was something to be found here, some clue to validate the boy's account, he was determined to find it. JP squinted at the window of Maverick's bedroom to see what angle he would have had.

The bush that supposedly concealed a violent act trembled violently with each gust of wind. JP circled it, his flashlight beaming and his eyes combing the area with practiced scrutiny. The deluge had washed the world clean of easy answers. He knelt beside a cluster of shrubs. A disturbance caught his eye—marks in the soft ground, erratic imprints that suggested a scuffle. Yet, there was no bloodstain to mark the violence, no discarded weapon or piece of clothing. It was as if the earth had absorbed the sin without leaving a scar.

Could be anything, he thought. *Animal... or a dang good cleanup.*

He followed the subtle trail, noting each irregularity with meticulous detail. His fingers traced the grooves in the mud, the displaced stones, and the broken twigs, all of which could have been made days or weeks ago. He stood and stepped back, analyzing the scene, trying to piece together the fractured story told by these silent witnesses.

Someone might've been here, but they left nothing behind.

JP was soaked through by the time the squad car's lights cut through the dark, and its tires hissed on the wet asphalt.

"Evening, DuBois," JP called out as the detective stepped out, a mix of impatience and disbelief obvious on his face, even in the half-light.

"You'd better not be disturbing our phantom crime scene," DuBois said, pulling up his collar against the downpour.

"Something happened here," JP insisted, motioning toward the side yard. "There are marks that show it."

DuBois surveyed the property with a powerful flashlight and a skeptical eye. "Where's the body? The blood? Any shred of evidence?"

"Absence of evidence isn't evidence of absence. You know that."

"Philosophy from a cowboy PI. That's rich." DuBois chuckled dryly. "Maverick McLaughlin is a kid with a vivid imagination. We've been down this road before."

"He didn't imagine the phone calls."

DuBois tipped his head to one side. "He could be lying about that too."

"Sabre has the phone records. He received the calls from unknown numbers."

"Let me know when she finds out who they're from." DuBois shook his head. "He could've had someone call him. He isn't necessarily doing this all on his own."

"The kid's scared out of his wits. He believes he saw something violent."

"The kid's just trying to get attention," DuBois shot back, his patience wearing thin. "We can't turn the department upside down every time someone cries wolf."

"Or murder," JP corrected him.

"Fine," DuBois conceded with a sigh. "I'll give it a once-over, but I'm telling you, it's a wild goose chase."

"Thanks for indulging me," JP said, as he turned to the side yard.

"All right, McCloud. Let's see what your keen cowboy eyes have found." DuBois followed JP to the big bush, the light from his flashlight dancing erratically across the ground.

"Look at these broken twigs, the way the mud's all churned up." JP pointed his finger tracing the lines in the dirt.

"Could be anything. A dog digging for a bone, maybe," DuBois offered dismissively.

"Since when do dogs wear boots?" JP countered, indicating a half-erased imprint.

"Unless you pull a rabbit—or a dead body—out of your hat, there's nothing here. No witnesses, no physical evidence. Nothing."

"Except for a teenager who's out of his mind with fear," JP insisted. "You gonna dismiss that too?"

"Listen, if we chased down every shadow in this city, we'd never sleep," DuBois said curtly. "I'm sorry, JP, but I'm not buying it."

"Then you're not looking hard enough!" JP's voice carried a rare edge of anger.

"Enough!" DuBois snapped. "We're done here. Call us when you have something more than a hunch and a handful of mud."

"Sure thing, detective. I'll call you when I find the truth," JP said, his gaze unwavering, even as DuBois turned to leave.

"Good luck with that," DuBois muttered over his shoulder. "I'm going to talk to Maverick."

JP's frustration was intense, but beneath it lay a burning determination as well as strong skepticism. The night was dark, the rain unceasing, but he would keep looking for Sabre's sake. As the officers behind him muttered indifferently, their footsteps sloshing through the thickening mud with an air of impatience, JP's keen eyes scoured the wet earth beneath the window.

"Find something, cowboy?" a younger cop sneered, as he loomed over JP with a flashlight.

"Every detail counts," JP replied without looking up. With gloved hands, he moved aside wet leaves and debris with precision. The large, thick bush kept some of the ground from being drenched. He traced the outlines of prints in the soil, measured the distance between them, and noted their depth, evidence of weight and haste. But much of it went beyond the bush and was lost with the rain.

The rain hammered down harder, relentless. The water-logged scene around him began to blur into a canvas of grays and blacks.

"Hey, you need some help there, or are you just gonna play in the dirt all night?" another officer called out, clearly bored. He leaned against the squad car, watching JP's meticulous movements with detached amusement.

"Thanks, but I prefer my evidence uncontaminated," JP shot back. He could feel the weight of their stares, their disbelief hanging heavy in the air.

"Damn stubborn, aren't ya?" an officer muttered as he walked by, shaking his head.

"Like a mule halfway home after plowin' all day."

The officer walked on and got into his car. JP felt the cold seep through his boots, numbing his toes, but his focus remained sharp.

"Wrap it up! We're calling it a night!" DuBois' voice cut through the storm, impatient and final.

JP rounded the corner to the front. "What did Maverick have to say?"

"Same thing as last time. The kid is seeing ghosts."

As JP edged closer to the street, something caught his eye. "Damn," he whispered to himself, kneeling for a closer look. Amidst the wet sheen of the sidewalk, broken twigs lay scattered, their jagged edges pointing haphazardly. He noticed how the mud from the adjacent flower bed had been smeared onto the concrete—evidence that someone or something had been dragged through here.

"Hey, DuBois!" JP called out as the detective retreated to his vehicle. "You might want to see this."

"I doubt it," DuBois responded, still annoyed. "There's nothing here. It's time to pack it in."

"These twigs, this mud—it's out of place," JP insisted. "Doesn't that strike you as odd?"

"Odd doesn't make it a crime scene," DuBois shot back, his hand already on the car door. "We can't arrest Mother Nature for making a mess. Goodnight."

The squad cars, with their bright lights, drove off, leaving the crime scene in darkness again. JP felt another surge of frustration. The evidence was right there, yet the very people who should be helping him investigate were turning their backs on potential leads.

"Fine," JP grumbled under his breath as he watched the last taillight disappear into the storm. He knew when he was beat, but he also knew when to trust his gut. And right now, his instincts screamed that something significant had happened here. *Or did he just need to find some clue, anything?*

JP's hand was steady as he pulled out his smartphone, the screen barely visible through the rain. He snapped several photos of the muddy sidewalk, capturing the irregular patterns and the broken twigs scattered across the concrete.

With resolute steps, he made his way back to his truck. As he sat behind the wheel, his wet leather boots creaked in protest. He pulled his phone again and called Sabre. "There's no more I can do here."

"I'll be right out."

Chapter 11

Monday morning

The cold metal of the handcuffs clicked ominously around Maverick's wrists, a chilling sound that seemed to echo down the quiet street. A police officer's firm grip on his arm was the only steady thing in the whirlwind of flashing lights, murmuring neighbors, and the scattered debris of a life turned upside down.

"Hey, Maverick!" a voice called from across the road. It was one of his neighborhood friends, skateboard hanging from his hand. "You didn't actually do it, right?"

Maverick wanted to shout back, to affirm his innocence, but the lump in his throat held the words captive. Instead, he offered a helpless shrug as he was led away from the only semblance of home he'd known—past the people who'd once believed in him, their eyes now clouded with doubt. He looked over at Gary and Edie Venable, wondering if they were happy to see him go.

But Gary approached him and said, "We'll call Sabre, son. She'll be there to help you."

Gary called him "son." That must mean something. Maverick's next thought was that he had let them down. How could he have been so stupid?

"I didn't see anything." He tried to convince himself as much as the officer, whose expression was unreadable behind mirrored sunglasses. "I was just telling a story, you know? I swear. I promise I won't do it again."

The officer didn't respond, as he guided Maverick into the back of the cruiser, where the world outside became a blur of judgment and confusion.

~~~

Sabre's heart pounded as she entered the juvenile hall, scanning the cold, sterile walls as she walked to the small interview room. Within minutes, Maverick was brought in, his face etched with fear and desperation. He collapsed onto the bench, his eyes pleading for salvation.

"I'm scared," Maverick said. "This place is awful."

"I know," Sabre said. "I hate that you have to be here, but I'll do everything in my power to get you out as quickly as I can."

A glimmer of hope appeared in his eyes.

Sabre explained the legal process, so Maverick knew what to expect. "They must hold a detention hearing within seventy-two hours. I'm hoping to get you released at that hearing."

"I have to stay here three days?"

"I know this is hard, but that's the best I can do. Even then, I can't guarantee anything."

"What chance do you think I have of getting out?"

"I think our chances are pretty good, but I don't want you saying anything more to anyone about what you saw or didn't see, not even your fellow detainees."

"I understand."

"The police report says you admitted to making everything up. Is that true?"

"It's true that I told them that. I thought they might let me go. It was stupid, wasn't it?"

Sabre tried not to react. Her thoughts were exactly that, but instead she said, "They will argue that you made a confession, and that's not a good thing, but we need to find some evidence that your account of events is true."
~~~

"They are true. Every one of them."

"I'm sure you can understand how farfetched it sounds that there were three murders with no bodies or traces of anything left behind."

"I know it sounds crazy. It's almost like it's a movie playing."

"What do you mean?"

"They're almost *ghost-like*. Sometimes people seem more like holographs."

"Why didn't you tell me this before?"

"Because it sounds crazy. I know I'm not seeing ghosts, and the first one was more life-like."

"We'll keep digging and see if we come up with anything that helps explain what you saw. In the meantime, do the best you can in here. Keep your head down, don't talk about your alleged crime, and stay out of trouble. I'll get your court hearing set as soon as possible."

The room fell into an uneasy silence as Sabre processed the legalities. Her heart ached for the young boy who had been thrust into this nightmare, but she knew she had a tough road ahead and so did he.

She took time to explain what Maverick's next few days would be like and encouraged him to be strong. Even with all the tough times Maverick had experienced in his life, he knew nothing of the real street life that existed beyond his home. He was about to live in a world that had a whole different set of rules. Sabre hoped he didn't learn too much.

She checked the time, told Maverick goodbye, and left the Hall. She had made an appointment to meet with Maverick's therapist, Dr. Reynolds. She had just enough time to get there.

~~~

Dr. Reynolds' office door clicked shut behind Sabre, enveloping them in a space that was small, yet somehow expansive in its promise of confidentiality. Bookshelves lined the walls, filled with volumes about psychology and human
~~~

behavior, while a plush couch faced two comfortable chairs. A tranquil painting of the ocean hung on one wall, its waves frozen in time.

"Thank you for seeing me, Dr. Reynolds." Sabre took a seat across from the therapist.

"Of course. I understand how important this is," replied Dr. Reynolds. "What exactly can I do for you?"

"As I told you on the phone, Maverick has been arrested for making false statements to the police. I'll need to defend him in court, but to do that, I need to understand Maverick better. You've been working with him for a while now. Do you truly believe that what he claims to have witnessed is genuine?"

The lines around Dr. Reynolds' eyes deepened as he considered his response. "Maverick is consistent in his accounts, which is generally a good indicator of truthful recall. His emotional reactions when recounting the events have the hallmarks of sincerity."

Sabre listened intently, absorbing his words like a sponge. The quiet hum of the air conditioner provided a soft backdrop to their conversation.

"Can you say with certainty that he isn't seeking attention? That this isn't a ploy?" Sabre was determined to explore every angle.

"Certainty is a rare commodity in my profession." Dr. Reynolds gave a gentle shrug. "But in my professional opinion, there's something authentic in his claims. Something that doesn't quite fit the pattern of a fabrication."

"If this goes to court, you will need to testify. Are you okay with that?"

"Of course."

"You will be asked what is authentic about his statements when they appear so preposterous. How would you respond?"

"I'm convinced that Maverick saw exactly what he says he saw the first time he reported it. After that, his mind could be replaying the incident. But, in my opinion, he saw something gruesome and very memorable."

Relief coursed through Sabre, but she simply nodded. She would fight for Maverick, but she needed something concrete to work with, not just the opinion of the therapist.

"Thank you, Doctor. Your insight is invaluable," she said, rising from her chair.

Chapter 12

Monday afternoon

Sabre worked on her cases while she waited for JP to join her. She had asked him to stop by her work office before he investigated further.

“Got somethin’ new for me, darlin’?” JP sauntered in a few minutes later.

"Maybe." Sabre tucked a strand of hair behind her ear. "Maverick gave me a more vivid description the second and third times. He said it felt like watching a movie unfold right in front of him."

"A movie?" JP raised an eyebrow. “You mean he didn’t think it was real?”

“He still believes it was real. And his therapist says it’s too detailed, too consistent to be a fabrication. Maverick spoke about specific lighting and angles. He even mentioned a sense of timing that felt rehearsed or staged." Sabre got up and closed the blinds against the bright sun.

"Staged murders, now that's a twist." JP stroked his chin. "And you think there's weight to his story?"

"Enough to consider it seriously."

JP's eyes narrowed as he processed the information. "The Andersons are back from their vacation, and their house has a direct view of the site where Maverick claims the murders took place."

"Surveillance recordings," Sabre felt a spark of hope. "If we could get our hands on them..."

"Exactly." JP nodded. "I'll pay the Andersons a visit. If there's anything in their security files, I intend to find it."

"Good," Sabre said. "I hope they cooperate."

"Leave it to me." A hint of a smile tugged at the corner of his mouth. "Sometimes a cowboy's charm can do wonders."

"It has certainly worked on me."

JP winked. "See you later at home."

~~~

JP parked his truck along the curb in front of the Anderson home. He climbed out and stood for a moment, enjoying the suburban stillness of the neighborhood. It was hard to believe a vicious murder might have taken place here just a short time ago. He approached the well-kept house with neatly trimmed hedges, blooming flowerbeds, but no vehicles in the driveway.

JP pressed the doorbell, and a dog barked somewhere in the recesses of the house. He waited, scanning the windows for any signs of movement. Maybe they were both at work. Moments later, the lock clicked, and Chuck Anderson opened the door. He was in his late forties, with salt-and-pepper hair and an expression that read like a mix of curiosity and cautious annoyance. "Can I help you?" He eyed JP's attire.

"Chuck Anderson, I presume?" JP extended a hand, which the homeowner accepted with a firm grip. "Name's JP Torn. I'm a private investigator looking into some incidents that occurred nearby while you were away on vacation."

"Is this about those ridiculous stories that kid has been spreading around?"

"Maybe not as ridiculous as they seem," JP replied. "There's a possibility your surveillance system caught something that could shed light on what really happened."

"Ah, yes, the boy who cried wolf," Chuck mused, but there was less disdain in his voice now—more intrigue.
~~~

"Maybe," JP said, locking eyes with Chuck. "He may be as full of wind as a corn-eatin' horse, but if he's not, this whole neighborhood could be in danger. Do you want to take that chance?" When he didn't answer right away, JP continued, "I get it. Privacy is a sacred thing, but consider this: there's a boy out there whose life has been nothing but chaos. Maverick's trying to hold on to some semblance of reality amid harassment he has received. And it's bigger than Maverick. It's about your neighborhood, your community. If there's a chance that what he saw was real, we need to act. Not just for his sake, but for the safety of everyone around here."

Anderson's stance softened slightly.

"Come in," he finally said, stepping aside. "Let's see what you're talking about."

JP tipped his hat in thanks and crossed the threshold.

The home breathed the sterile air of modernity, its walls adorned with abstract art and shelves that held a collection of blue and silver ceramic curios. Anderson led JP down a narrow hallway, the muted click of their shoes against the hardwood floor marking time.

"In here," Anderson said, gesturing toward a room with the door ajar. "By the way, call me Chuck."

JP followed him into an office, tailored to someone who appreciated technology. One wall was dominated by a large screen flanked by smaller monitors, each flickering with the ghostly images of various parts of the property. A sleek black console hummed beneath them, its surface littered with controls and LED indicators.

"Quite the setup you've got." JP surveyed the equipment, assessing its capability.

"It keeps an eye on things when we're not around," Chuck said with pride. "What do you need, exactly?"

"A closer look at last Monday night to start with, then two other nights." JP gave him the dates that Maverick had reported. "I can check that footage." Chuck approached the console, his hands deftly navigating the controls. As he cycled through the camera feeds, he pointed out the vantage points: the wide-angle view of the driveway, the tight shot of the side entrance, the infrared capture of the backyard.

"Let me see what I've got on the archived footage." Chuck started to search, then stopped abruptly. "We have a problem."

"What's that?"

"We can't get the first date. The system is set to keep the images for only thirty days unless I save them."

"Try the second date, please."

Chuck set the request for the previous Monday. The screen flickered, fast-forwarding through hours of inconsequential footage—cars passing by, leaves fluttering in the wind, the occasional nocturnal animal scuttling across the lawn.

"What should I be watching for?"

"Anything that doesn't fit the pattern of a quiet suburban street at night." JP kept his eyes locked on the monitors. "Maybe something that matches Maverick's account or even the slightest hint of something amiss."

Hours of footage rolled by in minutes, compressed into rapid sequences of normalcy until—"Wait!" JP snapped. "Back it up a bit."

Chuck reversed the feed slowly, painstakingly, until JP found the frame that had caught his attention. First, there was movement at the corner of the street, then a flash of light on the crime scene. Seconds later, a shadow seemed to detach itself from the darkness before melding back into it. It was creepy enough to make the hairs on the back of JP's neck stand on end.

"See that?" He pointed, but Chuck was already leaning in.

"Could be lightning," Chuck offered, although his voice lacked conviction.

"Could be. But it lasted longer than a flash."

"Is that what you were looking for?" Chuck's tone held an edge now, bordering on concern.

"Let's just say it's worth a closer look." JP's mind was already racing ahead to what they might discover next.

He squinted at the monitor. The grainy nighttime footage flickered with occasional headlights from a passing car or the flutter of wings. Everything seemed mundane, expected—until a shape coalesced from the periphery.

"Stop there." JP tapped the screen, where a figure appeared briefly near the fence line—a silhouette against the dim urban glow. It was the spot Maverick had described with detail, the scene of the alleged crime.

"Could be a stray cat, maybe?" Chuck hovered close enough for JP to catch the scent of his aftershave.

"Too big for a cat," JP murmured. "And cats don't walk upright. Rewind that please."

Chuck rewound the tape, the image jerking back to life in reverse. When he reached the crucial moment, he played it frame by frame. The figure was there again, distinctly human this time.

"See how they move? Deliberate. Purposeful." JP's voice was low.

"Someone from the neighborhood?"

"Maybe. Or someone who shouldn't be here at all."

The third night's footage rolled forward with an eerie sense of *déjà vu*. Again, the figure emerged at the same hour, their movements replicated with uncanny precision. The light appeared again too—a subtle luminescence that bathed the area in an otherworldly glow—but it was impossible to discern its source.

"Could be a reflection, perhaps? Headlights?" Chuck asked.

"Headlights don't hover. And they don't return night after night to the exact same spot. Something's going on here." JP finally relaxed and straightened up.

Chuck replayed the sequence again, and they both tracked every nuance of the shadowy figure and the inexplicable light.

"Good God," Chuck muttered. "I never would've thought..."

"Seems Maverick might not have been making up tales after all," JP said.

"Thank you for letting me take a look at these. Might just help us clear up this whole mess."

"Of course." Chuck's voice carried the tremor of a man who'd glimpsed something he couldn't explain. "We all want the truth. No matter where it leads."

JP extended his hand. "You've been a real help. Your cooperation means we're one step closer to getting to the bottom of this."

“I can do one better than that. I'll see if I can get some better images. I have a friend who's quite good at that.”

“Any chance you can give me a copy of those files?”

“Be glad to.”

“That would be great.” JP gave him his business card.

"Please keep those cameras rolling—especially if it rains again."

Chapter 13

Tuesday afternoon

Ron picked up Conner and Aiden from school. After they dropped Aiden off, Conner said, "I asked Aiden about Lily's condition. He said it was called Williams Syndrome."

Ron had never heard of it. "What exactly is that?"

"Aiden said it affects development across multiple systems in the body. She was born with it. That's about all I know."

"How does it affect her?"

"You can see what it's done to her face and leg, and I know she has some heart problems too. I think you'd better look it up to get a full picture."

"I will. Thanks for asking for me. I hope Aiden wasn't offended."

"He wasn't. In fact, I think he liked that I was interested."

~~~

When they reached JP's house, Ron sat down at Sabre's computer and searched for *Williams Syndrome*. The screen loaded with links. Medical websites, research papers, support groups—all beckoning with knowledge just a click away. He opened several tabs, each promising to shed light on the mysterious syndrome that had thrust itself into Lily's life—and now into his.
~~~

"Let's see what we're dealing with," he muttered, scanning the first website. The lead article took a deep dive into genetics and explained the deletion of material on chromosome seven, which apparently played a crucial role in the syndrome.

Ron clicked onto a foundation dedicated to Williams Syndrome and discovered a trove of resources: detailed descriptions of symptoms, personal stories, emerging research. He absorbed the text, his brain already sifting through the information, separating facts that could lead to action from those that were merely clinical.

He bookmarked sites with comprehensive guides and downloaded medical journals that contained the latest studies. Each fact and figure added another layer to his understanding of Lily's world.

Knowledge is power, he thought. And with that power, he would craft an act of kindness that transcended mere gesture; one that would ripple through the fabric of Lily's life and provide the support she and her family so desperately needed.

When he came across *intellectual disability* and *learning difficulties,* he took notes, underlining them for emphasis. It was crucial to understand these challenges if he was going to make a meaningful difference.

A beep from the computer signaled the download of a comprehensive study. Ron studied the graphs and figures that quantified cognitive struggles in terms of standard deviations and percentile ranks. But it was the personal accounts that tugged at him—stories of children like Lily, whose bright eyes and wide smiles belied the battles waged within their minds.

He took a moment to absorb it all. Each statistic was a life. Each case study was a family's hope.

Unique cognitive profile, another article highlighted, and Ron's attention snagged on those words. *Strengths in lan-*

guage and music. It was a glimmer of light amidst the darkness, and he clung to it, envisioning Lily not just as a beneficiary, but as a person with her own set of talents and dreams.

"Perhaps a scholarship for music therapy?" he mused, scribbling the idea next to the highlighted text. His thoughts raced ahead, imagining how music could be both a solace and a stepping stone for Lily to help her navigate a world that often seemed out of sync with her needs.

As he read his notes about cardiovascular problems— including something called supravalvular aortic stenosis—his heart clenched at the thought of that sweet girl facing such a serious condition.

Distinctive facial features, Ron read about the star-like pattern in their eyes, the broad forehead, and the small, upturned nose that marked those with Williams Syndrome. *Growth delays*, too. He pictured Lily, how these traits might shape her in the eyes of the world. It was one thing to know the facts, another to understand the daily reality they created.

With a deep breath, he clicked a link to a video, watching as children with Williams Syndrome laughed and played, their joy unmarred by the challenges they faced. They were like Lily – full of life.

Shifting gears, Ron searched for the social implications of Williams Syndrome. He was drawn to traits like *outgoing, empathetic,* and *engaging.* He leaned back in the chair, imagining Lily's future – her innate warmth drawing people in, her eagerness to connect with every soul she met. He smiled as he thought of her easy laughter, the way she'd reach out to others without hesitation.

But there was a flip side. Difficulty in reading social cues, vulnerability due to an unconditional trust in strangers – the risks were real.

Extremely sociable, yet easily taken advantage of, he read, the paradox not lost on him. It was a delicate balance, fostering that openness while safeguarding against potential exploitation. As he jotted down thoughts about intervention strategies and social skills training, he imagined standing before the board of trustees, presenting his case with the powerful simplicity of human connection.

"Everyone deserves a champion," he said to the quiet room. "And I need to step up for Lily."

He glanced at his phone. It was time. Ron called Dr. Helen Archer, a pediatric cardiologist renowned for her work with children with Williams Syndrome. As the phone rang, he steadied his voice, ready to delve deeper into the medical intricacies of the condition.

"Dr. Archer, Ron Brown here," he began when the call connected. "I appreciate you taking the time to discuss Lily's case with me."

"Of course, Mr. Brown. I received the information you sent me. I understand you're looking to gather information about treatment options for Williams Syndrome?"

"Exactly." Ron drummed his fingertips softly on the desk. "Particularly concerning the cardiovascular complications and any recommended interventions."

"One of the primary concerns is narrowing of the blood vessels," Dr. Archer explained. "Regular monitoring is crucial, along with an early and proactive approach to management. Depending on the severity, medication or even surgery may be necessary."

Ron scribbled notes as she spoke, a furrow forming between his brows. "What about support systems? Is there a network or a program that can assist families in navigating these treatments?"

"There are several foundations and support groups. They provide not just educational resources but also emotional support for families," she elaborated. "It's important to remember that while the medical treatments are vital, the family's wellbeing is equally so."

"Understood." Ron paused, considering how this tapestry of care would look for Lily. "One more question, if I may?"

"Go ahead."

"Are there therapies that can help?"

"Early intervention is key," Dr. Archer advised. "Speech and occupational therapy can help with developmental delays. Social skills groups are also beneficial."

"Thank you, Dr. Archer. This has been helpful."

"Happy to assist. And Mr. Brown?" Her voice held a note of warmth. "It's heartening to see someone so invested in the welfare of a child with Williams Syndrome."

"Believe me, the privilege is all mine." Ron replied, then ended the call.

He dialed another expert.

"Williams Syndrome Association," the woman answered. "Susan speaking. May I help you?"

"Absolutely, Susan. My name is Ron Brown. I'm looking for therapeutic programs that would be helpful to a child around five or six," he said, pen poised above his notepad.

"We have music therapy groups that stimulate language and emotional development," Susan offered. "And there are specialized education plans tailored to their strengths. I'll send over some literature."

"Music therapy... that sounds promising," Ron mused, already picturing Lily's response to such an approach. "Please do send that, and thank you."

"Remember," Susan added with a chuckle, "these kids might have challenges, but they have incredible gifts too. Their joy in music, their empathy—it's quite remarkable."

"Remarkable indeed," he echoed, a small smile lifting the corners of his mouth.

As he set the phone back in its cradle, Ron felt like he finally understood the significance of his mission. With each expert's guidance tucked away in his arsenal of knowledge, he was building a foundation not only for Lily's immediate needs but for her lifelong journey of growth and discovery.

He opened a file and pulled together his jigsaw puzzle of scattered notes and highlighted texts. He included every symptom, from intellectual disability to cardiovascular issues. The treatment options—music therapy, specialized education plans, physical therapy—were neatly categorized, each accompanied by potential providers and programs.

He knew too well the weight his words carried; they had the power to sway the trust members, to secure the crucial funding Lily needed for her dental work, heart surgery, and ongoing music and physical therapy.

"Time to rally the troops," he said, reaching for his phone to schedule a meeting with the other trust members.

"Rosemarie, it's Ron. Can you set up a conference meeting with the board? I have a proposal to discuss."

"Of course, Mr. Brown. I'll let you know as soon as I have a date."

"Thank you."

He no sooner hung up when Sabre came home. "What are you still doing here? Not that I mind. I always love seeing my favorite brother."

"You do realize I'm your only brother, right?"

Sabre smiled. "Staying for dinner?"

"Who's cooking?"

"JP."

"I'd love to."

Chapter 14

Tuesday afternoon

JP stepped out of his pickup truck, and the midday sun cast a sharp silhouette on the cracked pavement. He approached Mrs. Jenkins' modest house and rapped.

She answered the door, her eyes widening a fraction as she recognized him. JP didn't miss the flicker of something that crossed her face. Was it apprehension? Fear?

"Mrs. Jenkins." JP gave her a polite nod. "Hope I'm not catching you at a bad time."

"Mr. Torn." She forced a smile. "Not at all. Please come in."

"Please call me JP. Mr. Torn was my father."

She smiled. "Okay, JP."

He stepped inside and scanned the living room for any changes since his last visit. Everything appeared the same, down to the floral-patterned couch and the faint smell of lavender.

"Care for some tea?" She motioned toward the kitchen.

JP declined with a shake of his head. "Thank you, ma'am, but I'll get straight to the point." He noticed she was fiddling with the hem of her apron again. "I can't shake the feeling that there's something you're not telling me about this neighborhood."

Mrs. Jenkins avoided his gaze, her voice quivering slightly. "I've told you everything I know, Mr. Torn."

JP was going to remind her again to call him JP, but decided to let it go. "Ma'am, how long have you lived here?" JP's tone was gentle, yet insistent.

She hesitated before answering. "Nearly forty years now," she whispered.

"Forty years..." JP let the weight of those decades sink in. "That's a long time. A lot could happen in forty years."

"Indeed, it can." Her eyes darted away from his.

"Mrs. Jenkins." JP leaned forward. "I've seen the surveillance videos from the night Maverick claims the assault took place. Something strange shows up, but it's difficult to see what it is. Almost like a... "

She sucked in her breath and her hand flew to her mouth. Her eyes locked onto his, and for a moment, JP thought she might crumble under the weight of her own secrets.

"... like a ghost." She finished his sentence.

"I was going to say *person*." JP paused. "Why did you say *ghost*?"

She took a deep breath. "Surveillance videos?" she finally managed. "I... I didn't realize."

"Seems like there's something going on in this neighborhood that you don't want to talk about. "You sure there's nothing you know that might help explain what I saw?"

Mrs. Jenkins shook her head, but her uneasiness spoke volumes. She seemed to be waging an internal battle, torn between the desire to help and the need to protect whatever fragile peace she'd constructed over the years.

"Some things are best left undisturbed," she murmured, her hands trembling now.

"Respectfully, ma'am, if there's been an injustice, I plan to disturb it." JP spoke sternly, something he rarely did. "The truth has a way of coming out. We're analyzing the videos, and we'll get a better picture soon. It would help if you gave us somewhere to start."

Mrs. Jenkins stared at him, with a mix of resignation and fear. It was clear this conversation had unearthed something she wished had remained buried.

"Has anything like this happened here before?"

She shook her head. "I think you'd better go now."

"Thank you for your time." He turned toward the door. "I'll be in touch."

JP left her home, his mind swirling with unanswered questions. This case was more than it seemed, and he could feel the noose of the mystery tightening with every step he took towards the truth. He drove back to his own place, contemplating all that Mrs. Jenkins hadn't said.

Upon arriving home, JP found Ron lounging on his porch, flipping through a small notebook. "I was just about to call you," JP said.

"What's up?"

"I'm working on a complicated case, and I could use your help."

Once they were settled in the living room, JP dove into the details. He recounted Maverick's story—the uncorroborated claim of murder, the elusive evidence, and the surveillance files that added more shadows than light.

"The kid's adamant about what he saw." JP furrowed his brow. "But without something concrete, he's just crying wolf to a police department full of skeptics."

"Sounds like we're chasing ghosts through the fog," Ron said. "Anything I can do, JP, you know I'm in."

"Appreciate it, Ron. I've got a hunch there's more to this tale, something buried deep. Mrs. Jenkins hinted at past troubles, but clammed up when it got too real."

"Might be worth digging into the history of the area, see if any old bones resurface."

"Exactly my thought." JP stood up to pace. "I'll use my contacts, try to sniff out any previous crimes in the area. If there's a pattern, we'll find it."

"Meanwhile, I'll start with the location's history and look for anomalies or untold stories," Ron suggested.

"Good man." JP nodded. "Get this," he added. "The kid describes the assailant down to the scuff on his boots, but he never sees his face. Problem is, nobody else seems to have seen a man fitting the description."

Ron leaned in. "And the videos? Anything pop out at you?"

"Nothing concrete, but there's a shadow, a silhouette, a flash of light that doesn't match up with the rest of the movements—a glitch in the pattern. It's like trying to spot a rattlesnake in high grass, but it's there."

"Could be our smoking gun, or just a play of light." Ron opened his notepad and scribbled something. "We'll need to get tech guys on this."

"That's what I was thinking." JP was relieved that Ron's connections were already proving valuable. He shifted the conversation, his voice dropping a notch. "Mrs. Jenkins—the widow who lives two doors down from the crime scene—clammed up when I mentioned the shadowy figure in the video. She said something about leaving the past in the past."

"Sounds like she knows more than she's letting on." Ron's brow creased as he took notes. "History has a way of whispering its secrets if you listen closely enough. Maybe it's time we lend an ear to what the neighborhood has to say."

"I'll pull some strings," JP said. "I've got a few buddies who aren't strangers to the darker alleys of this town. If there's been trouble around that area, we'll sniff it out."

"And I'll dig into the archives, see what kind of skeletons the neighborhood's closet is hiding. Old police reports, news articles, maybe even a chat with local historians if need be."

"Good. Now let's go eat."

Chapter 15

Wednesday morning

The courtroom buzzed with nervous energy, like a hive disturbed. Every eye fixed on the sixteen-year-old boy who sat with shoulders hunched, trying to become invisible under the weight of the stares.

"Order," Judge Johnson commanded. As the robed older man took his seat on the bench, the room fell silent.

"This is the detention hearing for Maverick McLaughlin, charged with Penal Code Section 148.5, Making a False Report of a Crime. How do you plead Mr. McLaughlin?"

Maverick stood as Sabre had instructed. "Not guilty, Your Honor." He sat back down.

"What is the recommendation from the State for detention?"

The prosecutor rose, his posture rigid with confidence. He was the embodiment of authority, his suit crisp, his gaze unyielding as he surveyed the court. "Your Honor," he began, "Maverick McLaughlin stands accused of fabricating a tale so perilous, its ripples have tainted our community's sense of security. His claims" —the prosecutor gave the boy a pointed look—"have diverted precious resources and sown distrust among law enforcement and citizens alike. He did all that just to get attention. We must consider the potential harm caused by these allegations—unsubstantiated as they are—and weigh them heavily when we determine where he will be detained. He has reported the same crime three different times. The same exact crime, but without evidence. I repeat, no evidence was found to back it up."

"Thank you, Mr. Knowles," the judge acknowledged. "Ms. Brown."

Sabre stood. "Your Honor, Maverick McLaughlin is not the attention-seeking delinquent the prosecution would have you believe. He is, in fact, a victim of circumstances—a teenager grappling with the instability of a life spent in foster care, seeking only to tell the truth as he has witnessed it."

The prosecutor scoffed, shaking his head with a practiced air of disbelief. "Ms. Brown, let's not romanticize the situation. We're dealing with a boy who cried wolf, who relished the temporary spotlight afforded by his so-called *witness account*. Yet when pressed for details, when asked for evidence, the defendant's story crumbles like a house of cards."

"Really, Mr. Knowles?" Sabre locked eyes with the prosecutor. "Maverick's account of the crimes have been consistent from the start. The lack of physical evidence does not negate the possibility that he stumbled upon a crime most foul—a crime that someone went to great lengths to cover up."

"Consistent fabrications remain fabrications, Counselor," the prosecutor retorted, then turned to face the judge.

Judge Johnson, a seasoned adjudicator with decades on the bench, peered down at Maverick, his eyes narrowing behind thick-rimmed glasses. His expression was unreadable, yet the lines etched into his forehead betrayed a mind deep in thought.

"Ms. Brown." The judge's voice was measured and deliberate. "While I understand your insistence on your client's credibility, we cannot ignore the absence of corroborating evidence. What motivation would a young man like Mr. McLaughlin have for inventing such a tale?"

"Your Honor, if I may," Sabre replied. "Maverick has no history of deceit or misconduct. His account, while extraordinary, is detailed and vivid. It paints a picture only an eyewitness could render—not a fabrication from the imagination of a troubled youth. Also, we have recently discovered surveillance footage that has evidence of activity in that area."

"What does that mean, Counselor?"

"The videos aren't clear, Your Honor, but we're getting them enlarged so we can see more detail. However, there was definitely someone in that area on at least two of the occasions that my client reported."

"And you have these tapes?"

"Yes, Your Honor, and they will be entered into evidence at trial should that happen."

The judge leaned back, as he regarded Maverick once again. "And yet, Mr. McLaughlin's desire to impress his peers is well-documented. One might argue that the temptation to concoct a story for social gain could be quite compelling for someone in his situation."

"Respectfully, Your Honor," Sabre countered, "there is also ample evidence that Maverick shied away from the spotlight. This isn't about social currency; it's about a boy who believes he saw something horrific and had the courage to speak up."

"Courage, or a cry for help?" Judge Johnson glanced toward Maverick with eyes narrowed.

"Perhaps both," Sabre conceded with calculated honesty. "But that doesn't diminish the veracity of his claim. If there's even a sliver of truth to what Maverick has witnessed, do we not owe it to justice to investigate further rather than dismiss him out of hand?"

The prosecutor cut in. "The defendant is here because he is charged with reporting a false crime. Is Counselor actually suggesting we further investigate the alleged bogus crime?"

"Your Honor," Sabre said, "I urge the court to consider the absence of any prior delinquency in Maverick's record and to release him into the care of his foster parents. This will allow him to continue his education and receive the support he desperately needs during this trying time."

The judge peered down from the bench and tapped his gavel on the wood. "Very well, Ms. Brown. I am granting conditional release for Maverick McLaughlin. The pretrial hearing is set for next Thursday. The trial will take place the following Monday." He shifted his attention to the boy, who sat with an air of restrained hope. "Young man, you are to remain under the supervision of your foster parents, adhere to a curfew, and avoid any further trouble. Do I make myself clear?"

"Crystal clear, Your Honor," Maverick replied, the relief in his voice barely contained.

Johnson turned to the prosecutor. "Mr. Knowles, I believe you said, let me see, I wrote it down. Ah, here it is. 'Fabricating a tale so perilous, its ripples have tainted our community's sense of security.'" The judge shook his head. "Please don't pontificate in my courtroom. There's no jury to hear it—just me."

"Yes, Your Honor."

"Case adjourned."

As Maverick's handcuffs were removed, and he slowly walked out of the courthouse, the weight in Sabre's chest lightened. But the battle was far from over.

Chapter 16

Thursday morning

JP strode toward DuBois' desk, noticing that, with age, the lawman looked like he was molded from the grit of the streets he'd once patrolled.

"Got a minute?" JP leaned against the edge of the cluttered workspace.

DuBois squinted up at him through narrow eyes, a smirk on his face. "If it isn't McCloud. What's got you riding into my corral today? Looking for a ghost?"

"Something like that," JP replied, unamused. "I need to know about any unsolved murders in the Venables' neighborhood. I know something happened there. I just don't know what."

DuBois raised an eyebrow, shuffling papers. "You're digging graves now?"

"Let's just say I've got reason to believe there's more than dirt buried out there," JP said firmly.

"All right." DuBois leaned back, fingers steepled. "I'll look into it. But if this is some wild goose chase..."

"Thanks, DuBois. I owe you."

"Damn right, you do."

~~~

Across town, Ron hunched over a microfilm reader in a quiet corner of the library. The soft whir of the machine
~~~

filled the space as he scrolled through endless pages of old newspaper records. A musty scent clung to the air—the smell of secrets waiting to be unearthed.

He stopped abruptly, his heart thudding as he stared at the headline: *Local Woman Suspected Missing, Foul Play Feared.* The date was almost three decades ago, but the story was chillingly relevant. The woman had been last seen near the very spot Maverick had mentioned. No body was ever found.

This could be the break they needed—the link between Maverick's story and a cold case that had been collecting dust. He grabbed his phone and snapped a picture of the article, knowing JP would want to see it immediately.

~~~

JP tapped the screen of his smartphone, enlarging the image of the old newspaper article Ron had sent. He looked at DuBois, who was pouring over a manila folder that had seen better days.

"That unsolved case we've talked about, the Harrington case - it's got legs." JP said, leaning back in the creaky chair opposite the detective's cluttered desk.

DuBois raised an eyebrow. "You don't say? What did your archive rat dig up?"

"Thirty years back, a missing person, suspected dead. No body, just a trail colder than a well digger's feet in January." JP handed his phone to DuBois, who squinted at the article.

With a grunt, DuBois set down the folder and scrutinized the screen. As he read, minutes dragged by, filled only by the distant murmur of precinct activity. Finally, he nodded. "Checks out. I remember hearing about this one when I was a rookie. Thought it was just ghost stories, tall tales to scare the new blood."

"Looks like we've got a connection," JP remarked, retrieving his phone.

"Unless your client knows the old story and is just describing what he read."
~~~

"Maybe, but I don't think so."

"That case was quite a scandal," DuBois added. "If I remember right, the prime suspects were important people in town."

"Thanks. You've been more help than you realize."

"Just make sure to break it to me gently if you find a poltergeist."

~~~

Sabre looked up from her desk at home as JP entered.

"Got a minute?" JP asked, leaning over her shoulder.

"Always for you. What's up?" She put down her pencil and gave him her full attention.

"Ron found a newspaper clipping about a suspected murder from thirty years ago. Same area where Maverick saw the assaults." JP smiled as her lawyerly poise shifted to intrigue.

"Interesting," she mused. "And?"

"And..." JP paused for effect. "The suspected victim was connected to the Callahans, and the murder was never solved."

"The real estate moguls?" Her brows shot up. "That's quite the accusation. It could explain a lot."

"Could be it was swept under the rug. Money talks, and the Callahans have always spoken loudly."

"You're suggesting there was a cover-up of a crime that took place thirty years ago in the same place that Maverick saw the assault?"

"Yes. Maybe."

"And you think Maverick saw the ghosts of that crime?"

"No, but I'm saying it's quite a coincidence that a similar crime took place in the same spot."

"So, there may be a connection." Sabre's eyes sparked with determination. "We need more evidence. Something concrete."

"Agreed. If the Callahans are behind this, they won't go down without a fight." JP's stance was resolute.
~~~

"Then we'll have to hit them where it hurts—the courtroom." Sabre was calm, but JP could see the fire smoldering. "Justice for Maverick, and for whoever's been buried by time and influence."

"Unraveling three decades of silence won't be a small feat, but Ron's on his way over with more information. We'll see what he's dug up."

"Good. I ordered pizza so we could keep working."

JP took his beagle, Louie, out for a walk, and when he returned, Ron was there with his laptop all set up and ready to go.

"Find anything new yet?" JP tapped his fingers on the wooden table.

"Maybe." Ron didn't look up. "Apparently, a woman named Elise Harrington went missing. She was engaged to Thomas Callahan who was initially the prime suspect. Then the police focus switched to his father. It looks like she was caught in a web. One article suggests she wanted out, but feared the consequences."

"Like what?"

"Family ties. You know how these wealthy clans operate. She knew too much, probably." Ron turned his screen and showed JP a grainy photograph of a young woman with haunted eyes. "Her friends said that before she vanished, she'd been acting strangely, even paranoid. Afraid someone was following her."

"Sounds like she was scared for her life." JP furrowed his brows. "Then she just disappeared without a trace in the same spot where Maverick swears he saw a woman murdered? That's no coincidence."

Ron scrolled down for more information. "No body was ever found, and the case went cold quicker than it should have. I suppose that's no surprise with the Callahans involved."

JP studied the image of Elise frozen in time. It was like she seemed to be reaching out, begging them to uncover her story. "She was a stunning woman."

"What color is her hair?" Sabre asked.

"I think they call it strawberry blonde." He handed the photo to Sabre.

"Maverick said the woman or women he saw had reddish-blonde hair."

"Maybe he did see Elise's ghost," Ron said.

JP scowled at Ron. "Keep digging. There's got to be something we're missing," JP urged. "We owe it to Maverick—and to Elise—to piece this together."

"Will do." Ron nodded, determination set in his jaw. "If the Callahans are behind this, they've done a hell of a job covering their tracks. But everyone slips up eventually."

"Let's hope they slipped up thirty years ago," JP said, "and left us a trail to find now."

"Wow!" Ron exclaimed.

"What did you find?"

"Elise Harrington was going home the night she disappeared. She lived in the house where Maverick now lives."

Chapter 17

Thursday afternoon

JP stepped into DuBois' office, noticing that the chair he'd sat in an hour ago was now covered with files.

"McCloud. You're back," DuBois rolled his eyes. "Have a seat." He cleared the guest chair again.

"Thanks." JP settled into it.

DuBois held out a thin folder, its edges worn from frequent handling.

"Everything we've got on Elise Harrington," DuBois said.

JP flipped open the cover and scanned the pages for patterns in the chaos, for the thread that would help them.

"Anything jumping out at you?" DuBois asked.

"Still looking."

"Her friends and family were cooperative at the time, but nobody's seen hide nor hair of her since she vanished."

JP didn't respond, his focus riveted to the few pages of evidence. Every now and then, he made a soft noise of consideration.

"She apparently went out for the evening and never came home. Her father reported her missing the next day when he found her car parked out front, but no Elise."

"So, someone was probably watching for her to get home, and then nabbed her," DuBois said.

"And look here." JP tapped a forensic report. "No real evidence was found. It had been raining hard that night, and it probably washed away. This report did mention some trace elements found on a bush, fibers that didn't match anything related to Elise or her family. They could be from the perp, but we'd need something to match them to."

DuBois reached for the report, then scanned the highlighted text. "The fibers could've come from someone walking by, or kids playing, or any number of things."

"True enough," JP said. "There sure isn't much in this file."

"Because nobody saw anything." DuBois pushed up his glasses. "Except this one." He handed a witness statement to JP. " A neighbor claims she saw a man loitering around Elise's home the night she disappeared and an old car around the corner."

JP snatched the paper and read the report. A description caught his eye. "This part about the man she saw...tall, dark trench coat, well-built?"

"What about it?" DuBois responded.

"Sounds like Maverick's description."

"Could be. But it's still vague."

"Does the description fit Thomas Callahan?" JP asked.

"He's a wealthy guy with fingers in half the city's pies, so he's been on TV and in the papers a lot." DuBois raised an eyebrow. "I guess it fits his description, but it also fits a million other men."

"Where there's money, there's motive," JP said.

"Money has a way of complicating things," DuBois agreed.

JP picked up a police report and glanced through it. "Callahan's alibi says he was at a charity gala the night Elise disappeared. A room full of witnesses."

"That's convenient. But I'm sure someone with Callahan's resources could've slipped out unnoticed."

"I'll take a look at his past. If Callahan's hiding something, maybe I can sniff it out. Hidden motives have a way of clawing their way to the surface."

"Be careful," DuBois cautioned. "People like Callahan don't play by our rules."

"Never expected 'em to." JP grinned. "Makes it more interesting."

"You know what this means, don't you, McCloud?"

"No. But I'm sure you're about to tell me."

"Maverick is probably re-telling an old ghost story."

"How would he even know about it? He wasn't even born when this happened."

"You can find anything on the internet these days. Somebody probably told him there was a *murder* in his yard and he looked it up."

"That's one explanation."

"Got any others?"

"Not yet, but you'll be the first to know."

With a firm nod to DuBois, JP strode to the door. He squared his shoulders, extending a roughened hand toward DuBois. "Appreciate all this," he said. "I'll keep you looped in."

"Counting on it, McCloud," DuBois replied, grasping JP's hand firmly.

Releasing the handshake, JP swung open the door of the cluttered office. The hallway outside was quiet, the muted sounds of distant conversations barely creeping through the walls. He strode down the corridor. Once outside, the crisp air hit his face, a welcome slap of reality against the skin. The drive back home was a blur of stoplights and honking horns, the cacophony of city life. JP replayed the conversation with DuBois—the witness statements, the alibi—and had a gut feeling that if he solved the old crime, he would solve the current one. They had to be connected. There were too many overlaps. *Or, was Maverick just acting out some old unsolved crime?*

At home, he settled behind his desk and created a list of people who were connected to Elise Harrington and/or Thomas Callahan. JP tracked down their phone numbers and entered the data into a spreadsheet on his screen. He annotated each entry with probing questions he would use to peel back the layers of Elise's life.

Feeling ready, he picked up his cell phone and called the first person on the list, the witness who saw the man in the trench coat.

"Hello." A soft voice on the other end.

"Good evening. My name is JP Torn. I'm looking for a woman named Nancy Yates."

"I don't know anyone by that name. You've got the wrong number."

"I apologize. Do you mind telling me how long you've had this number?"

"About ten years, maybe."

"Thanks. Sorry to bother you." JP hung up and made a mental note to see if he could find more information about Nancy Yates.

The second call connected to a groggy voice, still tethered to sleep despite the mid-day hour. JP introduced himself and tried to ease the witness into wakefulness before delving into his inquiry. But the witness said she'd never known Elise, that maybe her grandmother had, but she'd passed on several years earlier.

"Thank you for your time." JP hung up. Two down, a dozen more to go.

Midway through punching in the third number, Sabre's name flashed on his screen. He cancelled the other call and took hers.

"Tell me you've got something good," Sabre said.

"Good afternoon, Counselor," JP said cheerfully. "As a matter of fact, I might be onto a lead. DuBois had a file on the Elise

Harrington case. Thomas Callahan's been scrubbed cleaner than a preacher's conscience, but I've got a hunch."

"That's the guy Elise was engaged to, right?"

"The one and only. His alibi's tighter than a drum, but there's a rhythm that doesn't match the music."

"Meaning?"

"It's too perfect. Like it was manufactured. I'm calling some folks who were at the gala to see what I can find out."

"That's great, JP. But even if we discredit Callahan's alibi, or prove who killed Elise Harrington, how will that help Maverick?"

"I don't know for sure, but it's all we've got to work with right now."

Chapter 18

Friday morning

JP parked in front of Mrs. Jenkins' weather-worn house again. He eyed the curtained windows for a sign of movement. He knew the old lady was wary of company, especially when it came to digging through the past.

"Mrs. Jenkins!" JP rapped his knuckles on the door. "It's JP Torn. We need to talk."

The door opened just enough for one suspicious eye to peer through the gap. "I told you everything I know the last time," she said, her voice frail.

"Ma'am, I wouldn't be here if it wasn't important. There are pieces missing, and I really think you can help. It's about Elise Harrington."

A long silence followed, punctuated only by the caw of a crow. Finally, the door swung open, and Mrs. Jenkins ushered him in.

"All right." She sighed, and gestured to the floral-patterned couch again. "I'll tell you what I can."

JP sat and pulled a notepad and pen from his pocket. "I assume since she lived next door, you knew her fairly well, am I right?"

"Elise was like a daughter to me." Mrs. Jenkins gaze drifted to a photograph on the mantelpiece of two beautiful, young women, one with dark curly hair, the other a strawberry blonde. "We were very close."

"How did you become so close?"

"She was best friends with my daughter, Katy."

"Is that them in the photograph?" He pointed to the mantel.

"Yes, that was their senior year. They had known each other since first grade and had big plans to go to college together, but that never materialized." She looked down at her feet.

"Because Elise disappeared?"

Mrs. Jenkins shook her head.

"What happened?"

"My daughter had an aneurism in her brain and died suddenly during her high school graduation ceremony."

"I'm so sorry."

"It's okay." But there was a deep sadness in her voice. "It was many years ago, and although you never get over something like that, time has helped dull the pain." She took a deep breath and went on. "Elise's kidnapping was a tragedy too."

"You think she was kidnapped?"

A pause. "I know there was a murder investigation, but I'd like to think she's still out there somewhere living a good life. I know it's silly, but it helps me."

"I've read that the Callahans may have been involved somehow. Do you think that's likely?"

"Maybe. There was something between Elise and Harper Callahan."

"I thought she was dating his brother, Thomas."

"Yes. Elise was engaged to Thomas, set to join the Callahan family and all their... influence. But when Harper came home from college that summer, he stole her heart." Mrs. Jenkins' twisted her hands in her lap. "They thought they were careful, but I saw them together several times—looks that lingered too long, hushed conversations when they thought no one was listening."

"Did she know that you knew?"

"I talked to her and tried to make her see reason, but Elise denied it all, at first. She said she was marrying Thomas and that she and Harper were just friends."

"Did Thomas know?" JP asked.

"Thomas was a proud man." A shadow crossed her features. "If he knew, he never let on. But the heart wants what it wants, and Elise wanted Harper."

JP could almost see the picture she painted—a forbidden romance blooming under the watchful eye of an imposing family dynasty. The kind of thing that usually ended in tragedy.

"You said she denied it at first, did she eventually tell you the truth?"

Mrs. Jenkins nodded, a faraway look in her eyes as she delved into a past laden with secrets. "Their affair was like something out of a novel. They'd slip away to the old boathouse by the lake, where they could be away from prying eyes." Her voice wavered. "They would take separate cars and meet there whenever they could. Only at night, when they were less likely to get caught."

"Was Elise with him the night she disappeared?"

"Yes."

"Do you think Harper could've been involved?" JP asked.

"No." She answered quickly, giving JP an earnest stare. "Harper would never hurt anyone. He's the only Callahan with a heart."

"Did anyone else know about Elise and Harper? Any suspicions?" JP probed.

"Only whispers," Mrs. Jenkins conceded. "But whispers can be as telling as shouts in a rich community like theirs. I don't think Elise told anyone else, and I never said a word," she said. "But the walls have ears, especially among the privileged.

Their passion was intense. You could feel the energy around them. I tried to tell her how obvious it was and that she needed to cut it off with one or the other."

"Why didn't she just break up with Thomas?"

"She was too afraid of what he might do if she humiliated him. As the eldest, Thomas was in line to be the head of the Callahan dynasty."

"But Harper was a Callahan too. Didn't he have any clout?"

"He wasn't like Thomas. He wasn't greedy and didn't really want the family fortune."

"So, why didn't they just run off together?"

"Harper was afraid of his father. He needed money for medical school, and his father was footing the bill. Old man Callahan was a tyrant, and Thomas was molded in his image. But eventually, Harper and Elise couldn't bear the secrecy any longer," Mrs. Jenkins continued. "They planned to reveal their relationship, consequences be damned. They wanted to be free to love each other without hiding."

"She told you that?"

"Yes. Elise came to my house the night before she disappeared and told me they planned to confront Thomas together in a few days." The old woman looked pensive.

"What is it?" JP asked.

"She said they would have more information the next day, and that would cinch it."

"Do you know what she meant?"

"Not really. I thought maybe they had something on Thomas. Maybe they caught him cheating or something, but she wouldn't tell me anything else."

"But they never revealed their affair because Elise disappeared before they could?"

"That's right."

"And Thomas was the prime suspect?"

"Not for long. After his alibi was verified, his father, Patrick, became the suspect for a hot minute, but that was hushed up really quick."

"And they never found Elise?"

"No." Her expression changed and her eyes darted to the window, then to the door, as if expecting shadows to spring to life.

"Your identity will be kept strictly confidential," JP promised. "You have my word on it."

She frowned. "I know you mean well, but Thomas Callahan is not a man to be crossed. Their family has so much power. And they use it to silence anyone who dares stand against them."

JP knew the kind. They wielded power like a preacher wields the Bible. The Callahans were more than just a wealthy family; they were a dynasty that could make or break the lives of those around them.

"Was Harper ever a suspect?"

"No. Once the Callahans squashed the investigation, it all went away."

"What happened to Harper?"

"He went back to college, then to med school. He comes home occasionally, but not that often." Mrs. Jenkins looked into JP's eyes. "Be careful. The Callahans have friends in places you wouldn't expect."

"Understood." JP paused. "I'm curious, Mrs. Jenkins. Last time I was here it was about the disturbance at the Venables' house. Why aren't you surprised that now I'm digging into the Harrington case?"

"I don't know what the kid saw." She shrugged. "But I used to see the ghosts all the time on rainy nights. I know it was just my mind playing tricks on me. Guilt maybe."

"Why would you feel guilty?"

"Because I should've done more to get Elise to stop her affair with Harper. Maybe that would've saved her."

“And maybe not.” JP took her hand. "Thank you, Mrs. Jenkins. Your bravery today means a lot." His assurance was cut short by the shrill ring of the landline telephone.

Mrs. Jenkins' eyes snapped toward the intrusive sound. She lifted a shaking hand to answer, her eyes never leaving JP.

"Hello?" Her voice was taut. As she listened to the caller, her face drained of color, her knuckles whitening around the phone.

"Mrs. Jenkins?" JP asked. “Is everything alright?"

She didn't answer, her focus pinned to the caller and her free hand gripping the hem of her apron. "Understood," Mrs. Jenkins whispered, her voice barely carrying. She set the receiver down with a gentle click.

"Who was that?"

Her eyes met his, swirling with a fear that hadn't been there moments before. "You need to leave. Now."

JP frowned, the pieces not yet aligning. "But we're not finished—"

"Please." The word was clipped, almost desperate. "Just go. And don't come back here. It's not safe—for either of us."

"All right, I'll go. But if you're in danger—"

"I'm not," she cut in sharply. "Just... take care, Mr. Torn."

"Call me if you need—"

"Go!"

Her urgency propelled him to get up. "Okay, I'm going."

In his truck, JP called Ron and asked him to come over and do some surveillance. Then he drove down the street a short distance and waited. He didn't want to leave Mrs. Jenkins unguarded. He feared that he had put the poor woman in jeopardy.

Chapter 19

Friday late morning

Sabre looked up as JP entered her work office. "I'm glad you're here."

"You call, I come, darlin'."

"Do you still think we should pursue the Harrington case?"

"What Maverick saw happened in the same spot Elise Harrington disappeared from. What are the chances that the crimes were committed in the same place—and aren't connected?"

It seemed unlikely to her too. "That means either there's a copycat killer or Maverick is seeing ghosts."

"Or, Maverick is aware of the earlier crime and is playing it for attention." JP took a deep breath. "But you don't believe that."

"It's certainly the simplest answer."

"Have you brought it up with him? Maybe ask him right out."

"No. I haven't."

"Do you mind if I do?"

"Not at all. I know it's a possibility, but we have to pursue his claims as if they were true."

"And it seems the only way to do that is to figure out why the current events are similar to the Harrington case.

The information from Mrs. Jenkins shed a lot of light on the situation."

"And the investigation starts with the Callahan family?"

JP removed his hat and ran a hand through his hair. "Yup. The Callahans are key. Elise Harrington's case being ice cold for nearly thirty years doesn't sit right with me. There's something they're hiding, something we need to dig up."

They turned their attention to the bits and pieces they had managed to learn about the missing woman. JP picked up an old news article with a photograph of the Callahan estate. "This place has seen more secrets than a confessional. Do you think we should dig into property records? See what kind of skeletons we can shake from the closets of this ancestral home?"

"Good idea."

Sabre turned to her computer and started scouring digital archives, combing through social media profiles with the smiling faces of the Callahans staring back. They dissected every image and post for hidden meanings or connections to Elise. They also scanned dozens of newspaper articles. Almost everything the Callahans did got media attention, but none of the information helped. There was very little published about Elise's disappearance.

"It looks like the media was squelched too," Sabre said.

"You'd think in a town this size, that wouldn't be so easy," JP said.

"If they have that much power, how are we going to find out anything?"

"There's more than one way to break a dog from sucking eggs."

Sabre smiled at the quaint expression. "Like what?"

"We'll find ex-employees and friends of the Callahans and start questioning them. Elise's connections too."

They put together a list and JP pocketed it. When he stood to leave, Sabre said, "By the way, my car won't be done until tomorrow. Please come back and pick me up when you're done."

"You got it, darlin'."

~~~

JP smiled at the woman sitting across from him in the coffee shop. "Ma'am, I understand that you used to work for the Callahans. Any insights you can share would be appreciated."

Darla, a former housekeeper with nervous eyes, fiddled with her mug. "I don't know much," she whispered, glancing around as if someone might be listening. "They were always kind to me, but there was... tension, secret meetings, late-night phone calls. I never asked questions."

"Did they ever mention someone named Elise?" JP pressed.

"Elise?" Darla's face paled visibly. "No. I never heard that name."

"Are you certain? She went missing about thirty years ago. Her name was Elise Harrington. It would've been at the time you worked there."

"I think I remember hearing something about that."

"Do you recall that she was engaged to Thomas Callahan?"

"Oh, yeah. But it didn't last long. If I remember right, she took off and basically dumped him. Look, I've got to get back to work. My break is up."

"Can we talk later?"

She shook her head, then in a stern voice said, "I don't have anything to say about the Callahans."

"Thank you for your time," JP called out as she walked away.

He moved on to the next name. Ida Quick lived nearby, so he drove over. She invited him into her home and quickly closed the door. JP settled into the worn leather chair across from her, noticing that her fingers were laced together so tightly that her knuckles had turned white. The blinds were closed and the air was stale with the scent of old coffee and anxiety.
~~~

"Ma'am, I just need to know about your time working for the Callahans," JP said.

Ida hesitated, glancing toward the door as if she regretted letting him in. "I signed a non-disclosure agreement."

"Which doesn't apply to criminal investigations," JP countered, sliding a document across the table. He was bluffing, but she didn't know that.

"The Callahans were very particular about privacy. I can't—"

"Elise Harrington's family has been without answers for thirty years," JP interjected sharply. "If you know something that could help you need to tell me."

"Okay." She exhaled sharply. "But I don't really know anything for certain."

"What do you know?"

"There were a lot of hushed conversations after Elise disappeared."

"Did Thomas seem upset that she was gone or possibly dead?"

"He claimed he broke up with her and started spreading the word that she was so upset she left town."

"Did you believe him?"

"It doesn't matter what I believed. I didn't really know anything for sure."

"Did Elise's name ever come up in family conversations? Any talk about her?" JP prodded.

"Once, I heard Mr. Callahan yelling about a mistake that couldn't be fixed. About 'the girl who disappeared.' That's all I know." Ida's words tumbled out.

"By Mr. Callahan, do you mean Thomas or Harper?"

"No. It was their father, Patrick Callahan."

~~~

JP's next stop was the lavish neighborhood where the Callahans resided. JP approached the only house that didn't have a fence around it, but it was just as lavish as the other
~~~

houses. The perfectly manicured lawn and gardens in the front yard looked like something out of a magazine.

He walked up to the neighbor's door and knocked.

"Good afternoon," JP greeted the middle-aged man who answered. "We're investigating an old case and wondered if you might be able to help."

"What old case?"

"Nearly thirty years ago, a woman named Elise Harrington disappeared. The authorities thought she might have been murdered. Do you remember hearing about it?"

"I do," he said. "Why? Did they find her?"

"No. But new evidence has come to light."

"What do you want from me?"

"I have some questions about the Callahans."

"I'm sorry I can't help you." He abruptly closed the door.

JP continued on his neighborhood quest, but he either got a similar response or the homeowner was too new to the area to know anything about the possible murder.

His last stop was at the home of Wendy and Harold Greer, friends of the Callahan family. The gate was open, so he drove down the driveway to a house big enough to be called a mansion. A fifty-something woman answered the door, blinked a few times when he introduced himself and his mission, then invited him in. Wendy summoned her husband, and the couple sat stiffly on an antique loveseat, their hands clasped together like a lifeline.

"Thanks for agreeing to talk with me." JP eased into an armchair across from them.

"Of course." Wendy's voice was tight. "Anything to help clear up this mess."

JP leaned forward. "I'm trying to understand the Callahan family dynamic a little better. You've been close to them for years, correct?"

"That's right," Harold chimed in. "Good people, the Callahans."

"Can you think of any reason someone would want to connect them to Elise Harrington's disappearance?" JP asked.

Wendy exchanged a quick glance with Harold before answering. "Certainly not. It was such a tragedy what happened to that poor girl. We all felt it here in the community, especially poor Thomas. He was devastated."

"I thought Thomas had broken up with her."

"But he still felt awful that she just left and never looked back."

"Indeed." JP noted the rehearsed quality of their responses. "Was there any talk about the Callahans having issues with Elise?"

"Nothing but normal neighborhood chatter." Harold shifted uncomfortably. "You know how people talk."

"Right." JP decided to push a little further. "Did any of that neighborhood chatter ever strike you as... odd?"

"Look, Mr. Torn," Wendy interjected, frustration in her voice. "We're not ones to gossip. The Callahans were good to us, and we've never seen anything that would make us think otherwise."

"Understandable." JP stood. "Thank you for talking with me."

He tried two more homes, but no one was there. It was time to meet with Thomas Callahan.

Chapter 20

Friday afternoon

JP drove his truck up to the colossal gate for the wrought iron fence that surrounded the Callahan property. He pushed the buzzer and announced himself, expecting to be turned away, but to his surprise, the gate opened. He stepped out of his truck and made his way to the front of the Callahan estate. The grandeur of the place didn't faze him; it was just another scene in a long career of digging through façades. He approached the entrance and pressed the doorbell. Moments later, the heavy oak door swung inward, answered by Thomas Callahan himself. Wearing a suit that cost more than JP's monthly mortgage, Callahan smiled smugly, like he'd already won some unspoken game. The Greers had probably called and warned him that JP was in the neighborhood, asking questions.

"Mr. Torn." Thomas' voice was smooth, almost slippery. "Please, come in. What brings a Texas cowboy such as yourself all the way to my humble abode?"

"Please call me JP." He stepped over the threshold, taking in the opulence of the foyer, then fixing his eyes on Thomas. "I expect you already know why I'm here, Mr. Callahan. After all, you allowed me in your home with little introduction, and I'm not all that well-known."

“There’s not much I don’t know when it comes to my family.” Thomas' smile faltered for a fraction of a second. "Let us discuss this further in the living room, shall we?"

"Lead the way.”

The space was vast, more a museum than a place of comfort, its walls adorned by oil paintings and shelves lined with first editions. JP's boots left faint impressions on the Persian rug as he followed Thomas Callahan inside. At the far end of the room Patrick Callahan, a once-formidable patriarch, now sat motionless in a wheelchair. The man had little muscle mass, but JP could tell by his frame that he had likely been quite a physical force as well. His eyes, sharp despite his silence, tracked every movement. The air seemed to hum with unspoken words around him. JP nodded in his direction, an acknowledgment of the old man's presence. A blond, well-built man in his sixties stood next to him.

"Ah, my father." Thomas mistook JP's attention for curiosity. "A stroke robbed him of his voice, but not his mind. He still watches over us like the silent guardian of this estate."

“And the man with him?”

“His long-time friend, Lars. He has become a caretaker of sorts, mostly just keeps him company.”

"I’m sorry to hear about your father’s stroke." JP settled into an armchair across from Thomas. "That’s not an easy thing for a family to deal with.”

“But you’re not here about my father, are you?”

“Let's talk about Elise Harrington.”

Thomas maintained his composure, but JP’s attention was on Patrick Callahan, the silent titan seated in the wheelchair. At the mention of Elise's name, something flickered across the old man's weathered features—a barely discernible twitch at the corner of his mouth, a slight narrowing of his eyes. It was gone in an instant, but to an experienced observer like him, it might as well have been a shout.

Thomas let out a sigh. "Elise ... yes. She was the love of my life. When she disappeared, it was as if the sun had been blotted out of my sky." There was a practiced sorrow in his eyes, too polished to be entirely believable.

"And nobody's seen her in nearly thirty years?"

"Quite right." Thomas' smugness seeped through his veneer of grief. "But believe me when I say I spared no expense in trying to find her. Private investigators, psychics, you name it. I've poured more into that search than most people earn in a lifetime." He gestured to the opulence surrounding them, as if to underline his point.

“Is there any chance she didn't want to be found?” JP asked.

“You mean, did she dump me?”

“People have lots of reasons for leaving,” JP said. “I'm not suggesting it was because of you.”

“At first, I couldn't admit that was a possibility. It hurt my ego, but I suppose you're right. She may have.”

“You were the prime suspect, correct?”

“I was until they checked my alibi. The cops always look at the one closest to the victim, don't they?"

“And where were you exactly?”

“I assume you already know the answer to that, JP, but I'll humor you.” Thomas waved a dismissive hand. "I attended a charity event that night at the Marston House. Hundreds of guests can attest to my presence. It was quite the affair." He smiled nostalgically.

“When did you leave the event?”

“Not until it ended. It was very public. My engagement with society is well documented. Elise Harrington—”

"Sorry I'm late," a jovial voice interrupted. A young man, not more than thirty, strode into the living room with an easy confidence. He extended a hand toward JP with a friendly grin. "Ian Callahan."

JP noted the firm grip and bright curiosity in Ian's eyes. "JP, private investigator." He glanced at Thomas, who watched the exchange with a hint of pride.

“I heard you mention Elise Harrington. Isn’t she the woman my grandfather was accused of killing?" Ian’s tone was laced with a mix of curiosity and concern.

Thomas let out a derisive chuckle, straightening the lapels of his expensive suit, as if to brush off the question along with any lint. "My father? Accused of murder? It's absurd," he said with a smug smile that didn't quite reach his eyes. "The police were grasping at straws. They thought it was me, then him." He gestured casually toward Patrick. "But they never even had a body. We still don’t know if she was killed. I pray every day that she was not."

“It is quite the mystery, Dad. You have to admit that."

"Indeed, it is," JP replied cautiously.

Thomas gave a nonchalant wave of his hand. "Ian's got a mind for solving things, a real hotshot in the tech world." He laughed softly, but JP caught a glimpse of something guarded behind his eyes. "He solves problems that most people can't even begin to understand."

"Is that so?" JP turned toward Ian with renewed interest.

"The truth is that my dad doesn’t quite understand what I do for a living, but I’ve been very lucky to become quite successful in my chosen field." Ian’s tone wasn’t arrogant like his father’s. In fact, he seemed almost humble. "But this mystery is far more complex than what I do. It's about people. And sometimes, people are the hardest puzzles to solve."

"Especially when they have secrets." JP glanced between the two men for a sign of discomfort.

"Everyone has secrets," Ian said smoothly. "Doesn't necessarily mean there's anything sinister behind them."

JP’s thoughts raced. "Sometimes secrets are kept to protect, and other times, to harm. Knowing which is which—that's the key."

"Speaking of keys," Ian said, "I should check on the old man before dinner." He gestured toward Patrick, who sat silently, his expression unreadable.

"Of course," Thomas interjected quickly. "Before he gets too tired."

Ian turned to JP. "It was nice meeting you. I hope you find what you're looking for."

"Thank you." JP watched Ian head toward his grandfather. A part of him hungered for a chance to speak with Patrick alone. But he would need to tread carefully; the Callahans were a clever bunch. JP pivoted to Thomas. "I'd like to speak with your father, if I may." His gaze drifted to the older man in the wheelchair, whose presence seemed to cast a long shadow over the room despite his silence.

Thomas stepped between JP and Patrick, blocking any possibility of communication. "I'm afraid that's not possible. My father's health isn't what it used to be. He's not up for questioning. Besides, he can't really communicate."

"Even a few minutes could—" JP began.

But Thomas shook his head, his charm replaced by cold refusal. "Non-negotiable."

Frustration knotted in JP's stomach. He suspected that Patrick held answers that could break the case wide open. But for now, Thomas' barricade was insurmountable.

"Very well," JP said. "I will respect your family's privacy."

As he turned to leave, he glanced at Patrick again and saw another flicker of something in the old man's eyes. Fear? Regret? Recognition?

"Let us know if you need anything further," Thomas offered, his voice smooth as silk but lacking warmth. "And good luck with your investigation. I've lived under this cloud of suspicion for too long, JP. I want this matter resolved just as much as you do."

"I'm sure you do," JP said, his gaze drifting momentarily back to the silent figure in the wheelchair. Patrick Callahan stared back at him, unreadable yet undeniably intense.

"Now, if there's nothing else, I have matters to attend to. You'll find your way out?"

"Thank you, I will."

"Take care now," Ian said with an earnest tilt of his head.

"Appreciate it, son," JP replied without turning back. The encounter had been sterile, too rehearsed.

Reaching his truck, JP took a last look at the grand façade of the Callahan home. He didn't have any more facts, but he now had a good understanding of the players. He climbed into the driver's seat and fired up the engine. The familiar rumble was comforting. As JP headed down the long driveway, the Callahan estate disappeared in his rearview mirror. But its imprint lingered, a nagging sensation that he had just walked over someone's grave. The case was more than cold; it was frozen in a block of ice that the Callahans had kept chilled for thirty years.

On the road, his phone buzzed with an incoming text from Sabre. JP pulled over and read the text: *How did it go?*

Like talking to a brick wall, he typed back. *I'll tell you about it when I pick you up. I'm on my way.*

~~~

Sabre was ready to leave when JP arrived at her office. On the ride home, he told her about each interview. "I learned very little, except that no one wants to talk against the Callahans."

The rest of the drive was silent, each lost in thought until Sabre's phone rang with an incoming call. She glanced at the screen—*Unknown Number*—and hesitated before answering.

"Hello?" She popped on the speaker.

"Drop the case," a voice hissed, distorted and unrecognizable. "Or you'll end up like Elise."
~~~

The call ended abruptly, leaving a chilling silence. Sabre tightened her grip around the phone, the threat echoing in her ears.

"Damn!" JP said. "I don't like this."

"We must be getting close to something."

"Yeah, too close. I don't want you in the middle of anything that puts you in danger."

She looked at JP with a steady gaze. "You know I'm not backing down. Especially not now."

Chapter 21

Friday afternoon

Ron adjusted his seat to be more comfortable as he watched Mrs. Jenkins' home. He checked his watch, noting the routine comings and goings of the neighborhood. A dog walker passed by twice and a mailman delivered letters, but nothing connected to the Callahan family or the cold case stood out. Ron kept his eyes peeled for anything out of the ordinary—a task made challenging by how ordinary everything seemed to be. A cat slinked along the sidewalk before disappearing into the shrubbery, and Ron noted the time in his head, though he knew it was inconsequential. No visitors, no mysterious packages—just the slow tick of time.

Ron's phone rang, and he recognized the name on his screen. "Hi, Rosemarie."

"Hi. We have Wednesday at ten o'clock for you to present Lily's case to the board."

"Do you think there will be any problems?"

"Just make sure you have all the facts, a treatment program laid out, and a plan to keep it anonymous."

"Oh, that's all," Ron said. "I've got this covered."

Ron ruminated over his presentation to the board as the afternoon wore on with little action. A few cars coming and going, mostly people appearing to be returning from work. Darkness came early this time of year, so lights started to flick on in the houses around him. The same with Mrs. Jenkins' home. It wasn't long before the lights downstairs went out and a light came on in the upstairs window. It wasn't that late, only five after seven, but she was an elderly widow, and maybe she went to bed early. Ron reached for his camera, ready to capture any fleeting evidence just in case she had a nocturnal visitor. He waited and watched, but never saw anything other than her occasional shadow through the curtain. Part of him hoped to see something, just out of boredom, yet he really didn't want the old woman to get hurt.

When the lights went out in the bedroom, he started to text JP and ask how long he should stay. Then, as if on cue, a car rolled down the street, its lights off, coasting silently until it stopped a few houses down. A figure emerged, glancing furtively around before hustling toward Mrs. Jenkins' house. Ron's pulse quickened. Camera in hand, he snapped a series of photos, capturing the stranger's profile. Then the young man stopped and stood against the wall of the house next door. A teenage girl came out from the back, and they got in his car and drove away.

Ron's phone vibrated against the dashboard, startling him. It was JP.

"I was just about to call you," Ron said.

"Anything exciting going on there?"

"Just a couple of teenagers sneaking out of the house next door. Other than that, not a thing. I think Mrs. Jenkins has gone to bed. Do you want me stay and watch?"

"No. You can't be there around the clock. We'll just have to do some random checks. You can go back tomorrow at a different time of day."

~~~

Sabre and JP settled into their regular routine at home—dinner, homework with the kids, then sending them off to their rooms. They sat down together on the sofa,
~~~

supposedly to relax, but Sabre opened her laptop and started another search.

"Anything from Ron's stakeout?" she asked without looking up.

"Zilch," JP replied. "Except for a late-night visitor to the girl next door. Ron got photos."

Sabre's attention reverted to the site she had loaded. "Look at this. Thirty years ago, the Callahans suddenly sold off a chunk of their property. No explanation, no follow-up investment."

"Before or after Elise vanished?"

"After. And they made a donation to a local foundation around the same time. It's like they were trying to cleanse something more than just their conscience."

"Maybe they were buying some silence."

"We need more on the family's past. There's something we're missing, something buried deep."

"I'm concerned about that threatening call. If it was from the Callahans, that's scary because they're pretty powerful."

"It could be any of my cases."

"That makes me feel better," JP said sarcastically. "Are you working anything sketchy right now?"

"Not really, but I ain't scared," Sabre said in a goofy voice.

"That's what bothers me. You should be."

"I promise I'll be careful."

"Regardless, you need to report it." JP said. "The problem is we don't even know who we're looking for. If the threat is from the Callahans, they probably aren't doing it themselves. We don't know what kind of henchmen they have."

"Or, who told them we were investigating."

JP looked through the list of people he'd interviewed. "My best guess is the Greers. They're close friends, and they skirted around questions and seemed too eager to dismiss any link to Thomas."

Sabre continued her search online. Her eyes scanned the screen, absorbing the endless list of legal documents and court filings associated with the Callahan family. "Speaking of Thomas. I've been researching the Callahans' history. Thomas is a big-time real estate mogul and developer. And apparently, major litigant. Look." She turned her laptop screen toward JP. "It's a legal swamp. Look at this—dozens of lawsuits, most of them settled quietly out of court. Huge payoffs, gag orders—you name it. It's his MO to cheat and silence. It's a mess. Lawsuits everywhere. It looks like he's made a habit of squeezing people dry."

With a skeptical frown, JP said, "Sounds pretty standard for big-time developers. They always have lawsuits."

"Not this many. And Tommy boy is following in his dad's footsteps. Patrick has the same kind of history."

"We knew we weren't dealing with a saint."

Sabre closed her laptop. "So, now what?"

"Now we go to bed. Tomorrow, I re-visit the Greer mansion."

As they stood, the ringtone from JP's phone went off. He fumbled to answer, putting the call on speaker.

"It's Vinny. I have news, but you might want to sit down for this."

They exchanged a glance. "Go ahead. We're listening."

"The evidence box for Elise Harrington's case is empty. Someone stole everything out of it."

Sabre's hand flew to her mouth. "The evidence ... "

"Gone." DuBois confirmed grimly. "Everything relating to Harrington or any evidence that the Callahans were involved—gone."

"Convenient timing," JP growled, his jaw tightening.

"Too convenient," Sabre agreed.

"When did it happen?" JP asked.

"We don't know. The last record of someone looking in the evidence box was years ago. No one has touched this case in nearly thirty years. It was only discovered because I tried to see it."

"So, you have no idea when it disappeared?"

"No. The evidence clerk has been questioned, and he's still under suspicion because it's his responsibility to keep every box safe. But there have been several clerks since that evidence was logged, and the original one has since passed away."

"Don't they ever inventory the boxes?"

"They do for a while after the initial investigation, but cold cases are often just forgotten about. There's just too much to keep track of."

JP sighed. "So, no one knows what was actually in there?"

"No. These days everything is listed in the database, but back then, that didn't happen. But whatever was in there, someone was afraid it might be incriminating."

"Thanks for the heads-up, DuBois."

"Wait, there's more," DuBois added. "There's a rumor that a suspicious character has been hanging around the precinct, asking questions about old evidence. He's a tall guy wearing cowboy boots and a black Stetson."

"Dang it! They're trying to frame me." JP clenched his fist.

"But it's all hype. You *have* been hanging around the precinct because you've been coming to see me. There's plenty of security cameras to show exactly where you went. It's not like anything is going to come of it. They're just trying to scare you off."

"I got the message, but I ain't scared."

"Be careful."

"I will. By the way, Sabre got a phone call that you should know about." JP told him what it said and then sent him a message with the time and date.

"I'll see what I can find out. And I'll call you if I get anything else." DuBois hung up.

"Someone's out to get us," Sabre said. "And they're not just covering tracks; they're counterattacking."

"Then we're hitting nerves and digging in the right graves," JP said, standing tall despite the target now on his back.

Chapter 22

Saturday morning

JP's pickup truck rumbled up the long driveway with towering oaks flanking the sides. He parked in front of the mansion, only a half mile from the Callahan estate.

Stepping out of the truck, JP squared his shoulders. As he approached the ornate double doors, they opened, and Mrs. Greer stood there in a tailored suit that spoke volumes about her wealth.

"Mr. Torn," she greeted. "This is an unexpected pleasure."

"Ma'am." JP nodded.

He was not surprised when she invited him in. That was the polite thing to do. He stepped into the opulent foyer. "We need to talk about Sabre's anonymous text."

Mrs. Greer's eyes narrowed." I don't know anything about that."

JP studied her closely. "What about the Callahans? Have you mentioned to them that I've been asking questions?"

"It may have come up."

"Why would you do that?"

"You *were* asking questions about them." She exhaled softly. "I didn't realize it was a secret, and it seemed prudent that they should be aware."

"Prudent because they're your friends, or because there's more to the story?"

"Mr. Torn," she said sharply, "my loyalties lie where they must. Now, if you'll excuse me..." She turned toward the door, signaling the end of the conversation.

"Mrs. Greer," JP said, his voice firm. "Elise Harrington deserves justice. If you know something—"

"Good day." Her dismissal was final. She opened the door and he stepped out.

As he left the estate, JP's mind raced. Wendy Greer had admitted to warning the Callahans, and that admission put her right in the middle of the tangled web he was trying to unravel. It put them one step closer to Thomas Callahan.

JP climbed in his truck and made his way back home. Sabre had taken the girls shoe shopping, and Conner was with his friend Aiden, so JP was alone except for their dog, Louie. JP sat down at his desk, booted his computer, and started looking through old newspaper articles for anything about the Callahans.

The family had spent a lot of time in the limelight. In his younger days, Patrick Callahan was often pictured with one of his prize-winning horses. JP read a couple of the articles, then quickly discovered a familiar name. Quaid Gearhart was a long-time employee, who managed Patrick's stables. With a little more research, JP determined it was the same Quaid Gearhart who lived on the street near Maverick.

"Interesting," JP said aloud, the gears in his mind turning rapidly. He leaned back, stroking his chin stubble thoughtfully. Why hadn't Gearhart told him that? Was it loyalty or fear that held his tongue? Time to find out.

~~~

The drive to Gearhart's place only took fifteen minutes. JP had been to the neighborhood often enough to know the route well. When he arrived, JP saw a faint glow in the living room. He rapped his knuckles against the heavy oak door, its aged wood groaning in response. A minute passed before Gearhart answered, scowling.
~~~

"Good afternoon," JP said. "Mind if I come in for a spell?"

"Why are you here again?" Gearhart snapped.

"Because I just learned you worked for Patrick Callahan, a detail you didn't bother to mention last time we talked."

After a brief hesitation, Gearhart stepped aside. "Come on in." JP followed Gearhart into the kitchen, where the old man put on a pot for tea. While it heated, they sat across from each other at the dining table.

"I appreciate your hospitality." JP wanted to ease into the conversation. "Mind if I ask why you didn't mention working for Patrick?"

"You never asked."

"But you knew that a crime had been committed in the same spot that Maverick reported seeing one. You'd think that might be suspicious, right?"

"To some, maybe. But you didn't ask about that. You gotta ask what you want to know."

"Fair enough. Now I'm askin'. What can you tell me about that night thirty years ago?"

Gearhart shifted uncomfortably. "Well, sir, I don't tell ghost stories."

That nonsense again. "Why would you call it that?"

"Because digging up the past is like calling out to spirits best left alone," Gearhart replied.

Intrigued, JP leaned forward. "I feel like it's my job to bring those spirits to rest. And now, I'm inclined to believe you saw something the night Elise went missing."

For a moment, Gearhart seemed lost in thought, then he whispered, "I did see something. And it didn't sit right with me."

"Go on," JP urged.

Gearhart swallowed hard. "There was a car ... one I recognized." His voice trailed off, and he swallowed hard.

"Whose car?" JP pressed.

"Can't ..." Gearhart hesitated, a shiver running through him. "I shouldn't say more."

"Mr. Gearhart, anything you can tell me could make a difference."

"Yeah, for both of us." Gearhart looked as though he might crumble under the weight of his secret. He opened his mouth, hovered on the edge of disclosure, then snapped it shut.

"Did the car belong to one of the Callahans?"

"Sorry, but I've said too much already. You should go." Gearhart abruptly stood.

Disappointed, JP rose as well, knowing when to retreat. "Think about it, please. If you change your mind, you know how to reach me."

Gearhart nodded mutely, then escorted JP to the front. As JP stepped out into the night, the door closed behind him with finality.

Chapter 23

Saturday afternoon

Ron drummed his fingers anxiously on the steering wheel, staring at Mrs. Jenkin's quaint front porch. The neighborhood was quiet. Ron had parked under a sprawling magnolia. He knew he stuck out, even here; his car mismatched among the family sedans and rugged SUVs lining the street.

A blue Hyundai SUV pulled up in front of Mrs. Jenkins' home, and a man climbed out. He appeared to be in his late forties or early fifties, with a salt-and-pepper beard and a wary look in his eye. His presence was unexpected, an anomaly in the routine Ron had been observing for two days.

He snatched up his phone from the passenger seat and called JP.

"We've got a situation at the Jenkins' place. A man just arrived and is going into her house. Could be nothing, but I don't like it."

"Describe him."

"Forties, about six feet tall, and looks like he's trying too hard to blend in." Ron watched as the man glanced down the street.

"Stay put. I'm on my way." JP's reply was curt, and the connection went dead before Ron could respond.

He leaned back, his eyes still locked on the man who had now reached the front door. He knocked, and Mrs. Jenkins let him in.

"Who are you?" Ron muttered under his breath.

~~~

JP pulled up and parked behind Ron, then stopped briefly to speak to him. "Any movement since we talked?"

"Nothing," Ron said. "What now?"

"I'll knock on Mrs. Jenkins' door and make sure she isn't in danger."

"Want me to go with you?"

"No. Stay here and keep an eye on us." JP handed him an envelope.

"What's this?"

"It's a subpoena for Quaid Gearhart to testify at Maverick's trial. You go serve him after I see what's going on with Mrs. Jenkins. I'd do it myself, but he may not come to the door if he sees it's me."

"Will do."

~~~

JP unsnapped his gun holster, then rapped on the weathered doorframe. "Mrs. Jenkins."

The door opened cautiously, and Mrs. Jenkins stood there, her face etched with worry. JP took in the scene, noting the man who hovered protectively behind her.

"Ma'am, are you all right?"

"Oh, JP. Yes, I'm fine." Her voice trembled slightly. "This is my son, Ford."

JP felt both relieved and a little embarrassed.

"Mr. Torn, nice to meet you." The man stepped forward with an open hand. JP realized Ford knew his name. *Had Mrs. Jenkins told him?*

"Sorry for the intrusion," JP said. "Just making sure everything's on the level here." His eyes never left Ford's, looking for the signs of deception he'd come to recognize in his line of work.

"Understandable." Ford nodded.

"Mind if we talk a moment, Mrs. Jenkins?" JP gestured away from the front door.

"Of course." She stepped outside, closing the door partway, leaving her son inside.

But he quickly followed them out. "Mom, is everything okay?" Ford hovered near Mrs. Jenkins, his body language protective but not overbearing.

JP watched them closely. He'd seen too many charades to take anything at face value. But as he observed the way Ford's hand touched his mother's shoulder, the way she responded to him, and the tenderness in her voice—it became clear they were bonded.

"Everything's fine, Ford," Mrs. Jenkins said. "This is the investigator I told you about."

"I figured that out when you called him by name." Ford turned to JP. "Mom has been scared ever since you talked to her. She is uncomfortable with what that teenage boy claims to have seen, and she doesn't want to be alone. And she's been getting a lot of strange phone calls. Maybe we need to hire you to check into those calls."

"What kind of calls?"

"Mostly hang ups, but they come at all hours of the day." He paused. "Anyway, I'm taking her home with me for a few days." He turned to his mother. "Everything's gonna be okay, Ma." The son's tone was warm and his posture relaxed.

"Are you sure?" Mrs. Jenkins' voice trembled again.

"Absolutely." Ford wrapped an arm around her.

JP watched closely, scrutinizing Ford's every gesture. The way his brows knitted together in concern, the slight tilt of his head as he listened to his mother—it all seemed genuine.

"Mom, look at me." Ford's voice softened. "You'll be safe. You can come back when this is over."

JP's practiced eyes searched for cracks in the façade, but none surfaced. As they spoke, he noticed the subtle exchange of familiar glances and the comfort that seemed to envelop Mrs. Jenkins like a well-worn blanket. JP had seen enough family reunions to recognize the signs—the authentic display of bonds that couldn't be faked.

"Thank you," Mrs. Jenkins murmured, a sigh escaping as she allowed her son to wrap her in a gentle hug.

"I apologize," JP said. "I just wanted to make sure your mother was safe. She seemed uneasy after we talked."

"No worries," Ford said. "We appreciate your vigilance."

"Would you mind giving me your phone number in case I need to reach you?" JP asked.

"You think she might be in danger?"

"Can't say for sure," JP replied honestly. "But I'd like to be prepared to reach out. Just in case."

"Sure. Give me your number and I'll call it." JP handed him his card.

When they finished, JP said, "Keep your eyes peeled and my number handy. Call me if anything—anything at all—feels off."

"Will do." Ford pocketed the card. "And thanks for watching over my mother."

JP walked past Ron's car to his truck, got inside, then called Ron. "I didn't stop in case they were watching. I think he's legit, but I want to make sure. Serve the subpoena, then stick around until they leave and follow them. Let me know where they go."

Chapter 24

Saturday late afternoon

Ron walked across the street and approached the small, weather-beaten house. Shadows spread across the cracked pavement as he climbed the steps to the porch. He paused for a moment, tightening his grip on the crisp envelope containing the subpoena.

He rang the doorbell, then waited, listening for movement inside. After a few moments, shuffling footsteps approached the door. It creaked open, and Gearhart appeared.

"Mr. Quaid Gearhart?" Ron asked, forcing himself to sound calm.

The door opened a bit wider, revealing a man in his late sixties, with a lined face and tired eyes. "Yeah, that's me," he replied.

Ron handed him the envelope. "You've been served."

"For what?" The envelope shook in his hand.

"It's for you to testify in Maverick's trial."

Gearhart's eyes flashed with fear and resentment. He stared at the envelope, still trembling, then tried to hand it back.

"I don't want to get involved," Gearhart muttered. "I didn't see anything worth talking about."

Ron took a deep breath. "Mr. Gearhart, I understand this is difficult. But what you saw could be crucial to the truth coming out. Maverick's future depends on it."

The old man's eyes darted around, as if seeking an escape. "I saw enough to know that getting involved will only bring trouble."

"It could go a long way to help an innocent kid."

A tense silence settled between them. The sounds of the neighborhood—children playing, a distant lawnmower—seemed to fade into the background.

"I'll be there," he finally said. "But I can't promise it'll help."

Ron offered a small, reassuring smile. "That's all we ask. Just tell the truth."

Back in his car, Ron called JP to let him know the paperwork had been served.

Twenty minutes later, Mrs. Jenkins came out and climbed into her son's car. Ford followed and shoved a large overnight bag in the back, and they drove off. Ron waited a minute, then got on the road, his gaze locked on the SUV ahead. He kept his distance, with two or three cars between them, blending into the traffic as if he were just another commuter on his way home.

As they left the bustling city center behind, the scenery shifted dramatically. They entered Rancho Bernardo, an idyllic suburban community with well-maintained houses and lawns so meticulously groomed they could have been green velvet.

Ron eased off the accelerator, letting the car coast along the peaceful streets passing one red-tiled roof after another. Each house looked more inviting than the last, their façades warm with the glow of the sun. It was the kind of place where neighbors held backyard barbecues and children played catch in the streets.

He checked his rearview mirror for any sign that he or Ford were being followed. Ron knew better than to let his guard down. He slowed as the SUV turned into a driveway. Ron coasted to a stop a few houses back, glancing between the rearview mirror and the house the Jenkins had stopped at. It was a beautiful home with more of the same Spanish tiles and a well-tended garden that spoke of affluence and care.

Ron squinted as he scrutinized every corner, every parked car that lined the sun-drenched street.

He killed the engine and waited. Suddenly, the front door burst open, spilling laughter onto the quiet street. A woman with chestnut hair stepped out, followed by two teenage girls, their ponytails swinging like pendulums.

"Grandma!" the girls chorused, their voices intertwining as they flung themselves into Mrs. Jenkins' open arms. A few seconds later, a young boy about ten years old shot out of the house with a similar display of affection for his grandmother. The woman's face transformed, her wrinkles becoming fault lines of joy as she enveloped them in her embrace. Their affection was substantial, the kind that spoke of Sunday dinners and shared secrets. Ron's heart was momentarily lightened by the scene. Then he retrieved his phone and called JP.

"It's Ron. The Jenkins are in Rancho Bernardo at what looks like Ford's home with his wife and kids."

"Got it," JP's voice crackled through the line. "Anything else?"

"Nothing suspicious and no one followed us," Ron replied.

"Good work," JP said. "But I think you've done enough there. Time to head back and keep an eye on Sabre."

"Is something wrong?"

"Nothing new, but I'm still concerned about the anonymous call she got." JP paused. "She's at her law office, and I expect she's there alone. Neither David or Hugh work much on the weekends. Go there, hang out, make sure she gets to her car safely, then follow her home. I'll be there when you get there."

"Do you remember last time we did that? Sabre was furious."

"And she'll be furious again, but she'll be safe and that's what counts, right?"

"Right." Ron couldn't keep the sarcasm out of his remark. "See you in a bit."

Chapter 25

Saturday evening

As the kids cleaned up after dinner, JP chatted with Ron and Sabre. They tried to stay away from talk about the case, but it kept coming up, finally interrupted by a call from DuBois.

"There's somewhere I need to take you." He sounded a little worked up. "It's not far from here and will only take about an hour."

"Tonight?"

"Yes. Trust me, it's important. You want to do this."

"Just tell me what it is."

"Nope. You gotta wait."

"All right. You want me to meet you somewhere?"

"Yeah. In your driveway. I'm already here."

JP pushed up from his seat, explained briefly where he was going, and went out the door.

The drive was quiet except for JP's occasional attempt to find out where they were going. Finally, DuBois pulled up to a small house on a corner lot in an aging neighborhood.

"Here we are." DuBois' voice carried a hint of nostalgia. "This is where I grew up."

"This is what you *had* to show me? Urgently?"

"You'll see."

JP surveyed the modest home, taking in the peeling paint and overgrown garden, and wondering what kind of life his friend must have had there.

"Come on." DuBois motioned toward the front entry. "Let's go inside."

As they approached, the door opened, and an old man stood in the threshold. He looked vaguely familiar, and JP suddenly realized he was DuBois' father, a retired cop he'd met long ago when they were both in the department. His gray hair had thinned, and a network of wrinkles etched deep into his weathered face. Yet, there was a steeliness in his eyes that hinted at the sharp mind beneath the frail exterior.

"Vinny!" His voice was gravelly with age but warm with recognition. "And you brought company."

"Pop, this is JP Torn," DuBois said. "JP, my dad, O'Neil."

JP tipped his Stetson. "I believe we met once when I was a rookie."

"Please, come in." O'Neil stepped aside with an inviting gesture. The living room they entered was a patchwork of memories and bachelorhood. Framed photographs competed for space with scattered sports magazines, and a lopsided recliner was the centerpiece of mismatched furniture.

"JP's working a case, Pop. It may be connected to the Harrington murder from thirty years ago," Vinny said.

"Chasing ghosts, are you?" O'Neil's eyes sharpened with curiosity. "Harrington. That's a name I haven't heard in years."

JP caught the glint in the old man's eyes. He had more than just a passing interest. "You remember it?"

"So well."

"Mind if we talk about it?" JP cut straight to the chase as he perched on the edge of a sturdy sofa.

"By all means." O'Neil plopped into the recliner. "I'm all ears, but I'm not sure how much help I'll be. It was a long time ago, and there wasn't much to go on."

"Let's start with the basics, Mr. DuBois," JP said. "What was your role in the Harrington investigation?"

"Please call me O'Neil. It makes me feel very old when a man your age calls me mister." He shifted in his recliner, the leather creaking under his meager weight. "I was lead detective on the case for about a minute." He shook his head. "But then they pulled me off."

"Reassigned?"

"Yep." O'Neil nodded, a note of bitterness threading through his words. "Just when I was getting my teeth into it, they yanked me. Threw me onto some drug-ring circus uptown."

"Any idea why?"

"Probably politics. I never got the full story. Of course, they claimed it was because I was needed so badly on the other case."

"Before you were pulled, what did you make of it?"

O'Neil's eyes narrowed. "I'm pretty sure Elise Harrington was murdered. And I'd bet my pension that Thomas Callahan had his hands dirty."

"You seem as sure as the sun sets in the west."

A smile ignited in O'Neil's eyes. "The evidence we started to pull together was pointing right at him. He was too cool, too collected. His alibi was backed up by all his friends, and there were inconsistencies—" The old man broke off, a cough rattling his chest.

JP waited it out.

"His family acted odd too. Like they were holding back. Protecting him, or hiding something themselves." O'Neil's eyes drifted, perhaps seeing the past more clearly than the present.

"Did you collect anything concrete?" JP asked.

"Enough to have 'em squirming. But then I got reassigned, and my replacement ... let's just say he wasn't as convinced."

JP's jaw tightened. "So, if you initiated the case, you must've written a report. I didn't see one with your name on it in the file."

O'Neil DuBois exhaled heavily, his breath sounding like the rustle of old parchment. He ran a gnarled hand through his thinning gray hair. "After I was pulled from the case, my notes, my observations ... all vanished. Only the clean, polished reports from my successor remained." His eyes clouded with suspicion. "Misplaced or accidentally discarded—that's what I was told."

JP's frustration simmered. "That report could've been key to understanding the Harrington case," he said. "Do you have any other notes? Anything you might have hung on to?"

"Back then, I kept everything. But without that report ..." His voice trailed off.

"Any personal notes? Records? Anything at all?" JP pressed.

A spark of recollection behind his sharp eyes. "I just might have something. Back then, we had to write all our reports by hand or type them. I wasn't much of a typist so I would write them immediately when everything was fresh in my mind. But my handwriting was terrible, so I would re-write them. The first version was a bit of a mess."

"Did you offer it when your file went missing?"

"No. I was too skeptical of the politics. And I had notes as well."

"You said *had*." Vinny spoke up. "Are they gone?"

"Nope. I never threw anything away from a case." He smiled at his son. "Don't you remember how your mother would complain about the extra junk, as she called it?"

Vinny smiled.

"Where are they?" JP asked.

The old man's hands, once steady and unyielding, now trembled as he gestured toward the back of the house.

"I kept all my notes in the shed out back."

"I'd be as happy as a hog in slop to help find them," JP offered.

"Me too, Pops." Vinny said. "Not quite the way McCloud said it, but glad to help." He looked at his dad with pride. "I knew you'd come through for us."

"Don't thank me yet, son. There's a lot of papers to go through to find what you need. Lots of boxes and lots of junk. They've been buried for years."

"When would be a good time for you?"

"Tomorrow. First light."

"That works for me," JP said.

"I can do that." Vinny nodded.

"Good. Because I'm at my sharpest in the mornings."

"Then it's settled." JP rose from his seat.

As JP reached the doorway, the old man called out, "Thanks for not letting this go. It's haunted me for years."

JP nodded solemnly.

Chapter 26

Sunday morning

The first light of dawn was barely brushing the sky as JP stepped out of his truck. The air was crisp, just the way he liked it. He glanced at his watch, which read 0600, military time. When he left the Marine Corps years ago, he used military time for a year or so. It made more sense to him, so he was trying it again. He wasn't so sure it was going to be comfortable now.

"Right on time," Vinny called from his dad's porch.

"Wouldn't want to keep you city folks waitin'," JP replied.

O'Neil appeared at the door. "I hope you're ready to get dusty." His laugh triggered another coughing spell.

The trio made their way to the shed tucked away at the back of the property. It was an old structure, its wood siding weathered by years of neglect. A graveyard of discarded items—rusted garden tools, broken chairs, and boxes swollen with moisture—littered the path leading up to it.

"Looks like we've got our work cut out for us," JP muttered.

"Yep," Vinny agreed. "Let's hope Elise Harrington's secrets didn't get buried under all this mess."

They pushed open the creaking door, and the musty smell of neglect washed over them. Inside, chaos reigned. Decades of accumulated debris lay strewn about. Camping equipment, boxes filled with who-knew-what, and various junk formed a formidable barricade between them and their goal—the boxes at the back containing notes from a case nearly as old as the shed.

JP surveyed the clutter. "Dang!"

Vinny took one look and just shook his head.

O'Neil followed them inside. "Good lord. This is worse than I remembered." His cough punctuated the stillness.

"Take it easy, Pops," Vinny advised. "We can handle the heavy lifting." Vinny clapped a hand on his dad's shoulder.

"Thanks, son, but I'll be damned if I'm not going to help find those notes."

Vinny cracked his knuckles. "Let's see what secrets this tin can holds."

"Looks like we'll have to dig a path," JP said.

"Careful where you tread," Vinny warned. "Wouldn't want to stumble on a nest of rattlers or rats."

JP pushed aside a stack of old newspapers, their headlines faded into obscurity.

"You sure you need all this stuff?" Vinny grunted as he hoisted a worn-out patio table onto its side. "Feels like half of this could go straight to the thrift store or the dump."

"You're right, son," O'Neil wiped his brow. "But for now, let's focus on clearing enough space to find those boxes."

JP glanced at the pile of junk amassing outside. "I'd be glad to help carry this away."

Vinny surveyed the mess with a critical eye, then turned to JP. "What say we clear out some of this junk first? Make our lives easier. I can swing by later with a trailer and get rid of it."

JP gave a nod. "My truck's outside. We may as well load her up, and I'll take care of it today."

"Good idea."

They moved into action, working in tandem, a silent rhythm developing as they heaved an assortment of discarded memories into the bed of JP's truck. Each item approved by O'Neil.

The old man pitched in where he could, despite the cough that rattled ominously in his chest. The morning sun climbed higher, spilling light through the cracked panes and illuminating the dust motes that danced in their new-found freedom.

Vinny paused to check his watch, then sighed. "Time's ticking. Let's hustle."

With a final heave, the last of the junk was loaded onto the truck, revealing a path to the back where the boxes lay in wait like slumbering secrets.

"Hey, Vinny, remember the Robertson case?" O'Neil wheezed out between coughs, as he leaned against a workbench littered with old paint cans.

"How could I forget? You chased that lead like a bloodhound."

"Turned out to be nothing," O'Neil said, his eyes distant. "The killer was someone we never even considered until the last minute."

"Often the way, isn't it?" JP remarked, sliding an old lawn mower onto the bed of the truck with a grunt. He straightened up and looked at O'Neil, the concern evident on his rugged face. "You need to sit this one out, partner?"

"Nope. I'm good," O'Neil rasped, pushing off from the bench to prove a point. He let out a series of coughs, each one seeming to steal another piece of his vigor.

JP pulled a tarp off a stack of boxes, revealing more potential hiding spots for the elusive notes they sought.

From the threshold of the shed, O'Neil's eyes lit with excitement. "Just like the old days, eh? Digging through the muck for the glint of gold."

"I'm sure you were in your element," JP said.

"Ah, but the stories!" O'Neil exclaimed. "Every case, every piece of evidence ... they're all chapters in the grand book of justice. That reminds me of ..." O'Neil launched into another story about the old days that made them all laugh.

"Almost there." JP eyed the corner of the shed where the evidence boxes awaited. He noticed the tremor in O'Neil's hands as he pointed to another stack of boxes. "Take a break, O'Neil. We got this."

O'Neil shook his head stubbornly.

As they moved stacks of newspapers, the old man's movements slowed. A bead of sweat trailed down his temple, and his laughter had a hint of strain.

"All right, O'Neil, that's enough," JP placed a supportive hand on the old man's shoulder. "We'll pick up where we left off tomorrow."

"I'm good for a little more." O'Neil said, but he was struggling to catch his breath, his chest rising and falling more rapidly with each movement.

Concerned, JP encouraged him to sit. "You did good today, but we'll handle it from here."

The old man's face suddenly drained of color. Vinny rushed over, but his dad abruptly collapsed, taking down a shelf of paint.

"Call 911!"

JP was already on it.

The two men kneeled next to O'Neil, who was conscious, but slow to respond.

"How do you feel? Is it your heart?" Vinny sounded scared for the first time JP had ever witnessed.

"Uh ... I'm ... just a little dizzy."

"Probably dehydration or exhaustion," JP suggested. "I'll get him some water."

For eight minutes they waited, feeling helpless to do much. Finally, the ambulance arrived, and paramedics loaded the old guy into the back and started an IV line.

"I'll meet you there," Vinny called to his Pops before they slammed the back doors.

"Do you want me go with you?" JP asked.

"Thanks, but no. He's tough, and as you said, it's probably just dehydration. He hates water, but he can't drink beer anymore." Vinny laughed, but it was a hollow sound. "We'll finish up in the morning," Vinny said.

Chapter 27

Sunday early afternoon

JP climbed into his truck, the scent of dust and leather mixing as he settled into the driver's seat. He glanced back at the load of junk that once cluttered the shed they'd been sifting through for clues.

The drive to the VA thrift store was short, and JP spent most of it worrying about DuBois' dad. Upon arrival, the volunteer staff greeted him with smiles and grateful nods as he helped unload the items.

"Appreciate ya, sir," said a young volunteer.

"Happy to help," JP replied, tipping his hat. "You folks do good work here."

Back in his truck, JP drove to the dump. One by one, he tossed the remnants into the designated areas, the sound of breaking wood and clattering metal punctuating the end of their usefulness.

With the day's physical labor behind him, JP returned to the sanctuary of his home office. He sank into his desk chair, wondering what to do next on Maverick's case. He was stumped. He cast a long, contemplative look at the cluttered desk, his eyes settling on a copy of Gearhart's subpoena. He decided to check in with him and pin down his testimony. He headed back to his truck.

Within twenty minutes, he pulled up to Gearhart's home. His sharp eyes immediately caught the change in the atmosphere—most of the curtains that were once open to let in the morning light now were drawn.

He got out of the truck and hurried to the front door. A pair of mockingbirds chattered in the nearby oak tree, their melodic duet hanging in the otherwise quiet air.

"Gearhart," JP called out, with a firm rap on the wooden door. Seconds ticked by without a hint of movement from inside the house. He knocked again, louder this time.

"Dang it, Gearhart." He grabbed the doorknob and gave it a turn. Locked. He briefly entertained the possibility that Gearhart had simply stepped out for an errand, but a nagging in his gut told him otherwise.

JP took several steps back and surveyed the windows, searching for a sign that might betray Gearhart's presence—a shifted curtain, a fleeting shadow. It occurred to him that Gearhart might be avoiding him.

He circled the home's perimeter, pausing at each window with an open curtain and pressing his face close to the glass, each view offering fragmented glimpses of Gearhart's life—a half-empty coffee cup on the kitchen counter, a newspaper spread open on the couch. It was as if the man had vanished into thin air, leaving behind only the ghost of his daily routine.

A sudden chill ran down JP's spine. This case had already taken its share of twists and turns, but if Gearhart has disappeared ... that was more than even JP had anticipated. Now, standing outside the locked home of a key witness, JP realized the stakes had risen.

He reached into his pocket, retrieved his cell phone, and called Gearhart's number. As he did, he could hear the phone ringing inside the house. "Come on, pick up," he coaxed.

But the call slid into voicemail, and JP spoke into the digital void. "Gearhart, it's JP. I'm outside your house, and I need you to call me back pronto. There's something we gotta go over about the case. It's urgent."

With no answer forthcoming, JP scrolled through his contacts and called DuBois.

"Miss me already, McCloud?"

"You sound chipper. Is your dad all right?"

"Yeah. I just took him home and got him settled in. He pushed too hard and didn't hydrate. You know, like a real man."

JP laughed, then got back to his own predicament. "I'm at Quaid Gearhart's house. He's a prime witness on the McLaughlin case. I saw him a few days ago, and Ron served him with a subpoena. And now, he's gone. The house is locked up tighter than a drum, all but three of the curtains are drawn, and there's no sign of the man. I've got a bad feeling, DuBois. Could be he just skipped town, but with this case, I don't trust that he's safe."

"Or maybe he just went to the store?"

"I don't think so."

"Or maybe he's left town, so he doesn't have to go to court."

"That's possible, but something doesn't feel right."

"Sit tight. I have to pass by there anyway. I'll be there in ten, and we'll take a look together."

"Appreciate it." JP ended the call, then paced in front of Gearhart's silent house. He cast another long glance at the drawn curtains, imagining scenarios that might explain the sudden disappearance of their key witness. *Had he fled? Was he inside but unable to answer the door or the phone? Or had someone gotten to him?*

DuBois soon pulled up in an unmarked cruiser and joined JP on the porch. "I hope you didn't get me out here on a wild goose chase."

"I hope I did."

DuBois fished out his badge and rapped sharply on the door. "Police!" His authoritative bellow broke the eerie quiet, yet the house offered no reply.

"Something ain't right here," JP said.

"Let's not jump to conclusions." DuBois' hand rested on the doorframe, his keen eyes scanning the perimeter. When no one answered, DuBois said, "Try his phone again."

JP called and they heard the ring, but got no response. They stepped off the porch to circle the perimeter of Gearhart's home again. The curtains remained drawn. JP's hand hovered near his gun, concealed beneath his jacket—a habit from years on the job.

"See anything?" DuBois kept his voice low as they approached a side window.

"Nothing." JP peered through the glass where he'd found the curtain open earlier.

"Let's try the back entrance," said DuBois, leading the way.

"I already did. It's locked." They approached the back door, its stoop empty and unwelcoming.

"No signs of tampering on the frame or lock."

"Everything seems too ... normal."

"Because maybe it is."

"Over there." JP gestured to a small wooden shed tucked into the corner of the backyard. Its door was slightly ajar. "Maybe he's holed up in there."

DuBois nodded, and together they approached the shed.

JP grabbed the cool metal of the shed's handle. With a hard pull, he swung the door wide open. They stepped inside, scanning for any sign of Gearhart.

The interior was a jumble of shadows and shapes. JP stepped inside first, the musty scent of earth and old wood filling his nostrils. He glanced around, noting the rusted garden shears and a tangle of hoses coiled like serpents in the corner. A dusty tarpaulin draped over something large and formless in the back. Together, they cautiously pulled back the tarp to find an old motorcycle that looked like it had not moved in at least a decade.

As they sifted through the clutter, the sudden trill of DuBois' phone sliced through their concentration. He glanced at the caller ID before answering.

"Detective DuBois."

JP watched the lines deepen around his eyes as he listened.

"Understood." DuBois ended the call, sliding the phone back into his pocket with a deliberate motion. He turned to face JP.

"Gearhart's daughter just reported him missing. He hasn't been seen since yesterday evening."

"Has she been in the house?"

"Yes. Last night and again this morning. He hasn't been here."

"Dang it. Do you still think I'm chasing ghosts?"

"Something's up for sure," DuBois said.

"Gearhart's our key witness, the only one who can add some credibility to Sabre's case. Besides that, he may have seen what happened to Elise that night. We can't let this trail go cold."

"I know, but there's not a lot I can do. Gearhart is a missing person, not a homicide investigation, and I'm not officially on the Harrington cold case. Although, I did get permission to have a look at it. There'll be very few resources, and my time is only allotted to when I'm not working on something else. That doesn't happen very often."

"His phone," JP mused. "If we can get Gearhart's phone, there might be information from recent callers."

"I'll try to get a warrant and see if we can get in."

Chapter 28

Sunday early evening

Unwilling to quit for the day, JP tried to figure his next move. He was out of prospective witnesses to either Maverick's sighting or the actual crime thirty years ago. He decided to see Maverick again. There were holes in the kid's story that needed filling, details that seemed just beyond reach, yet crucial to understanding what truly happened.

Driving to the Venable home where Maverick lived, JP rehearsed his questions, hoping to ensure he got the information he needed.

JP noticed the well-tended rose bushes as he walked up to the house and made his way to the front door. He knocked and the door swung open.

"Please, come in," Edie said, stepping aside as her husband appeared behind her. Gary Venable, a sturdy man with a demeanor that spoke of both kindness and a life of labor, extended his hand. JP clasped the offered hand, noting the callouses of someone not afraid to work hard. "Sit down, JP. Would you like something to drink?"

"Thank you, no," JP replied

"What brings you here this evening? I assume it has something to do with Maverick."

"Possibly. I have some questions about a crime that took place here thirty years ago. Does the name Elise Harrington mean anything to you?"

"That's a name I haven't heard in a long time. Why would you be bringing up something like that now?"

"Never thought I'd hear that name again," Gary murmured, shaking his head.

"Were you living here when it happened?"

Edie shook her head. "No, we moved in much later."

"We knew about the incident, though. It was quite the talk of the town—even after all these years. The folks who sold us the house made sure to mention it. Said it was only fair we knew what had happened here."

"Disturbing piece of history," Edie murmured.

Gary leaned back into the couch, his hands clasped together. "It was unsettling to hear, no doubt. But I don't believe in ghosts or curses so it didn't deter us from buying the place."

"Didn't think twice about it," Edie affirmed with a quick nod.

"Have you ever talked to Maverick about what happened here thirty years ago? About Elise Harrington?"

Gary exchanged a quick glance with Edie. "No, we haven't," Edie said.

"Do you think he could've heard about it somewhere else?"

"I suppose it's possible. It has become a bit of a neighborhood legend." Gary paused. "And you're thinking Maverick is telling an old 'ghost story' to get attention."

"I'm not saying that exactly. I'm trying to find out if that is even a possibility. And maybe if he's heard the story in the neighborhood, he actually thinks he saw it."

"I suppose that's possible. I can see why you'd ask. There are some similarities to what Maverick saw and the old crime, but it's not really like Maverick to make up stories like that."

"Where is Maverick now?" JP asked, standing.

"Upstairs, in his room," Gary answered, pointing towards the staircase. "I can call him down if you'd like."

"No, that won't be necessary." JP ascended the stairs.

At the top of the stairs, JP found Maverick's door ajar. The boy was slouched on the edge of an unmade bed, headphones on, lost in the world of music and adolescent dreams. JP knocked gently on the doorframe, and Maverick looked up, startled, pulling off the headphones.

"Come in," Maverick said.

"Evenin', Maverick," JP greeted. "Mind if we talk a bit?"

Maverick shrugged. "Guess not. I just don't know what else I could tell you."

"Have you ever heard about someone named Elise Harrington?" JP watched Maverick closely, searching for any flicker of recognition, any telltale sign.

"Elise who?" Maverick furrowed his brow, confusion etched across his young face. "No, I don't think so."

"Have you heard about a crime that took place near here many, many years ago?"

"How would I know that? I've only been here a few years."

"Sometimes kids in the neighborhood pass around ghost stories. Have you heard about any in this neighborhood?"

Maverick looked puzzled. "No. Why? What does this have to do with me?"

JP studied the boy's expression, looking for the micro-expressions that usually betrayed a lie. But Maverick's confusion seemed genuine, his eyes wide with curiosity rather than deceit. "Probably nothing."

JP pulled a chair up close to him. "I need you to think real hard for me. That second night you saw something—can you remember any details? Anything at all that might've seemed out of place?"

Maverick chewed on his lower lip, his forehead creasing with concentration. "It's just ... it was dark, ya know? And raining hard. And there was these shapes, like people, but they didn't move right. Kinda floated."

"Like a ghost?" JP pressed.

Maverick shook his head, frustrated. "I don't know what I saw! I don't believe in ghosts, but I swear I saw something weird."

"Take your time," JP encouraged.

"Wait!" Maverick suddenly looked up. "There was a sound, like a chain dragging."

"Good." JP jotted down the detail. "Anything else?"

Maverick sighed, sinking back. "No. Just sounds and shadows."

"All right." JP stood. "If you remember anything else, you call me, okay?"

"Sure," Maverick agreed, but his eyes were distant—caught in the memory of that night.

Leaving the room, JP felt frustrated. He needed a breakthrough, something concrete to go on. He glanced at his watch. Sabre had been checking more into the Callahans' lawsuits. Maybe she had some fresh perspective.

~~~

The house was quiet when JP entered, the clock on the wall ticking away the seconds with mechanical indifference. He found Sabre in her office wearing comfortable jeans and a loose shirt, her brown hair cascading over her shoulders.

"Hey," she greeted, looking up from a stack of files. "How'd it go with Maverick?"

"More shadows than light," JP admitted, pulling out a chair and sitting across from her. "Kid thinks he heard chains. It's something, but I don't know what to make of it."

Sabre pursed her lips, considering. "Chains could mean a lot of things."

"How about you?" JP asked. "Did you learn anything new about the Callahans?"
~~~

"Nothing that helps us here. Just more of the same. Just when I think I can't find anything worse on the Callahans, something pops up."

JP looked at the information Sabre had brought up. "That man is so crooked he could eat nails and spit screws."

She shook her head. "How about we set it all aside for the evening and enjoy some time with the kids."

"Good idea. Where are they?"

"The girls are in their room, and Conner went to pick up food. He wanted tacos from Maritza's, but it isn't open on Sunday, so the girls got what they wanted, Thai food. I don't care which, just so we can avoid cooking and clean up."

"That works for me."

"Good. How about movie night with popcorn? The kids always like that."

Before JP could respond, Conner walked in and set to-go bags on the table.

"Thanks, Conner," Sabre said.

He shrugged. "Any time I can drive your BMW is fine with me."

JP stood, ruffled the boy's hair, and said, "Get the girls, please."

"Morgan! Dené!" Conner bellowed. "Food's here!"

JP frowned at him. "I could've done that. I meant for you to go get them—quietly."

"Oops, sorry." Conner grinned sheepishly.

They all sat down to dinner, Morgan chattering through most of it.

"No wonder you're so skinny," Conner said to her. "You talk while the rest of us eat."

"I'm not skinny," Morgan retorted and continued with her chatter.

After dinner and much debate about which movie to watch, they finally settled on one. Conner gave in to Morgan's choice, which Dené also wanted.

"That was nice of you to let the girls choose," JP said.

"I mostly did it to get Morgan to stop talking."

JP squeezed his shoulder affectionately. He knew how kind Conner was, and how he would do anything for his little sister. He was also starting to treat Dené like a sister as well, which pleased Sabre.

After the kids went to bed, Sabre and JP relaxed on the sofa for a while, then headed for their bedroom. JP went to sleep almost immediately, only to be awakened by the shrill ring of his phone. He glanced at the time: 0415, and the caller ID read *Vinny DuBois*.

JP snapped up his phone. "What's goin' on, Vinny?"

"It's Pops. He's back in the hospital." Dubois was frantic, breathless.

"Oh no! What happened?"

"Someone set fire to his shed, and he collapsed again trying to put it out."

"I'll be right there."

Chapter 29

Monday early morning

JP pushed through the double doors of Scripps Hospital. The scent of antiseptic hung in the air.

"McCloud," a voice called softly as he entered room 217. Vinny sat slumped in a chair beside the hospital bed, looking as worn out as the man lying in it.

JP clapped a hand on his shoulder. "How's the old bull?"

"Been better." Vinny sighed. The elder DuBois was hooked up to an array of beeping monitors. "The fire took more out of him than we thought. He had a mild heart attack."

"I'm so sorry. He's gonna recover though, right?"

"Yeah. But we both know what this means."

"Talk to me," JP leaned against the wall, arms crossed.

"Darn shed went up faster than a tinderbox. Pops went after it with a hose before the fire department showed up." Vinny's voice was steady, but the tightness around his eyes betrayed his concern. "The smoke got to him, and with his lungs already in bad shape, he started coughing, then panicking."

JP understood the gravity of O'Neil's preexisting lung condition. "Any idea who would've set the fire?" He had his own idea, but wanted DuBois to get there first.

"Working on it." Vinny stared at his father's unconscious form. "He has ticked off a lot of people."

A long moment of silence.

Vinny turned to JP. "You think it's about the evidence we were looking for, don't you?"

"Seems rather cause and effect, right on the face of it."

"Yeah. We'll question the Callahans at some point. But right now, I'm just hoping he pulls through."

O'Neil's eyelids fluttered like moth wings against a lantern, then finally opened. JP noticed the subtle shift in his breathing, a sign of returning consciousness. The old man's eyes were cloudy, but they sharpened as soon as they saw his son.

"Vincent," O'Neil rasped.

"Take it slow, Pops." Vinny pulled his chair closer to the hospital bed. "You gave us quite the scare."

"Scare?" O'Neil chuckled, the sound turning into a cough. "You should've seen those cowards run."

"Tell me what you witnessed," Vinny urged. "But only if you're able."

"Two of them ... outside, at the shed." O'Neil lifted his hand, a weak effort, and pointed at the window, as if he could see the crime scene. "They had gas cans, and I shouted. Told 'em I'd shoot." He curled his fingers into a feeble imitation of a gun.

"Did you get a look at their faces?" JP asked.

The old man turned to him. "Sorry. Didn't see you there. Thanks for coming." After a moment, he remembered the question. "They were wearing ski masks. One had a torch. He threw it inside the shed as I came to the back door." O'Neil paused. "Torch guy was wearing gloves." O'Neil took a breath. "The other idiot wasn't. Dropped his can when I threatened to shoot him."

"Good," JP said. "Maybe he left us a fingerprint or two."

O'Neil's chest heaved with a sigh, and his head sank back against the pillow. "Scared rabbits. That's what they were."

"Cowards," Vinny said.

"I tried to stop them." O'Neil's voice was now barely above a whisper, as he turned to his son. "I wanted to stop them."

"You did what you could." Vinny reached out and touched his dad's hand. "Now rest. We'll take it from here."

"Didn't waste a second," O'Neil rasped, his voice dry as the desert air. "As soon as those cowards took off, I was on the phone with the fire department. Then I grabbed the garden hose and tried to beat back those flames."

"Any chance you remember something else about those two?" JP asked. "A build, height, anything?"

"You know I do. The stupid one with the can was six-foot, with long hair coming out of the back of his mask. He weighed about one-eighty, but ran like a girl." The old guy stopped to breathe. "The other was a short little scumbag. Five-eight at most, weighed about a hundred forty. And he threw the torch with his left hand."

"You didn't miss much."

"Even in the dark, they moved like they knew the land ... like they'd been there before." O'Neil's voice rasped as he resumed his tale. "They both wore dark clothing. Hoodies up, faces covered. Chickens."

"Your actions," JP said, "may not have saved your shed, but you kept it from spreading. Kept your house safe, your neighbors too."

"Wasn't about to let those bastards burn down my house," O'Neil growled defiantly. "Not without a fight." His hand quivered as he reached for the cup of water on the bedside table, his movements slow and deliberate. As he worked the liquid down, the room was quiet except for the rhythmic beep of the heart monitor.

"I'll head out and let you get some rest. You were very brave," JP said. He turned to leave, but not before a final, concerned glance at O'Neil, who had closed his eyes, exhaustion claiming him.

Vinny stood. "I'll walk you out." He turned to his dad. "Try to sleep, Pops. I'll be right back."

Out in the hall, Vinny said, "His shed is gone, JP. Burned to the ground. Everything in it is ash. The reports, my father's old notes ... anything that might've led us somewhere. It's all destroyed."

JP felt the room sway as he grasped the gravity of their loss. The boxes in the shed had been their best hope, the key to unlocking a cold case and hopefully saving Maverick. "Seems targeted and purposeful."

"You know it was," Vinny said. "They seem to know everything we're doing and they're attacking us from every angle. Sabre's anonymous phone call, the rumors about you at the police station, the disappearance of Mr. Gearhart, and now the destroyed evidence in the shed. It's not coincidental."

JP sighed. "I know you're right."

"Do you think it's Thomas Callahan?"

"That's my first choice," JP said. "He has a lot of clout and is so crooked he could hide behind a corkscrew."

"Thomas didn't set the fire himself—neither of the descriptions Dad gave fit him. But I wouldn't expect him to get his own hands dirty."

"That's good for us. If he's hiring people to do his dirty work, we have a better chance of catching them. The more they know about him, the more evidence we gather. I know he consistently gets away with things because of his power."

"Not this time." Vinny was adamant.

"Nope. He's messed with the wrong grizzlies!"

Chapter 30

Monday afternoon

JP Torn pushed through the automatic glass doors of Kohl's department store, the hum of commerce enveloping him. He scanned the bustling aisles for the manager, Shelby Williams. He had seen a photo online, so he had an idea of what she looked like, a beautiful woman with coal black hair, long eyelashes, bright red lipstick, and both arms heavily tattooed. Catching sight of her at the jewelry counter, he made his way past racks of discounted clothing.

When she finished speaking to an employee, JP approached. "Ms. Williams, I'm JP Torn. I'm a private investigator working on a case that involves your father."

She hesitated at first, then said, "I'm due for a break. Let's go somewhere we can talk privately." She slipped off her name tag and led JP out of the store. They walked in silence until they reached a Starbucks just across the parking lot, the aroma of roasted beans promising sanctuary from the outside world. Shelby chose a secluded table on the shaded patio, they sat opposite each other, the traffic's noise a distant murmur.

"What is this about?"

"Your father. I went to see him yesterday and he wasn't around. Then I was with Homicide Detective DuBois when he got the call that you had reported him missing."

"Why are you looking for him?"

"I'm working for an attorney who is representing a teenager accused of a crime he didn't commit. Your father has information that could clear him. We gave him a subpoena, but now it looks like he won't appear."

"Who's the kid?"

"Maverick McLaughlin."

Shelby seemed satisfied that JP was one of the good guys. She nodded, her eyes brimming with worry. "He hasn't answered any calls or texts for over twenty-four hours. That's not like him. He always lets me know where he is."

"Any idea what might've happened to him?"

She shook her head, strands of black hair falling into her anxious gaze. "Nothing. He just ... vanished. And now I don't know what to do." Her voice broke slightly.

"I understand this is tough," JP said softly. "Can you tell me about his recent activities or anyone he might've been in contact with before he disappeared?"

"He kept to himself mostly, but he mentioned some tension about something that happened years ago. He wouldn't tell me more, he just said it was 'nothing to fuss over.' But then ... he's gone." Her voice cracked on the last word.

"Did he mention any names? Anyone who might have had a motive to harm him?" JP was gentle but persistent, hoping to get her past the surface details.

"Callahan," she whispered, as though saying the name out loud would summon further misfortune. "They had a falling out years ago."

"Did he say which Callahan?"

"No. And he wouldn't tell me anything else."

"Did you tell the detective in Missing Persons?"

"Yes. Please, find my father." A desperate plea.

"We're doing all we can."

"I'm grateful for your help."

"I'll keep you updated with any progress. Should you hear anything at all, please call me right away."

"Thank you, JP. I just want him back."

Chapter 31

Tuesday morning

JP paced his quiet house, unsure of what to do next. He'd run out of leads, his only evidence had gone up in flames, and his star witness had disappeared. Determined to make progress anyway, JP reached for his phone. He thumbed through his contacts and found the number he'd added the other day and called it. He resumed pacing while he waited for Gearhart's daughter, Shelby Williams, to answer.

Each ring was a tick against his patience. Finally, the line clicked.

"Hello?" The voice on the other end was tentative.

"Ms. Williams? It's JP Torn," he said, his tone reassuring.

"Have you found my father?"

"No. I'm sorry. I was just checking in to see if you have."

A pause. "No, nothing," she finally replied, her voice quivering. "I've been carrying and checking my phone day and night, hoping for any word, but it's like he vanished into thin air."

"I know this is hard," JP said softly. "I'll check in with you later."

JP clicked off his phone and slid it into his jacket pocket. He headed out to his truck and drove to the hospital.

JP went directly to Room 217. Pushing open the door, he found Vinny slumped in a chair beside his dad's bed, his eyes weary but vigilant. The rhythmic hiss of oxygen punctuated the gap between the beeps of the heart monitor.

"McCloud," Vinny said, acknowledging JP with a nod that seemed to carry more exhaustion than greeting.

JP approached the bedside. "How's he holding up?"

"Much better. Docs say they'll release him with oxygen. Maybe a pacemaker down the road. Stubborn old man wants to go straight home instead of staying with me."

"Thinks he's still got nine lives, huh?" JP's gaze lingered on O'Neil, whose chest rose and fell with the help of the clear tubes beneath his nose.

"Something like that." Vinny's chuckle was devoid of humor.

"Got plans for getting him settled?"

"Workin' on it," Vinny said. "I'd like to get him a caretaker for a few days."

"Don't need no damn babysitter." The old man opened his eyes.

"Nothin' wrong with his hearing," JP said.

"Hi there, JP."

"You look a lot better than you did yesterday," JP said.

"Feeling fine." O'Neil coughed. "Ready to go home."

"All right. Let's get you home."

It took hours to get the paperwork done and O'Neil released, but by late afternoon, they arrived at his house. Vinny and JP maneuvered O'Neil's wheelchair across the threshold, and the old man breathed an audible sigh of relief.

"Let's get you comfortable, partner." Vinny guided the chair toward the living room.

JP followed, surveying the house for potential hazards that might complicate O'Neil's recovery.

Vinny stared out the window at the backyard. "I can't believe the shed is just gone."

"Whoever started that fire knew what we were after," JP said. "It's such a shame it's all lost."

"Not all of it " O'Neil's gravelly voice cut through the tension. "I grabbed the Harrington box before the fire caught it."

"What are you talking about, Pops?"

JP's heart surged with adrenaline. "Yeah. How did you pull that off?"

"I rested for a while after I got home from the hospital on Saturday, then I went out to the shed to look around. With the junk out of the way, I thought I could find it easily. And I did, so I brought it inside."

"Where is it, Pops?" Vinny's eyes were wide with hope.

"Behind the sofa."

Vinny retrieved the box and opened it.

"Is it the right one?" JP asked.

"Of course, it's the right one," O'Neil grumbled. "I ain't senile."

"We'll see." Vinny rifled through the contents, setting things aside. Finally, he pulled out a small notebook marked *Elise Harrington*. "Got it."

"That's it?" JP's hopes fell.

"That's all there is," O'Neil said. "Remember, I was only on the case a few days. All I have is the notes I took, but if I remember correctly, they were pretty extensive."

"Let's see what we've got." Vinny scanned the pages, reading aloud. "Elise Harrington's purse ... found at the scene, and there's a detailed list of the contents."

"Anything stand out?" JP asked.

"Standard stuff, mostly." Vinny ticked off the items. "Lipstick, tissue, hairbrush, keys." He moved his finger down the list. "Wallet with a Visa credit card, a photo, and forty dollars cash."

"Any ID on the keys?" JP interjected.

"Nothing noted. But this is interesting." Vinny's eyes sparked. "The notes say the photo is of Elise with another girl about her age." He squinted at the handwritten name. "Katy Jenkins—deceased."

"Elise's best friend growing up was a girl named Katy Jenkins, who lived next door," JP said. "She passed away at their high school graduation."

"How?" Vinny asked.

"Brain aneurysm," JP said, recalling his conversation with Mrs. Jenkins. "Katy's mother, Mrs. Jenkins, was very close to Elise," he added. "I think they brought each other comfort during their grief over Katy's death. Mrs. Jenkins lives next door to Maverick. I've questioned her, but she claims she didn't see anything thirty years ago, or even recently. What else you got?"

"This is interesting. It says there was an envelope in her purse with a sonogram in it and a note that reads *Elise...pregnant?* Do you remember that, Pops?"

"I had forgotten, but I do recall it now. I was trying to find out more, and that's when I was suddenly removed from the case. I never heard another word about it. And there was never anything in the news about it."

"Elise pregnant," JP mused aloud. "That changes the game."

"It sure does." Vinny raised his eyebrows, almost comically. "The question is, who was the baby daddy?"

Chapter 32

Wednesday morning

In the austere boardroom, Ron stood at the head of the polished mahogany table, his palms resting on its cool surface. He looked around, noting the stoic faces of the people who held the fate of his proposal in their hands.

"Thank you for considering my proposal today," Ron began. "I haven't requested a gift this large before, but I want you to give it your full consideration. It will give Lily Armstrong a chance at a much better life."

"Your proposal is quite different than anything your Aunt Goldie ever presented to us, Mr. Brown," one board member said, peering over her glasses. "But we're certainly willing to entertain it."

"Indeed, it is," Ron admitted. "But sometimes, unorthodox methods are what lead to the most extraordinary outcomes."

The members exchanged glances. Ron took a deep breath. "Let me explain why this isn't just a gift—it's an investment in hope." As Ron delved into the heart of his plea, the mood in the room seemed to shift. His words carried weight, each sentence imbued with his earnest desire to make a difference.

"Anonymous acts of kindness can transform lives," Ron concluded. "I believe we have the power to change Lily's life for the better, and I'm asking you to help me do that."

A silence enveloped the room as the board contemplated his proposal. Ron waited, watching their faces for a sign of their decision.

Worried, he tried again. "Williams Syndrome isn't just a diagnosis; it's a life sentence that Lily never asked for. But we have an opportunity to rewrite a part of her story."

The room was silent save for the hum of the air conditioner. "I want you to see something." Ron displayed photos on the projection screen showing Lily trying to maneuver in her limited world. In all of them, she wore her sweet smile.

"Imagine a world in which Lily can receive the medical procedures she needs, where her condition doesn't define her limits." He paused, meeting each gaze. "We can be the architects of that world."

"Exactly what are you proposing, Mr. Brown?" Rosemarie Doyle, the acting chairwoman, leaned forward.

"An anonymous donation that will cover all the costs for the facility willing to undertake her treatment." Ron didn't mention the amount, but the massive sum was in the document he'd handed out. "It's our shot to give Lily a fighting chance at a normal life."

"Do you have a personal interest in Lily?" Mrs. Harrow exchanged a look with Rosemarie.

"Every act of kindness is personal, don't you think?" Ron countered deftly. "She is the sister of my nephew's best friend. I've only seen Lily twice, but my heart reached out to her the minute I met her. But no, my interest in Lily's case is purely out of compassion."

"Your proposal is compelling," Mr. Anderson conceded after a moment.

"Thank you, sir. With your approval, we could change the course of a child's life. Isn't that worth our best effort?"

"Very well." Rosemarie's tone carried the weight of decision. "We agree to approve the gift for Lily. Since you know the recipient personally, you need to take extra care to make sure the gift remains anonymous."

"I've already made arrangements for the treatment facility to contact the family directly with a cover story," Ron said. "And thank you very much. I'll get it in motion right away."

Chapter 33

Thursday morning

Sabre sat upstairs at juvenile court in the office of Landon Knowles, the Deputy District Attorney who was assigned to Maverick's case. This was their last attempt to settle the issue before trial. They would try to come to an agreement, then meet with the judge and either set the case for a sentencing hearing or continue to trial.

"Summary probation, Ms. Brown," the DDA offered. He leaned back with a confidence that irked her. "We'll drop two of the counts if Maverick pleads to one. It's a generous offer, considering the circumstances."

She could see the efficiency of his offer—a shortcut through the legal proceedings that lay ahead. But Maverick was innocent, and she still had hope that Mr. Gearhart would surface.

"Generous?" Sabre laced her voice with incredulity. "My client saw what he saw. He's been unwavering in his testimony. You're asking him to admit to something he didn't do for the sake of convenience."

"He wouldn't do any time. It's a misdemeanor. He can have his record expunged before long."

"But he's innocent."

"Think it over, Sabre. Talk to your client. The clock's ticking."

Sabre left the office to confer with Maverick, who was sitting in the hallway. His hands were clasped together, knuckles white.

"They're offering a plea deal," she began. "One count, summary probation, the other charges dropped. It would mean no custody, and you would be on a light probation."

"But I'd have to admit to one count of lying?"

"That's correct."

"And if I don't take the deal?"

"Then we go to trial," Sabre said.

"Can we win?"

"Maybe. We're still trying to figure out how to explain your visions. There's never any guarantee with a trial."

"How much time would I do if I'm convicted?"

"You could get six months for each count, but there's a chance the judge would have them run at the same time. Although, the DA will argue against that."

"But with the plea deal, I'd have to say I made it up?"

"I'm afraid so."

"But I didn't." He shook his head, a mix of adolescent obstinacy and a steadfastness that seemed beyond his years. "I saw weird stuff, Sabre. How can I say I didn't?"

"Listen." She squeezed his hand. "If you take this deal, you avoid the risk of a harsher sentence. That might be worth the risk. But it also means admitting to something you insist you didn't do. I know that doesn't seem fair, but you have to make that decision."

Maverick met her eyes, but didn't speak.

"Can you live with that?" Sabre's own heart felt conflicted.

"The judge is ready to hear your case," intoned a guard from the doorway, signaling an end to their conference.

The heavy doors of the courtroom groaned open, a familiar yet always disconcerting sound that signaled the start of another battle. She recognized the usual clerks and bailiffs, but today, there was an anomaly—a new face above the judicial robe.

The last-minute substitution of judges was not uncommon, but it added an extra layer of unpredictability to the proceedings. She knew little about this judge, except his name, Gerald Feldman, and that he was a transplant from Superior Court downtown. She had him on one other case a while back and he seemed fair and impartial.

Sabre sat at the defense table and arranged her notes with precise movements. Her senses were heightened, attuned to every sound, every shift in the room's atmosphere.

"Good morning, Counselors," Judge Feldman boomed as he took the bench. He was in his late fifties, with a receding hairline and a horseshoe pattern of dark hair sprinkled with gray on the back of his bald head and a salt-and-pepper goatee. "Let us begin the pretrial conference for the State versus Maverick McLaughlin. Are both parties prepared to proceed?"

"Ready for the State, Your Honor," the DDA responded, rising smoothly from his seat.

"Defense is ready, Your Honor." Sabre stood too, her voice steady despite her whirlwind of concerns.

"Very well." Judge Feldman nodded, then glanced down at his notes. "The purpose of today's conference is to ensure a fair and efficient trial. I expect directness and professionalism from both sides. I've reviewed the case files, and I'm aware of the plea deal offered. Ms. Brown, has your client come to a decision?"

"Your Honor, we appreciate the State's offer, but my client maintains his innocence and opts to proceed to trial." It was Maverick's decision.

"Understood." The judge acknowledged with a tilt of his head. "I trust you're both aware of the implications should this matter go to trial and I find otherwise."

"Yes, Your Honor." Sabre tried to sound confident. "We believe the evidence will speak for itself."

"Very well." Judge Feldman set down the gavel that had yet to strike its foreboding note. "Are there any motions to be heard?"

"None from the State, Your Honor," DDA Knowles said.

"None for the defense, Your Honor."

"This pretrial conference is adjourned. See you all at trial on Monday morning, nine o'clock sharp. Don't be late."

As the courtroom began to empty, Sabre collected her materials, her thoughts already racing ahead to the next phase. Just as she was about to exit the courtroom, her phone vibrated.

New evidence on the McLaughlin case—keep looking, the text read. Sabre's heart skipped a beat. *Who had sent it? And what could it mean?* She called JP to let him know.

Chapter 34

Saturday morning

JP sat at his desk, hunched over his laptop. Sabre, skeptical about the new judge, had asked him to investigate Feldman's background. He hated this kind of research, mostly because he was stuck in a chair. But he scanned pages of text, legal filings, and social announcements, looking for a thread that might connect Judge Feldman to the influential Callahan family. JP knew that in the web of high society, affiliations were often more than they seemed; hidden alliances were the unspoken rule of the game.

A breakthrough came in the form of an archived newspaper article. The headline read, *Callahan Family Hosts Annual Charity Gala,* and halfway down the page was a photo of Feldman, a glass of champagne in hand, surrounded by the Callahans. His mid-laugh posture was too relaxed for someone who was merely an acquaintance. The date on the article placed the event years back, but still, it was a potential relationship or affiliation.

He printed out the article and added it to their file folder. It was a start, but he needed something more personal, or at least closer to the present time. JP went back to his search.

Finally, an archived legal notice loaded on the screen, confirming that Feldman had once been more than just a guest at a Callahan event. He'd been their family lawyer. JP jotted down the details. This was the kind of connection that created a conflict, not just the appearance of one. He printed out the finding and added it to the file.

A few minutes later, Sabre returned from visiting a client in a group home. Her friend Bob Clark also had a minor in the home, so they'd gone together. Now they were stopping by Sabre's house to pick up a file. Sabre had texted JP earlier to let him know.

"Hi, Sabre. Hi, Bob," JP said, standing to greet them. "How did the visit go?"

"Better than we thought it might." Sabre smiled. "Those two kids spend more time in trouble than they do out of it." She grabbed a folder from her desk. "Did you learn anything about Judge Feldman?"

JP reported what he had found.

Bob raised an eyebrow, then turned to Sabre. "A charity event isn't exactly a smoking gun."

"It is, *if* you're the Callahans' family lawyer," JP countered.

"That's definitely a conflict of interest," Sabre said.

"I get where you're coming from," Bob cut in. "But this case is not about the Callahans. It's about what Maverick reported. Which has no direct ties to the Callahans—unless you can prove that they are somehow involved in Maverick's claims. If you challenge Judge Feldman and fail, which is likely, you'll end up with a ticked-off judge presiding over Maverick's trial."

"I know what you're saying." Sabre's expression was grave. "But I also know the Callahan family is connected somehow. And I've been so sure of it, I lost sight of the fact that there's no actual evidence."

Bob shook his head. "I've seen judges retaliate for less. If you challenge Feldman, he could find a way to keep information about the Harrington case out of court."

"Which he is probably going to do anyway. This judge comes from downtown, supposedly to get some experience in juvenile court, and just happens to get this case. I don't think so."

"You think the influential Callahans pulled some strings?" Bob looked skeptical.

"I'd bet on it," Sabre said. "But we need to be absolutely certain before I can make that accusation."

"Exactly." Bob nodded emphatically. "You need something irrefutable. Otherwise, it's just conjecture."

JP cut in. "While you two figure that out I'll go see what I can dig up on Elise's sonogram."

"We have to get going too," Sabre said as he walked out.

~~~

Sabre took a deep breath, feeling the weight of the decision on her shoulders. *Would challenging Judge Feldman lead to a fairer judge and trial, or simply put Maverick in greater peril?*

Sabre turned to Bob. "You're right."

"I'm always right, but about which part?"

"I can't challenge Feldman." She started toward the door and Bob followed.

"Because of Maverick or because you don't have enough basis?" Bob asked.

"Both," she confessed. "I'm worried about the ammunition it might give Feldman."

"You think he'll bury you and be harder on Maverick?"

"Exactly." Sabre climbed into the passenger seat of Bob's car, and he got behind the wheel. Sabre had driven last time. "There's more at stake here," she added. "Elise Harrington's cold case is now intertwined with Maverick's trial. If Feldman senses us poking around, he might suppress anything linking to it."

"Isn't that more reason to push forward?" Bob countered. "To shine a light on potential bias?"
~~~

"Normally, I'd agree, but we're not dealing with *normal* here. We have a powerful family likely leaning on a judge. And if he decides to retaliate ..."

"Then Maverick doesn't stand a chance." Bob started the car and backed out.

"Right." Sabre sighed. "So, for now, I hold back. I protect my client and keep digging—quietly."

Chapter 35

Saturday afternoon

JP pushed through the glass doors of Kaiser Hospital on Zion with a purposeful stride. The sterile scent of antiseptic hung in the air as he navigated the maze of corridors, heading straight for the records department.

The woman stationed behind the counter wore a nametag reading *Linda*. "Ma'am." JP tipped his hat. "I need to retrieve medical records for Elise Harrington, from an incident that dates back almost thirty years."

The administrator peered at him over the rim of her glasses. "Do you have a court order for those records?"

JP leaned in, trying to bridge the gap with his well-worn charm. "The information is critical for an investigation I'm working on. A murder that might've been overlooked all these years."

"Sorry, mister." Linda was unimpressed with his Texan drawl and unfazed by the urgency in his voice. "Hospital policy is clear—no court order, no records. No exceptions."

Undaunted, JP flashed a wry smile. "Surely there's something we can do. An arrangement that respects both the law and the urgency of justice for the victim."

"Justice or not, I can't hand over confidential information." She shuffled papers, a fortress of bureaucracy between them.

"Then think of it as helping tie up loose ends on a cold case." JP's tone was firm yet respectful.

She shook her head and spoke sharply. "I get that you think you're doing something important, but unless you have legal paperwork, I can't help you."

JP sighed. He'd known it was a long shot, but other people had given him information they shouldn't have, so it was always worth a try. "Thank you for your time, ma'am."

On his way out, he called Sabre. "Any chance we could get a court order to see the medical records for Elise Harrington?"

"Not likely. We don't even know where the sonogram was done. There are a lot of medical facilities in San Diego. No judge will give us a court order for each one until we find it. Besides, unless we can tie Elise to our case, it's totally irrelevant as far as the courts are concerned."

"Right. I guess it's pretty hard to argue that the murder Maverick saw was Elise getting killed thirty years ago."

"Yeah, judges don't take well to ghost stories." Sabre chuckled. "You need to find someone Elise may have confided in."

"Like Mrs. Jenkins," JP said.

He drove to the address Ron had given him after he followed Mrs. Jenkins and her son. A boy about ten answered the door. JP asked for Mrs. Jenkins.

"Grandma!" the kid called out.

Mrs. Jenkins came to the door. She sighed, then said, "Hello, Mr. Torn." But she opened the door wider. "Please come in."

"Thank you, ma'am." JP entered, removing his hat out of habit. Her son's house was bright and filled with life, quite different from her own home.

"I don't know how I can help." Mrs. Jenkins led him to a breakfast nook, away from where teenage girls were watching TV.

"We have reason to believe Elise was pregnant." JP watched her expression as he spoke.

Mrs. Jenkins sighed again but didn't respond.

"It's important, ma'am." He watched her expression. "She told you, didn't she?"

"She came to me a couple of days before she disappeared. She had confirmed her pregnancy and had a sonogram scheduled for the next day. I never saw her after that."

"Did she tell you who the father was?"

"No." A hesitation. "She didn't."

"Do you think it was Harper Callahan?"

The old woman shook her head. "I don't think so."

"Why not? You said she was in love with him, right?"

"Elise asked me an unusual question that would've excluded Harper."

"What was it?"

"She asked if I thought she could love the child if she hated the father. Of course, I told her she would love him or her no matter what. Again, I asked her who the father was, but she wouldn't tell me. She said she'd have it all worked out in the next few days."

"Did Elise have a friend or family member she might have confided in?"

"No. Her mother passed away when she was twelve. She had an older brother, Ted, but he moved north right after high school. They were never close, and I don't think she ever saw him again after he moved."

"And her father?"

"He left the neighborhood not long after Elise's disappearance. I heard he passed away a few years back."

"Thank you, Mrs. Jenkins. If anything else comes to mind, please let me know." JP stood to leave.

"Wait." She hesitated, struggling with a decision. "There was one person she might've confided in.

"Who?"

"Harper Callahan."

"Even though he wasn't the father?" JP mulled it around. "Do you think Elise may have told Harper *he* was the father?"

"I doubt it. They weren't just in love, they were good friends. If she told anyone the truth, it was Harper."

"Do you know where he is now?"

"Orange County, and he's Dr. Callahan now. He's been practicing for years and really likes his work."

"It sounds like you've kept in touch."

"We have. He stops to see me when he comes to visit his family, which is only a few times a year. We also send Christmas cards, and he never misses my birthday."

"Do you talk about Elise?"

"Just the good stuff. We never mention her disappearance. It's too painful."

She gave him the doctor's address and phone number, and JP left, knowing what his next move would be.

Chapter 36

Sunday morning

As JP's truck ate up the freeway miles to Orange County, he realized he had finally gotten used to living in the busy, concrete landscape of suburban California. Although, he wouldn't mind a few days in the peace and quiet of the countryside.

As he turned onto the tree-lined street where Harper Callahan resided, JP slowed the truck to a crawl, absorbing details of the neighborhood that might later prove significant. The houses were pristine, with manicured lawns and expensive cars parked in driveways. They weren't extravagant, however, like his family's estate.

Pulling up outside Harper's place, JP cut the engine and sat for a moment, assessing the scene. The garage door stood open, and inside, he glimpsed a man obscured by shadows, the rhythmic sound of a wrench turning bolts punctuating the air. Harper Callahan, a doctor by trade but a tinkerer at heart, seemed engrossed in his work. It was clear from his collection of tools that Harper found solace in mechanical tasks.

Stepping out into the sunshine, JP strode toward the garage. The man didn't notice him until he was only a few feet way. Startled, Harper straightened up to assess the unexpected visitor, a sheen of sweat glistening on his forehead.

"Dr. Callahan?" JP called out.

Harper wiped his hands on a rag and peered curiously at JP, the corners of his eyes crinkling. "Can I help you?"

"I hope so." JP stepped into the brightly lit and well-organized garage.

"JP Torn, I presume?" Harper's voice carried a hint of resignation, tempered with a professionalism born of his medical training. "I was told you might be stopping by."

"Mrs. Jenkins?"

"Yes. She called right after you left. She wanted me to know that she gave you my information."

"I expect I'd have done the same." JP extended his hand, which Harper shook without hesitation. "I'm looking into Elise Harrington's disappearance. I understand you knew her quite well."

"Indeed," Harper replied.

"Mind if we talk?" JP asked, adjusting the brim of his Stetson with a practiced motion.

"Not at all. Please, come in." Harper gestured toward the interior door leading into the house. "We'll be more comfortable there."

As they stepped inside, the garage door closed behind them.

Harper led the way into an elegant living room, with tasteful, but minimal furnishings and a few artistic wall hangings. JP noticed a medical textbook on the coffee table and a framed medical degree on the wall—but no family photographs anywhere. The décor suggested a man dedicated to his profession, perhaps to the exclusion of all else.

"Let's get down to brass tacks," JP said as he took a seat opposite Harper. "Elise Harrington was pregnant when she disappeared. The million-dollar question—were you the father?"

Harper's face remained stoic, but his eyes reflected a sorrow that suggested intimate knowledge of the tragedy. "No, JP, I was not." His certainty left no room for doubt.

"You seem quite sure."

"Elise and I never had sex."

"Never?" JP's voice was sharp. His experience told him people often hid behind half-truths.

Harper met his eyes squarely. "Never."

"But you knew about the pregnancy?" JP probed.

"Yes, I did." Harper clasped his hands tightly together, as if holding back a tide of memories.

JP eyed Harper Callahan with a renewed intensity. "So, if you weren't the father, who was?"

"Thomas, I imagine."

"You're not sure?"

"I can't say for certain," he admitted. "Because I didn't ask her, and she never volunteered."

"Why didn't you ask?"

"Because I didn't think it was a question that needed answering. She was engaged to Thomas, and she was a good woman. I just assumed he was the father. She wasn't seeing anyone else."

"Except you?"

"Correct, but I knew it wasn't me."

"What were the dynamics like between the three of you?"

Harper hesitated, casting his eyes to the floor before meeting JP's again. "It was ... complicated," he said slowly. "Thomas and Elise seemed happy on the surface, but there were tensions. Like any couple, I suppose."

"I need specifics please," JP insisted. "Were there arguments? Something that might suggest trouble in paradise?"

"Elise was ambitious, spirited." Harper's admiration was evident. "She and Thomas would clash at times about her career and their future. She wasn't the type to settle for a quiet domestic life. Not easily, anyway."

"Did those clashes ever turn violent?"

"No, nothing like that," Harper replied, almost too quickly. Then he added, "Thomas can be possessive." Harper paused, then seemed to choose his words with care. "Elise highly valued her independence. It was a constant balancing act for them."

JP looked around the room again. "Are you married?"

"No. I've never taken the plunge."

"Because you never got over Elise?"

"Probably. Elise and I ..."—Harper's voice was barely above a whisper—"we had something special."

JP cocked his head, doubtful.

"Thomas is my brother, and even though I don't like him much, I found it hard to betray him. But what Elise and I shared was real."

"Real enough to keep it hidden?" JP watched Harper's reaction closely.

"Elise was afraid of how Thomas would react." Harper swallowed hard. "We planned to tell him, together. But before we could, she disappeared."

"Regrets?" JP's tone was softer now.

"Every damn day," Harper admitted. "I should've protected her. She didn't deserve what happened. And I ..." His voice cracked.

"You loved her very much, didn't you?"

"We loved each other." He looked pleadingly at JP. "I'm glad someone is finally looking into her disappearance. Justice for Elise. That's all I want now. For the truth to come out, no matter how much it costs me."

JP had a wild thought. "Did you fake the murder scene to prompt someone to investigate?"

Harper laughed. "No. That's not my style. But whoever did it, I'm grateful. I've hired several investigators in the past, but got nowhere."

"Thomas told me the same thing."

"I sincerely doubt that he spent any money on a search for her. He was married within four months of Elise's disappearance. I don't think he was grieving that hard."

"Do you think he had something to do with her disappearance?"

"It doesn't really matter what I think."

JP tried another approach. "Is it possible he found out about you and Elise?"

"Maybe. If he did, he never let on. He just played the part of the grieving fiancé, for a few minutes."

"Thank you, Doctor, for your insight."

"Thank you for stirring all this up."

"Do you have any idea who might be behind the *ghostly scenes*?"

"I don't have a clue. But if I did, I'd be glad to tell you and to shake their hand."

JP headed toward the door. Harper followed, stopping when they reached it.

"JP." Harper's warning came low and urgent. "Watch your step with Thomas. He's got influence that reaches further than you might expect. And he's not above using it to derail your efforts."

"Is that a threat or a prediction?"

"Consider it advice from someone who knows Thomas well," Harper replied. "He doesn't like loose ends. And right now, you're pulling on one that's been tied up for nearly three decades."

"Thanks for the heads-up." JP gave him a tight smile. "But if there's one thing I learned growing up in Texas, it's how to handle a bull by the horns."

Chapter 37

Monday morning

Sabre entered the courtroom with Maverick beside her, his jaw clenched. She placed a reassuring hand on his shoulder as they approached the defense table.

When the clerk called the case, the judge asked for any preliminary matters. Both parties declined.

"Very well. Mr. Knowles, would you like to make an opening statement?

"Yes, Your Honor." The prosecutor, a tall man with a hawkish nose and sharp eyes, stood with an air of confidence. "The state will prove beyond a reasonable doubt that Maverick McLaughlin knowingly reported a false crime, in direct violation of PC Section 148.5."

"We have forensic reports indicating no physical evidence at the scene consistent with the accused's description of a violent altercation. No blood, no signs of struggle—nothing."

"Furthermore"— the prosecutor cast a glance in Maverick's direction— "we have a witness who will testify they were with Maverick at the time of the second incident, and saw nothing that Maverick reported."

Sabre turned to her client and whispered, "Was someone at your house?"

He grimaced. "My friend, Zoey. I snuck her into the room. She wasn't supposed to be there."

Sabre was upset that Maverick hadn't been honest with her, but now was not the time.

"Your Honor," the prosecutor said with a slight pivot toward the judge. "We intend to demonstrate that Maverick sought attention and validation from his peers through fabricated heroics. To show that he's a troubled youth, who sought to belong, using any means necessary—including crafting tales of crime."

Sabre noticed the subtle emphasis on Maverick's unstable upbringing, a psychological portrait painted with broad strokes intended to sway the judge's perception.

"Through meticulous examination of the timeline," the prosecution continued, "it will become evident that Maverick had both the opportunity and the motive to concoct this story. And let us not forget," he added, his tone shifting to solemn gravity, "that false reporting diverts precious resources and undermines public trust in law enforcement. The implications of such actions are far-reaching and severe."

Sabre listened, keeping her expression unreadable, as the prosecutor continued to detail the accusations with a theatrical flair, painting Maverick as a troubled youth who craved attention so desperately he fabricated a murder.

"Thank you, Mr. Knowles." The judge nodded gravely. "Ms. Brown, your opening statement, please."

"Your Honor." Sabre stood tall with her shoulders squared, making eye contact with the judge. "What we have before us is not a case of attention-seeking or deceit. Maverick McLaughlin is a young man who has faced more adversity in his sixteen years than many do in a lifetime, but that has not made him unstable."

She paused. "He reported what he genuinely believed to be a crime—a murder, or at the very least, an assault. And while his friends may have cast doubt, waffling between support and skepticism, Maverick has remained steadfast in his testimony. We will present a psychologist who will testify to Maverick's stability and state of mind."

"Furthermore," Sabre continued, her gaze now sweeping across the room, locking briefly with Maverick's own anxious eyes, "we will present a witness who can corroborate much of what happened at that corner. A witness who, until recently, was afraid to come forward."

The judge's raised eyebrows indicated interest. Maverick leaned forward, a glimmer of hope in his eyes.

"The evidence will show there was no malicious intent on behalf of Maverick, but rather a genuine concern for the safety of himself and others." Sabre sat down. She sounded confident, but she wished she knew what that text she received was all about. She could use some new evidence right now.

"Very well," the judge said. "Proceed with your case, Mr. Knowles."

"Thank you, Your Honor. The State calls Officer Mendoza to the stand."

Mendoza had responded to Maverick's call on the night of the first reporting, and recounted the fruitless search for evidence at the scene.

"Furthermore," he continued, "we found several inconsistencies in Mr. McLaughlin's statements over time."

Sabre made a note that he didn't actually testify to any of those inconsistencies, so she could deal with it on cross examination.

The prosecutor continued to question the officer to establish the details of what Maverick had reported seeing, often commenting on the absurdity of his statements. Each time Sabre objected, and each time it was sustained.

"No further questions for this witness," Mr. Knowles said.

"Counselor?" The judge looked at Sabre. "Any questions?"

Sabre stood. "Officer Mendoza, Maverick told you he saw a crime being committed, is that correct?"

"Yes."

"He described a man in an overcoat hitting a woman on the back of her head, correct?"

"Correct."

"And could he see either of their faces?"

"No. He said their backs were toward him."

"And then he saw the man drag the woman around the corner, correct?"

"That's what he said."

"At which time, he said they were out of his sight, correct?"

"Correct."

"You testified earlier that there were *inconsistencies* in his story, but he gave that same account to you and to the detective who came a little later, correct?"

"He said he couldn't see very well, but he essentially gave the same story."

"In fact, you wrote that…" Sabre picked up the report and read from it. "*Maverick was certain about what he saw and retold the same account each time.*"

"If that's what it says, then I wrote that."

"In fact, you believed him when he told you that he had witnessed an assault, correct?"

"I had no reason not to, so I called to get a detective out there."

"Mr. Mendoza, what was the weather like when you went on that call?"

"It was raining."

"In fact, there was a storm, right?"

"It was raining hard, making things difficult to see."

"There was thunder, correct?"

"Correct."

Sabre felt comfortable that she had sufficiently established that there were no inconsistencies in Maverick's first statements to the police. So, she took a different tack.

"Maverick told you he received a phone call from an unknown number telling him to look out the window, correct?"

"That's correct."

"Did you investigate to see if he had in fact received those calls?"

"No. I did not."

"Do you know if anyone else in the department looked into it?'

"Not that I'm aware of."

"No further questions."

As the prosecution moved through its list of witnesses, each piece of testimony seemed to tighten the net around Maverick. But Sabre didn't waver, challenging each point with legal precision. Then came the twist. The prosecutor stood, a smug tilt to his mouth as he addressed the court.

"Your Honor, we would like to submit into evidence this series of text messages recovered from the defendant's phone." He handed a sheaf of papers to the bailiff, who passed them to the judge. "These texts suggest that Mr. McLaughlin was indeed fabricating the story to impress his friends."

Sabre's objection was swift. "Your Honor, these messages have not been authenticated and thus are not admissible evidence."

"Mr. Knowles?"

"The State will call a witness later who can vouch for their authenticity."

"Very well." The judge looked over the rim of his glasses. "I'll reserve judgment on the admissibility of this evidence until it's properly authenticated."

Returning to her seat, Sabre exhaled silently, her mind already racing through her defense strategy.

"Let's recess for lunch," the judge said. "We'll reconvene at 1:30." He stood and left the bench.

A moment later, Knowles handed Sabre a paper. "This young woman has been added to our witness list. We can call her tomorrow if you need time to investigate."

"I appreciate that. I'll let you know in the morning if we've had enough time."

"Fair enough."

Sabre and Maverick walked out of the courtroom and down the hallway. Outside the earshot of anyone, Sabre said, "Tell me about the witness who was in your room." When Maverick didn't respond, she added, "They're calling a witness named Zoey Olson to the stand tomorrow."

"I'm sorry," Maverick said quietly.

"Is Zoey the girl who was in your room the first time you saw the murder?"

"Yes."

"This is a problem because you lied to the police and that makes you look suspicious. Our whole case is based on your credibility. On top of that, you lied to me, and I can't afford to be blind-sided."

"I'm really sorry."

"Tell me what she saw."

"Nothing."

"That's unfortunate. Please explain where each of you were, and tell me exactly what happened."

"Zoey wanted to come over and play video games, but I'm not allowed to have anyone over, especially a girl, after nine o'clock. I told her no, but she showed up anyway. So, I snuck her in. That's why I didn't tell because I didn't want to get into trouble."

"So far, that's not working too well for you," Sabre said.

"She was going to leave early, but then it started to rain. We were waiting for the rain to let up, but it went on for hours."

"What was she doing when you saw the assault?"

"We were playing video games, and I got a phone call, so I hit pause and answered it. The voice said to look out the window. So, I did." Maverick took a deep breath, then went on. "When the man hit the woman the first time, I called to Zoey. But she had her headset on and was playing the game, so she couldn't hear me. And I couldn't yell because I would've woken my foster parents. So, I don't think she realized how upset I was. By the time she came to the window, they were gone."

"Did she seem to believe you when you told her what you saw?"

"Yes. But I don't think she believed me the second time. None of my friends did. Not even Darius."

Chapter 38

Monday afternoon

The court reconvened after lunch, and the prosecutor continued to call witnesses. He began with the technician they used to retrieve the text messages from Maverick's phone. The tech guy talked about digital timestamps, encryption locks, and cellular towers.

"Each message bears the unique digital signature of the defendant's device," the technician claimed with confidence.

Knowles continued, "Does this list include all the messages between Maverick and Zoey Olson from the night of the first reporting of the *phantom murder*?"

"Objection, Your Honor," Sabre called out. "Leading and misstating the facts."

"Sustained," Judge Feldman said.

The DDA rephrased the question. "What time period does this list cover?"

The technician stated that the list covered the six weeks between Maverick's first reporting of the crime and his arrest.

"And who were the messages between?" Knowles asked.

"Most were between Maverick McLaughlin's phone and Zoey Olson's phone. The rest were between Darius Hendrix and Maverick."

"Is this a complete list of the messages between Maverick and the two youths, Zoey and Darius?"

"Yes. It includes every message."

The DDA once again offered them into evidence as Exhibit A and the judge accepted them.

"Any questions of this witness, Ms. Brown?" the judge asked.

Sabre stood and approached the stand. "You have no way of knowing who actually sent the messages, correct?"

"I can only tell what phone they were generated from and what phone the message went to."

"So, someone other than Maverick could've sent any of those messages to Zoey or Darius, correct?"

"That's right."

"No further questions, Your Honor."

The next witness, Officer James Newman, was called to the stand. With over two decades on the force, he had made the walk many times. His uniform was impeccably pressed, his badge polished to a shine.

After some preliminary questions, establishing that he was the arresting officer, the prosecutor said, "Please tell the court what Maverick McLaughlin said to you upon his arrest."

"He admitted to me that he had made up the story about witnessing the assault."

Maverick seemed to shrink into his chair.

"And how did you come by this admission?" Knowles continued.

"I approached Maverick with care and professionalism," Newman stated. "I asked him questions pertaining to the incident, and it became apparent that his narrative did not align with the evidence at hand. I placed him under arrest. After being presented with the inconsistencies in his story, he confessed to inventing the tale."

The prosecutor nodded, satisfied with the response. "No further questions."

Maverick's eyes remained fixed on the floor.

"Officer Newman," Sabre began, as she approached the witness stand." At what point during your interaction with Maverick did his supposed confession occur?"

"When I told him to get in the police car," Officer Newman replied.

"Were there any other officers present at the time?"

"Only myself."

"When you told him to get in the car, did he say anything else?"

"He said he was scared and didn't want to go to jail."

"And you had told him several times to confess to the crime and things would go easier, correct?"

"Not exactly."

"What exactly did you tell him?"

"I told him to tell the truth. That if he was lying, things could go bad. That he could go to the Hall."

"The truth was that he was going to the Hall no matter what he said at that time, correct?"

"That's correct."

"Isn't it likely that he felt intimidated by your statements, and if he admitted to the fabrication, you might let him go?"

"I don't know what his thoughts were, but intimidation was not my intention. My approach was by the book," Newman insisted.

"Let's talk about *by the book*." Sabre sharpened her tone. "Did you take notes during this interview?"

"Standard procedure requires—"

"Answer the question, Officer," Sabre cut in. "Did you take notes at the time?"

After a brief hesitation, Newman conceded, "No. I wrote my report after I booked him."

"How much later was that?"

"A couple of hours."

"Thank you, Officer Newman. No further questions."

"Re-direct, Mr. Knowles?"

"Thank you, Your Honor." The DDA stood in front of the witness. "Did you at any time during your arrest try to intimidate the defendant?"

"No. I did not," Officer Newman said.

"Did you at any time offer to let him go if he confessed?"

"No. I did not."

"In your opinion, did he voluntarily make the confession?"

"Objection, speculation," Sabre interjected.

"Sustained."

"Did you threaten him in any way?" Knowles continued.

"No, sir."

"No further questions."

"Re-direct, Ms. Brown?"

Sabre stood, addressing the witness from the defense table. "And yet you testified that Maverick was scared, correct?"

He hesitated, then said, "Yes. That's correct."

"No further questions, Your Honor." Sabre sat down.

"We will adjourn for the day," the judge announced. "Court will resume tomorrow morning at nine o'clock sharp." His gavel signaled the end of the day's proceedings.

Outside the courtroom, Maverick left with his foster parents.

As Sabre walked away, Bob joined her. "Done for the day, SOBs?"

"Yes. How about you?"

"Won and done." Bob grinned.

"Good for you. We're just getting started."

"How did it go?"

"It could've been worse. But we need..." Her phone rang, cutting into her thoughts.

She reached into her pocket for her cell. The caller ID flashed *JP* and a photo of her cowboy filled the screen. "Excuse me, Bob." She held up a finger as she answered. "Hi, baby. I was just walking out. I'll be home in fifteen minutes or so."

"We've got a big problem," JP said.

Sabre's grip on the phone tightened. "Is it one of the kids?" she asked, her belly filling with dread.

"No. They found Gearhart. He's dead."

"Oh no! How did it happen?"

"I don't know. I have very little information. Hold on. I have another call. Maybe it's about Gearhart."

While Sabre waited, she told Bob her best witness had been found dead.

JP came back on. "It was Gearhart's daughter. She wants to see me, said it's important."

"Did she say why?"

"No. But I sense it wasn't just a courtesy call. She might know something that can help us."

"When are you going to see her?"

"She said she'd call tomorrow and set up something. She sounded cryptic."

"Please be careful, JP. We don't know what we're dealing with here."

"Always am."

Chapter 39

Tuesday morning

In the familiar courtroom, the bailiff called out, "All rise for the Honorable Judge Feldman." Sabre stood and smoothed out her black skirt. She'd worn her favorite teal jacket this morning too, needing today to go better for her client.

As the judge took his seat, he gave a curt nod, signaling everyone to be seated. "In re the State of California vs McLaughlin."

After asking for preliminary matters, the judge said to the prosecutor, "Please call your next witness."

"The State calls Zoey Olson," Knowles announced.

The bailiff went out and momentarily returned with a timid teenage girl in tow. The door clanged behind her, and she jumped.

Zoey Olson's nervousness was obvious. Wide-eyed, she walked with hesitant steps, hands fluttering. Her blonde hair lay limp and tucked behind her ears, revealing a face drained of color. The courtroom lights accentuated the dark circles under her fearful eyes.

As she approached the witness stand, her gaze flitted about the room, touching briefly on Maverick's anxious expression before darting away. She seemed to shrink into herself, shoulders hunched, as if trying to become invisible.

"Thank you, Miss Olson. Please be seated." Knowles gestured toward the witness chair.

"Please raise your right hand," the clerk instructed. Zoey complied, her arm trembling visibly. "Do you swear to tell the truth, the whole truth, and nothing but the truth, so help you God?"

"I do," Zoey whispered.

"Please state your name for the record."

"Zoey Anne Olson." Her voice was barely audible.

"Miss Olson," the prosecutor began, his tone gentle yet probing, "thank you for being here today. I know this is difficult, but all we ask is that you tell the truth."

Zoey nodded mutely.

"How do you know the defendant?" Knowles' pen was poised above his legal pad.

She glanced again at Maverick. "We go to school together."

"Where were you on the night of January 8th around ten o'clock?"

Zoey shifted uncomfortably. "I was at Mav's house."

"Mav?"

"Sorry. Maverick."

"Are you referring to the defendant, Maverick McLaughlin?"

"Yes, sir."

"Why were you there?"

"Because he's my friend."

"Can you please tell us what you were doing around ten o'clock?"

"We were playing video games."

"What happened next?" Knowles asked.

"Maverick suddenly stopped playing. I think his phone rang or something." Zoey swallowed hard. "Then he jumped up and ran to the window."

"Did you hear anything?"

"No."

"Then what?"

"Mav called me over. He was pretty upset."

"Did you see anything when you looked out?" the prosecutor asked, peering over his glasses.

"No," Zoey replied. "Except a lot of rain."

"Yet Maverick claimed to have seen a crime occur?"

"Yes, he did. He was sure of it."

"Miss Olson, how did you feel about Maverick's claim that night?" Knowles queried.

"I believed him," Zoey said. "Mav wouldn't lie about something like that, not to me." She glanced at Maverick.

"Has your opinion changed since then?"

Zoey hesitated, her eyes darting away for an instant. "Now, I'm not so sure." She drew in a shaky breath. "It's just that when he saw it happen two more times, it didn't make sense to me. I don't know what to think anymore."

"Thank you, Ms. Olson. No further questions." The prosecutor stepped back.

Sabre approached the witness stand. "You weren't supposed to be at Maverick's house that night, were you?"

"No. I snuck out after my parents went to bed."

"And the Venables, Maverick's foster parents, didn't know you were there either, did they?"

"No. They would've called my parents, and I would've gotten in trouble."

"And you swore your friend, Maverick, to secrecy about that, right?"

"Yes."

"He wanted to tell the Venables, but you convinced him not to, correct?"

"That's right. He promised he wouldn't tell anyone."

"You testified that Maverick called you to the window on the night in question. How much time elapsed before you actually looked outside?"

Zoey fidgeted with her hair. "It was probably three or four minutes."

"Why didn't you go when he first called you over?"

"I was into the video game, because I was almost to the next level."

"Did you make it to the next level?"

Zoey smiled. "Yes. I did."

"You said it took three or four minutes before you went to the window. In those few minutes, isn't it possible the event Maverick claims to have seen could've occurred without your knowledge?"

"Objection, Your Honor!" Knowles stood abruptly, his face flushed. "Calls for speculation."

"Overruled," Judge Feldman replied. "The witness may answer the question."

Swallowing hard, Zoey nodded. "Yes, it's possible."

"Thank you, Miss Olson. When you did look out the window, what exactly did you see?" Sabre continued.

"Just a lot of rain," Zoey said. "I didn't see what Mav did, but it took me a while to get there."

"Regarding your change of heart about Maverick's story. Is it true that your doubt only arose because Maverick saw the same thing more than once?"

"Yes."

"So, you didn't witness anything firsthand that would discredit his account?"

"That's true."

"Thank you. No further questions." Sabre returned to her seat, relatively confident with the testimony.

Chapter 40

Tuesday morning

Following Shelby Williams' instructions, JP scanned the parking lot for a tail. Convinced he hadn't been followed, he sauntered toward the rear of the Kohl's department store, eyeing the back door.

"Mr. Torn?" The voice was hushed as the door opened.

"Call me JP." He stepped into the cool air of the service corridor. Gearhart's daughter, wearing a manager's vest and nametag, quickly ushered him into a tiny office that smelled of printer ink and stale coffee.

"Thank you for coming." She locked the door behind them.

"Sorry for your loss, ma'am." JP's words were genuine.

"Thank you. It's been hard. I appreciate your support."

"Anything you need, you just let me know," JP said. "Do they know what happened to him?"

"He was beaten to death and left by the side of the road."

"I'm so sorry," JP said, as he took a seat in a wobbly metal chair. The office was cramped, the walls lined with filing cabinets and motivational posters.

"My father didn't just run off." Her voice was hushed and strained. "He knew dangerous things about what Maverick saw. So, he went into hiding."

Finally! A bolt of eagerness shot through him. "Tell me everything."

She swallowed hard, fidgeting with a pen. "My dad called to say he was going away for a while. He said he was afraid for his life."

"Did he tell you where he was headed?"

"No. He didn't want me to know for my own safety. He instructed me to wait for a day, then report him missing. That way, it would look like I didn't know anything about his disappearance."

"Did he tell you why he was so afraid?"

"He said it was tied up with what he knew about Maverick's case and Elise Harrington. He also said if anything happened to him, or if I hadn't heard from him before Wednesday, to contact you and tell you everything."

"Why Wednesday?"

"Because he didn't want Maverick to be convicted of something he didn't do, and he figured that still gave him time to testify."

JP wanted to get to the real information. "So, what do you know?"

"The night Maverick first reported the crime, Dad was home and witnessed a lot, even though it was storming." She paused for a breath. "He saw two people get out of a car—a man and a woman. At first, he thought they were arguing, but then he realized they were probably trying to be heard above the rain. The man set something on the hood of the car, then they headed straight for the wall near the bushes, where Elise ..." Her voice trailed off.

"Where Elise Harrington was assaulted, thirty years ago." JP finished for her. "They were there to reenact the crime. Is that right?"

Shelby nodded, her face pale under the fluorescent lights. "Yes. The whole thing was deliberate. The man—who was tall and muscular—pretended to strike her on the head with such force that she crumpled to the ground. Then he swung at her again."

"Could your dad see the weapon?"

"He wasn't sure what it was. It was dark and raining heavily." Shelby swallowed hard. "But he thought it was a pipe. He said it was shiny, because, it would catch light from the streetlamp."

"What happened next?" JP prompted.

"The man dragged the woman around the corner, out of view for a few moments. But here's an even stranger thing." She paused, biting her lip. "They came back around the corner, grabbed whatever was on the roof of the car, and drove away."

"You and your father were brave to share this. Thank you." JP stood to leave. "I'll get to the bottom of this. You have my word."

"Thank *you*. I want my father's killer to be caught."

Chapter 41

Tuesday afternoon

The prosecutor called two more witnesses, then rested his case. Sabre breathed a sigh of relief. Neither testimony had done much damage.

She rose from her chair. "Your Honor, I move for a summary judgment. The evidence presented by the prosecution does not establish intent, which is a key element for this crime. The evidence is not only circumstantial but also woefully inadequate. There is simply no proof that Maverick had the required intent to commit this crime."

Sabre continued, "Maverick McLaughlin respectfully moves this court for a summary judgment in his favor on the charge of violating California Penal Code Section 148.5. The prosecution has not provided sufficient evidence to establish the essential elements of this offense beyond a reasonable doubt. Consequently, there are no genuine issues of material fact, and the defendant is entitled to judgment as a matter of law. California Penal Code Section 148.5(a) states: *Every person who reports to any peace officer ... that a felony or misdemeanor has been committed, knowing the report to be false, is guilty of a misdemeanor.*"

Sabre paused for a second. "To secure a conviction under this statute, the prosecution must prove beyond a reasonable doubt that, one, the defendant reported to a peace officer—"

The judge interrupted. "I know the elements of the crime, Counselor."

"Sorry, Your Honor. We're not disputing that Maverick reported the crime, and on more than one occasion. However, there is no proof that Maverick had knowledge of the falsity of the crime. In fact, some crime has very likely been committed, even if it is just a trespass. Someone was on that property. The prosecution has failed to establish that Maverick knew the report was false. Mere speculation or circumstantial evidence suggesting Maverick's potential motives or state of mind is insufficient. There must be concrete evidence demonstrating Maverick's awareness of the report's falsity at the time it was made. The evidence presented does not rise to this level of certainty, failing the requirement of proving knowledge of falsity beyond a reasonable doubt."

Sabre took a deep breath before continuing. "The prosecution must also demonstrate that Maverick made the alleged false report with the specific intent to cause action by a peace officer. The evidence shows no clear indication that Maverick intended for the police to take specific actions based on his report. In fact, there is no proof that Maverick was the one to make the call. Even the police report states that the Venables had to encourage him to tell the police what he saw. The prosecution's case rests on conjecture and lacks definitive proof of Maverick's specific intent, thereby failing to satisfy this crucial element."

The judge shuffled through some papers, and Sabre wondered if he was even listening. "In summary, the prosecution has not provided sufficient evidence to prove the elements of California Penal Code Section 148.5 beyond a reasonable doubt. There is no credible evidence that Maverick made a false report, knew it was false, or intended to cause action by the peace officer. Therefore, the defendant is entitled to summary judgment as a matter of law. The defendant respectfully requests that this court grant his motion and dismiss the charges."

The prosecutor showed a flash of annoyance.

Sabre sat down and awaited Judge Feldman's response.

"Ms. Brown," Judge Feldman's voice echoed through the chamber. "I have listened carefully to your motion for a summary judgment. However, after reviewing the evidence presented by the prosecution, it is my belief that there is sufficient cause to proceed with this trial."

Sabre kept her expression and posture stiff. She had expected the denial, yet the sting of disappointment was fresh. She tried not to let her client see it.

"Your Honor," Sabre said. "I'd like to request a continuance to prepare our defense further. We've suffered an unforeseen setback—the death of Quaid Gearhart, our key witness. This unfortunate event requires us to regroup and adjust our strategy accordingly."

"I'm sorry to hear that, Ms. Brown," Judge Feldman said.

The prosecutor stood. "Your Honor, the people are prepared to proceed. Ms. Brown has a host of other witnesses at her disposal. There's no need for delay."

Judge Feldman regarded him coolly, then turned to Sabre, who stood, poised for rebuttal.

"Your Honor, the unexpected demise of Mr. Gearhart has left a chasm in our defense that cannot be filled by simply calling another witness. We request time to realign our strategy, to ensure justice is done."

"Is how he died pertinent to this case?"

"Possibly, Your Honor. He was murdered."

The judge looked startled. "Your motion to continue is granted."

When Knowles started to object, Feldman gave him a stern look. "Really, Mr. Knowles?"

"Thank you, Your Honor," Sabre said. "I assure you, this opportunity will not be squandered. We will use this time to fortify our defense and ensure that Maverick receives the fair trial he deserves."

Judge Feldman nodded and turned to the prosecutor. "I sincerely hope the witness' murder had nothing to do with this case. Court will resume Monday morning at nine. Dismissed."

As the judge rose from his seat, the courtroom buzzed with whispers and speculation. Sabre collected her papers, then left the courtroom to call JP with the news.

"I'm glad you got the continuance," JP said, "but I'm terribly sorry about Gearhart. It was my call to bring him into this mess. If I'd been more careful—"

"We couldn't have known," Sabre interjected.

"Still, I should've seen the risks."

"How? This is a misdemeanor, not some high-powered murder case. It shouldn't be that volatile." Sabre took a deep breath. "Let's channel that energy into finding something we can use. We don't have much time to turn this around."

Chapter 42

Wednesday morning

JP again entered Kohl's store through the back door and followed Shelby Williams into her private office.

"Thank you for coming on such short notice." She motioned for him to take a seat, then sat there quietly.

"When you called, you said you needed to tell me something else." JP didn't have time to spare. "What is it, Shelby?"

"I didn't tell you everything before. My father's confession hit me hard, and I was ashamed." She looked away for an instant, then refocused. "It's about the night Elise Harrington disappeared."

"Go on."

"My father was a smoker back then, you know? He always went out onto the porch for a cigarette after dinner, then again before bed. The night Elise vanished he saw something."

"What exactly?"

"A car that was very familiar to him drove up." She glanced down at a notepad. "Dad said it was a black and burgundy 1940 Rolls Royce Phantom limo. It's an extremely rare car, and it belonged to Patrick Callahan."

"So, Patrick was there that night?"

"Or one of his sons. No one else was allowed to drive that car."

"Did your dad see Patrick?"

"He never said that it was Patrick. He wouldn't tell me who it was."

"Then what happened?" JP prompted.

"Elise drove up and got out. The man was waiting near the bushes. Elise walked up to him willingly, so she probably knew him. Dad said they talked for a minute, then Elise started to walk away. According to my father, the guy grabbed Elise, threw her into the Rolls Royce, then sped off."

"He's sure it was Elise Harrington?"

"That he was certain of. The streetlamp lit up her face when she got out of her car."

"Why didn't your father report what he saw?"

"He was too afraid." Her voice broke. "Patrick Callahan was a mean and powerful man. Dad worked for them and needed to keep his job. He was afraid for his family."

"Did you know any of this growing up?"

"Nothing. I'm sure Mom didn't know either." Shelby paused. "There's something else."

"What?"

She leaned in, her voice low. "The night Maverick claims he saw the crime reenacted ... that same Rolls Royce was parked on the street."

~~~

Back in his home office, JP booted his computer up and accessed a subscription database of information. It didn't take long to discover the new registered owner was Thomas Callahan. He called Sabre. "Your *smoking gun* might just be a luxury car," JP said. "Gearhart saw Patrick's Rolls Royce at the scene of the crime the night Elise disappeared, and again the first night Maverick reported his poltergeist. The Rolls Royce now belongs to Thomas Callahan. It's the same one tied to both scenes."

"That's huge. If we can place Thomas at the scene, we'd have exactly what we need to clear Maverick."
~~~

"I don't think that will be an easy task." JP shared the other information he'd learned from Shelby.

"Now what?" Sabre asked.

"I'll call DuBois and update him. Maybe he can help us."

JP decided to see if he could catch DuBois at the precinct. He was successful. When he walked into his office, DuBois said, "What now? More ghosts?"

"Sort of."

"Have a seat. This I gotta hear."

JP told him everything he'd just learned.

DuBois shook his head. "So, let me see if I've got this straight. You're telling me that your dead witness is accusing an old man in a wheelchair of a crime that may or may not have been committed thirty years ago."

"Yeah. That's pretty much it." JP smiled.

"Seriously, McCloud, I appreciate the information. Maybe it'll lead to the men who tried to kill my father."

Chapter 43

Thursday

JP was outside with his dog, Louie, when he heard the doorbell ring. He went inside and through the house to answer the door and let Ron in. "Thanks for coming over," JP greeted.

They moved into the kitchen and sat down at the table. "We've gotta figure out how to get close to Callahan's Rolls Royce without raising red flags."

Ron shook his head. "I don't think he'll let you back onto his property."

"Nope. And we don't want him to think we know anything about the car. We need a way that doesn't shout *investigation*. I was thinking, we need to figure out his schedule, see where he might show up the next few days. Then you can accidentally bump into him."

"Why me?"

"Because he knows me. You won't raise much suspicion."

"How do we figure out where he's going to be?"

"Lana." JP grinned. "She can dig up the information through her unconventional methods. I hate to ask, but we need it soon, or we won't have it in time for the trial."

"Right." Ron pulled out his phone and made the call. He dialed Lana's number. The line trilled twice before a click signaled her answer.

"Hey, Lana," Ron said, and then continued with some small talk before he said. "Sabre has a court-related emergency, and we need your help. I'm putting you on speaker so JP can hear."

"Hi, Lana," JP said. "Can you do us a favor?"

"Whatever you need."

"Can you find out the schedule for a man named Thomas Callahan? He's the CEO of a large real estate company and probably has a calendar online."

"I can try. What exactly do you need to know?"

"Somewhere he'll be that Ron can bump into him and chat about his car." JP gave her Callahan's business name and number, then realized she had probably already found it online.

"Give me a sec," came Lana's crisp reply, the sound of keystrokes punctuating her words. After a brief pause, they heard more clicking keys, then she said, "Got something. He's attending a charity event tonight. But heads up, it's swanky – a thousand dollars per plate."

Ron laughed. "Got anything more within my budget?"

"Let me have a look," Lana said. "I'll call you back."

JP and Ron tossed around other ideas to meet up with Thomas Callahan but didn't come up with anything promising.

Finally, Lana called back. "Got a bit of good news. I can snag you a ticket to that event."

"Seriously?" Ron's eyebrows shot up in surprise.

"Consider it done. I'll email you the confirmation details."

"Thank you, Lana. I owe you."

"I'll collect," she said. "Check your inbox."

Seconds later, Ron's phone pinged with the arrival of an email. Ron opened the attachment and showed JP a sleek, electronic ticket adorned with the charity event's ornate logo.

"Even the ticket looks expensive," JP said.

"Got it," he said to Lana, scanning the document. "You're on speaker again."

"Listen up." Lana's tone shifted, the playfulness giving way to stern efficiency. "Don't go there to enjoy the caviar. Your mission is to get close to Callahan, not to indulge in fine dining. In and out. If you're thirsty, drink water."

"Understood," Ron said.

"By the way, your name is Franklin Stevens, and you're a long-time car collector. You might want to brush up a little on your knowledge."

"I'll start right away."

"Good luck."

Ron hung up and turned to JP. "Looks like I'm going to a charity event tonight."

JP smirked. "Like she said, play it cool. We're after the truth, not a socialite badge. But keep your eyes open, Ron. This rabbit hole goes deep."

Suddenly, the door swung open, and Conner burst into the house.

"Ron!" he called out.

In the living room, JP and Ron Brown sat comfortably.

"Hey, Conner," Ron greeted. "You look like you've just won the lottery. What's got you so fired up?"

Conner's breath came in short bursts.

"Yeah, you're smilin' like a goat in a briarpatch," JP said.

"I've got news," Conner said. "Big news."

"Out with it, then," Ron urged.

"It's about Lily."

"Is she alright?"

"More than alright," Conner said. "She's been given a chance of a lifetime. She's going to get the treatment. Physical therapy, surgery for her heart—everything she needs."

Ron's eyebrows lifted in surprise, and he stood up from the armchair, stepping closer. "That's incredible, Conner," he said. "How did this come about?"

Conner paced the length of the living room, his hands animated as he spoke. "So, it turns out that the clinic reached out to Lily's mom directly. They offer this program where they select a few kids each year for ongoing therapy and surgeries—completely pro bono. It's like winning the medical lottery!"

Ron arched an eyebrow. "That's incredible news, Conner."

"Yes, it is," JP added. "But how did they pick her specifically?"

"Ah, that's the million-dollar question, isn't it?" Conner looked at Ron skeptically. "It seems random, but they must have some sort of selection process. I mean, what are the chances, right? And they're covering everything."

"Sounds like a guardian angel stepped in," JP said, giving Ron a quick wink.

A flicker of uncertainty passed over Conner's face. "Are you sure you don't know anything about it?"

Ron shrugged. "How would I know?"

Conner gave him another quizzical look.

"Don't look at me," Ron said. "This is just one of those strokes of luck—a fantastic break for Lily."

"Whatever you say."

Chapter 44

Thursday evening

The grand ballroom at the US Grant was a sea of tuxedos and evening gowns, each attendee looking better than the next. Ron's suit was tailored to perfection for a wedding he'd attended a few years back, and he hoped to blend into the high-society crowd like a chameleon. But the crystal chandeliers and ornate table settings were a little intimidating.

He glided toward the bar. "Ice water, please," he murmured to the bartender, who quickly filled his simple request. Ron added a skinny straw and a slice of lime so it would look like a vodka tonic.

As he meandered through the room, the conversations around him fluttered between stock market fluctuations and gossip about overseas vacations. He sidestepped invitations to chat with a polite nod or a deflective smile.

Across the room, Thomas Callahan's silver hair caught the light. As Ron neared, he summoned his new persona, a car enthusiast who would be welcome in Callahan's world.

"Mr. Callahan?" Ron maneuvered himself into the man's path. "Excuse me, sir." Ron offered a hand. "Franklin Stevens. I thought I recognized a fellow connoisseur of fine automobiles."

"Nice to meet you," Callahan replied, his handshake firm. "Actually, I was never into antique cars. Expensive cars, yes.

Old cars, not so much. However, I did learn to appreciate their value at a young age. My father used to have at least a dozen priceless cars, but the family no longer owns them."

"Have you seen the latest DB11?" Ron asked, his tone casual. "Aston Martin has really outdone themselves this time."

Thomas Callahan's eyes lit up. "Now that's a car I'd love to have."

"It's pretty amazing. But there's something about the classics that always draws me back. Speaking of which, I hear you've got quite the gem in your collection—the 1940 Rolls Royce Phantom limo, if I'm not mistaken?"

"How do you know that?"

Ron gave him a knowing smile. "Word gets around among the collectors' circles. Every enthusiast dreams of getting their hands on a car like that."

Thomas chuckled. "Yes, it's quite the machine. But if I'm honest, it's more my son's pride than mine."

"Your son has an eye for excellence then." Ron feigned a casual curiosity. "Would you ever consider parting with it?"

"In a heartbeat." Thomas sipped his drink. "But Ian, my son, loves that car. He's the only one who drives it." Thomas smiled. "It will be his one day."

"Ah, to be young and have such taste," Ron mused.

"Indeed," Thomas agreed. "He's got quite the eye for it."

As the velvety voice of the emcee announced the commencement of the dinner—a signal for guests to take their seats—Ron excused himself and made his way toward the exit.

Outside, rain had started to fall, and Ron was glad he had valet parking. He handed the ticket to a man dressed as well as he was. Then he called JP.

"Got something juicy, partner." Ron spoke in a hushed tone, ensuring privacy amidst the limousines and idle chatter of valets.

"Spill it," JP said.

"Callahan's Rolls Royce—it's not just a pretty toy. It's his son Ian's pride and joy, practically his birthright." Ron unbuttoned his jacket with his free hand. "According to Thomas, Ian is the only one who drives it."

"Interesting," JP said. "Means the kid might be more involved than we thought."

"Do you want me to go back in and see if I can get more information?"

"Never follow good whiskey with water, unless you're out of good whiskey."

"Is that a *no*?"

"Correct. You did good, Ron. Tomorrow I'll have a chat with young Ian. See if he sings the same tune as Daddy Dearest, but first I'm going to see a ghost."

Chapter 45

Thursday night

The relentless drumming of rain on his roof provided a constant backdrop as JP backed his truck into Gearhart's driveway. Across the street lay the ghost of an unsolved tragedy, what used to be the Harrington residence, where echoes of Elise's screams seemed almost audible in the downpour. The weather seemed to weep for Elise, its tears washing over the world in a torrent of sorrow.

He slumped in his seat to be less obvious, and kept his key in the ignition, ready to leap into action. But for now, patience was his ally and observation his weapon. "Thirty years," he muttered under his breath. "And not a dang clue to Elise's whereabouts." *What he had just learned from the Gearharts was the first bit of real evidence they had.* JP scanned the area, searching for anything out of place, any sign that might lead to a break in the case. He willed the universe to throw him a bone, to help unravel the mystery that had brought him here. And still, the rain poured, like the steady ticking of a clock each minute stretching longer than the last.

JP glanced at his watch. "Three hours," he grumbled, his frustration mounting. "And not a dang thing to show for it."

He prided himself on being the kind of man who could out-wait any suspect, outsmart any defense attorney in court, but tonight, patience felt like a game for fools.

"Time for a little pick-me-up." JP reached into the bag resting on the passenger seat and pulled out the thermos, the familiar coolness of stainless steel a small comfort. He unscrewed the cap and poured steaming coffee into the lid. He took a careful sip, letting the warmth spread through him. With his free hand, he rummaged through the bag until he found the sandwich. It was nothing fancy—just ham and cheese on sourdough—but it was sustenance, something to keep his body fueled.

JP took another swig of the bitter coffee, then decided it was time for a different vantage point. He grabbed his binoculars and exited the vehicle, his boots splashing in the puddles as he crossed the front lawn.

Reaching the front porch of Gearhart's house, he eased into the shadows. The darkness enveloped him, with no lights to betray his presence. He nestled into a corner, the rough texture of the wooden planks pressing against his back. At least he was out of the rain.

Through the binoculars he diligently maintained a clear line of sight, scanning the area Maverick had reported. The rain acted as a curtain, distorting shapes and casting misleading shadows, making JP wonder what Maverick actually saw. Or if Gearhart had seen things as clearly as he claimed.

Suddenly, JP's phone vibrated. He flinched and fumbled for the device, squinting at the bright screen. The message was nothing but an advertisement for a mattress sale —automated digital junk.

He shoved the phone back into the pocket of his coat. The false alert had spiked his adrenaline. *Was this just another night wasted on a wild goose chase?* Yet, he continued to scan the darkness, searching for something, anything that might break the monotony of the relentless drizzle and shadows.

The street was a monochrome palette, shades of grey and black coalescing in the downpour. JP moved the binoculars methodically from one house to the next, lingering on the windows where diffused light suggested life within. A curtain twitched—or had it? He focused on the window, but saw no further movement.

"Patience, old boy," he muttered. "It's all about the long game."

He rubbed his hands together, seeking warmth that was quickly being sapped by the cold night. *Time to get back in his truck.*

As he settled in, he fumbled for the keys in his pocket. *Maybe it was time to call it quits, to admit that tonight was a waste.*

Then, from the corner of his eye, he saw movement. His heart skipped a beat, and he grabbed the binoculars from the passenger seat. As the scene came into focus, the silhouette sharpened into the form of a stray cat, that darted across the street.

"Son of a gun." The adrenaline rush left as quickly as it had come, and he was left once again confronting a silent, empty street.

JP squinted at his watch—0237. Hours had dribbled away with the rain, yet not a single lead had emerged from the murky night.

Then he saw it. A flash of light on the bushes outside of Maverick's window. Two figures moving across the lawn. He started his engine and drove down the street toward the light, but abruptly, it disappeared. *Had he seen Maverick's phantom?*

Chapter 46

Friday morning

JP sat at his desk, staring at his computer. He sifted through the digital strata for any trace of Ian Callahan. The search results were frustratingly sparse—a few scattered mentions in local news articles and a LinkedIn profile that hadn't been updated in years. No Facebook page, no Twitter handle, not even an Instagram feed.

"Guy's not too social," JP said out loud. With a final click, he shut down the computer and stood, feeling a familiar creak in his knees. He grabbed his hat and headed out. *Time for some good ole' fashioned legwork.*

On the drive to Pacific Beach, he watched the landscape change from urban sprawl to coastal beauty. Upon arriving, JP parked his truck a block away from the condo complex where Ian reportedly lived. He climbed out onto the pavement, the salt air clinging to his senses. The complex was upscale, with security cameras discreetly placed above the entrance.

Around him, Pacific Beach thrummed with life—joggers, dog walkers, the distant laughter of children playing. He observed the ebb and flow of the residents, hoping one would be Ian.

Casually leaning against a tree, JP kept one eye on the building's entrance while pretending to fiddle with his phone. Before long, an older man walked up, keycard in hand.

JP seized his chance and followed him in before the gate closed.

As the resident headed down the walkway, JP hurried to the mailboxes in front. He ran his finger down the list of names until he found *Ian Callahan, 207*. Now he just had to find the condo without arousing suspicion. JP made a couple of turns, watching the numbers until he saw the unit he was looking for.

As he walked to the door, he noticed several surfboards locked to the iron railing. He knocked, but no one answered. He waited a few minutes and tried again. Still nothing.

JP left the complex and wandered down to the beach, where he watched surfers jostle for position in the swelling waves. He scanned the water, shading his eyes against the glare. He spotted a tight group of surfers cheering a rider slicing up and down a curling wave. As the surfer kicked out, JP caught a glimpse of his face—it was Ian.

JP kept his eye on him until Ian returned to the sand and sat down next to several other surfers. JP waited for a few minutes, then when the other young men left, he seized the moment to approach Ian. "Hey man, great riding out there!" he called out.

Ian squinted up at him. "Thanks." He stared at JP. "Hey, I know you. You're the investigator who was at my grandpa's house last week."

"Yep. That's me. JP's the name." He squatted to be on Ian's level.

"Are you here to question me?"

"Naw. I had some business to take care of down here, and I thought I'd watch the surfers a bit. Then I realized you looked familiar." JP smiled warmly. "You guys fascinate me. It's like ridin' a wild horse, only wetter."

"There's plenty of waves for everyone today."

One of the surfers walked up and asked questions about a video game that JP didn't recognize. At least, that's what he thought the guys were talking about.

When the kid walked away, JP said, "You seem pretty knowledgeable on that subject."

"You could say I'm the resident expert on that game, since I'm the one who created it."

JP now remembered that Ian was a successful tech guy. "What do you mean, you created it?"

"That's what I do for a living. I make games. I do the graphics. I've always been a gamer, to my father's disappointment. He used to yell at me to stop playing, because I could never make a living at it. I decided to prove him wrong and created a successful business."

"Is he okay with it now?"

"No. Even though I make a lot of money, which is always a driving force for him. But it's not enough." There was no bitterness in his voice, just pride. "He still tries to tell people that I do something else for a living. It's become quite funny, actually."

Someone called for Ian and he stood up. "Stick around. I'll be back shortly." Ian paddled back out after an impressive ride, flipping his board around and straddling it while he caught his breath. He went out again, then came back. Two more of Ian's fans followed him across the sand, asking questions about his latest game, then they walked away chatting about how amazing it was.

"The graphics in the game you're working on sound insane," JP said. "It must take some serious programming chops to make things look that realistic."

"Yeah. It's definitely challenging," Ian replied. "I've always loved pushing the boundaries of what's possible. The more lifelike I can make it, the more immersive the experience."

Feeling satisfied that he had what he came for, JP said goodbye and left.

Chapter 47

Friday late morning

Sabre paced the length of Karl Edward's cluttered office, her thoughts keeping pace with her steps. The walls were lined with monitors and an array of blinking lights. She assumed it was like that in every tech expert's lab.

"Sorry, Sabre. I've had a lot of personal issues. My brother passed away last week and it really set me back."

"I'm so sorry, Karl."

"I should've let you know, but it took longer than I expected to get you these results." Karl, a man in his mid-thirties with spiked hair, stood behind a desk piled high with hardware components. "It's not good footage, and the rain makes it even more difficult to get clarity. But I did find something."

She stopped pacing. "I understand. Let's see what you've got."

With a few keystrokes, he pulled up the surveillance footage the neighbor had captured the second night that Maverick saw the assault. The camera had caught a section of the road where a car was barely visible through sheets of rain.

"Can you enhance that?" Sabre pointed toward the dim outline of the vehicle on the corner.

"Already on it," Karl replied.

The image slowly sharpened under Karl's deft manipulation, and the car started to become more distinguishable. The shape was there, but the details were still muddied by the downpour that had blanketed the neighborhood that night.

"Anything?" she pressed, scanning for a discernible feature.

"Patience, Sabre," Karl murmured. "Enhancing isn't magic, but let's see what we've got here."

"Sorry."

"Wait a second." Karl abruptly paused the footage. "Does that look like a tail light to you?"

"It might be."

The grainy image of the dark sedan jolted to a halt on the screen. "That's the best I can do."

"Can you tell the model?" Sabre asked.

"No. But I'm not good at that sort of thing. I can get a still shot of it and text or email it to you."

"That would be good."

"And look at this," Karl said. "Thirty-two seconds after you see the car, you see something flash on the bushes. It looks like some kind of figures, probably people. I can't tell for sure because the camera is at a bad angle to get a clear shot. But I can tell you this much—they're one dimensional."

"Like ghosts?"

Karl chuckled. "I was thinking more like a projection from a mechanical device."

"I'm sorry." Sabre smiled. "This case has just been so bizarre."

"It's different for sure." He made a wild-eyed face. "The same thing happens on the second file. First, the vehicle at the corner, then the *ghosts*. Except it was twenty-seven seconds between the car and the lights."

"Do you have any explanation for the difference in time?"

"Nothing that means anything to me." Karl brought the second video up on the screen. "Have a look for yourself."

"Those flashes can't be random," Sabre said. "Could it be a malfunctioning streetlight, or perhaps the reflection of emergency vehicle lights?"

"Definitely not. The rhythm was too deliberate. Look at the pattern." Karl pointed at the screen where the lights now seemed to dance purposefully across the dense foliage. "It's too systematic. It seems designed to catch attention—or perhaps to divert it. My best guess is that it's a projection."

"And this second one is exactly like the first?"

"No. But it's very close. Under the assumption that it was from a projection, I did some experimenting and discovered that the movement of the ghosts was exactly the same, but the angle was slightly different. Since the surveillance camera didn't move, the change had to come from the source."

"Meaning the projector was in a slightly different spot?"

"Correct."

"Please send still shots of those sections. My brother is somewhat of an old car expert. I'll see if he can determine the make. And my investigator may have another take on what you found."

~~~

Later at home

Sabre and Ron huddled in front of her laptop examining the still shots Karl had sent.

"Look closely at the snippets of the car." She displayed the images side-by-side. "Are they the same car?"

"They look like it to me. I can tell by the taillight that it's an older vehicle. I'd say forties or early fifties at the latest."

"Could it be the Rolls Royce?"

"It could, but I can't say for sure," Ron said. "A real expert might be able to tell."

JP entered the room, gave Sabre a quick kiss, and asked, "Whatcha lookin' at?"

"The footage from Anderson's surveillance cameras. I met with Karl earlier today."
~~~

"Anything good?"

Sabre showed him the still shots of the car and summarized what they knew. Then she showed both men the video clips with the ghosts.

"What does that look like to you?" Sabre pointed to the one-dimensional images on the screen.

"It looks like someone was projecting a video onto the wall and the bushes," Ron said.

"That's what Karl thinks too."

JP cut in. "I know exactly who would have the know-how to do that."

"Who?" Sabre asked.

"Ian Callahan." JP explained what he had learned and how realistic Ian's video games were.

"With the rain and the correct angle, I bet they looked real," Ron said.

"Gearhart told his daughter that he saw the man put something on the hood of his car," JP said. "What if that something was a camera?"

"Exactly," Ron added. "If the first reenactment was filmed, then subsequent ones could've been projected. That would explain the eerie consistency across scenes."

"But why would Ian do that?" Sabre scowled. "What possible motive could he have?"

"People do lots of things for bizarre reasons." JP finally sat down. "Clearing his father or grandfather's name could be a powerful motivator. The Callahans have always been protective of their legacy."

"But pride doesn't explain the risk he's taking. No." Sabre shook her head. "I don't think this is just about family honor. There has to be more."

"What if it's about setting the record straight?" JP suggested. "The Callahans have skirted the law for generations. Perhaps Ian's sick of the cover-ups."

"But why go to all this trouble to bring justice to Elise Harrington now?" The case still made no sense to Sabre. "Ian wasn't even born when it happened."

"Unless Ian found out something about Elise, something personal." JP's voice was low. "Maybe he discovered a connection we haven't."

"Or maybe Ian wants to expose the truth about his family's dark history because it's the only way to absolve himself from it," Sabre said.

"But why would he need to absolve himself? Just because he carries the Callahan name?"

Ron jumped into the mix. "Or maybe he's just one fry short of a Happy Meal."

Sabre almost laughed. "Whatever his reasons, he's playing a dangerous game."

"And we need to find out what he's up to," JP said. "I'll go back and see him. Maybe I can get him to fess up."

"And I'll get a subpoena. Whatever his reasons, we need him at the trial Monday."

Chapter 48

Saturday morning

The Pacific Beach sun was shining brightly as JP approached Ian Callahan's condo. A wet suit hung from the balcony wall, and a damp surfboard leaned against the wall.

JP knocked sharply. The door opened, and Ian looked at JP with acceptance—as if he'd been anticipating this moment.

"Mornin'," JP said. "You don't seem surprised to see me."

"You're good at your job. I knew you'd figure it out." Ian stepped back. "Come on in."

They walked inside and took a seat at the dining table.

JP laid it out. "We both know you've been staging those ghostly reenactments. My question is simple: Why bring Elise Harrington back from the dead?"

"Was she murdered though? They never found a body. There's reason to believe she was alive for months after she went missing."

A surge of excitement ran up his spine. "What evidence? What do you know that I don't?"

"A lot. Elise's murder was a tragedy. A young life cut short, a story unfinished."

"Unfinished stories have a way of haunting us," JP said. "Especially when they're resurrected for reasons other than grief."

"What about the truth?" Ian asked. "Shouldn't we give the dead their day in court?"

"Let's not wait for court." JP's patience frayed as he thought of Maverick—and the charges he faced because of this man's antics. "Tell me now, Ian. What's your endgame?"

Ian's eyes locked onto JP's, then flickered with something undefinable. "All in good time," he murmured.

"Ian!" JP snapped. "You've admitted to staging those visions. Why? And what are you hiding?"

"I have my reasons," he said. "Reasons that will only be disclosed in the courtroom."

"Dammit! " JP growled, frustration mounting. He remembered the mix of confusion and fear as Maverick recounted what he thought he'd seen. "Your little charade has put an innocent kid in hot water. Maverick is facing serious charges because of your games."

"I'm sorry about that."

"If there's a shred of decency in you, give us something to work with. The truth needs to come out. His trial is almost over."

"You'll get the truth," Ian promised.

"How do I know you'll even show up?"

"Because I've worked too hard to get this close. I wouldn't miss it for the world." Ian's façade abruptly began to crack. "I never meant for any of this to fall on the kid." His hands, which until moments ago had been balled into fists of defiance, now opened and shook slightly.

"Regret's a start," JP said. "But it doesn't change what you've done. You set up an elaborate hoax that's costing a boy dearly."

Ian swallowed hard. "I know. It spiraled out of control. I thought I could manage it. I was wrong. But I promise you, I'll be in court."

"And you'll testify that you created this whole crime scene?"

"Yes. I have no reason to deny it."

"Even if you face criminal charges?"

"That's the least of my concerns."

"Actions have consequences, Ian." JP reached into the interior pocket of his leather jacket, pulled out an envelope, and handed it to Ian. "You've been served."

"Thank you." Ian smiled.

"I've never gotten that reaction before when I served papers." He stood to leave.

"It'll all be worth it in the end. You think you know what's happening, but this trial will blow the lid off everything. Secrets have a way of crawling out of the darkness when you shine light on them."

"You had help when you reenacted the scene. At least the first night. Who's involved in this with you?"

"No one you know. I hired it done. It's easy to find someone for a gig like that. Lots of hungry actresses out there."

"One more thing," JP said. "Did you send the text to Sabre saying there was new evidence to be found?"

He nodded without speaking.

JP stepped out into the brisk ocean air. The click of the door locking behind him echoed a finality to their strange exchange. Yet it opened a floodgate of uncertainties. *What did Ian stand to gain by orchestrating those ghostly visions of Elise's murder? And why wait until trial?*

Chapter 49

Monday morning

With Maverick at her side, Sabre waited nervously in the courtroom. This trial could go any direction, and she hated the uncertainty. Finally Judge Feldman took the bench.

"Did you get a chance to regroup, Ms. Brown?"

"I did, Your Honor. Thank you for the time. It was most helpful."

The judge turned to the DDA. "Are you ready, Mr. Knowles?"

"Ready, Your Honor."

"Very well. Ms. Brown, please call your first witness."

Sabre rose from her seat. "The defense calls Shelby Williams."

A woman with nervous eyes took the witness stand.

"Ms. Williams." Sabre started by building a foundation for her strategy. "What is the address of your family home?"

Shelby gave the information and explained that she lived in Lakeside now, but that her father had lived in the family home until his death.

"And how close is that house to where Maverick lives?"

"It's across the street, catty-corner from our house in plain view."

"Did your father ever discuss with you anything strange he saw happen at the Venables' house?"

"Objection," Knowles said. "Hearsay."

"It's a yes or no question, Your Honor," Sabre countered.

"Overruled. Please answer the question."

"Yes, he did."

"When did he share that information?"

"The day before he was murdered."

"Did anything he told you have relevance to this case?"

"Yes, it did."

"Can you tell the court what your father confided to you?" Sabre knew what was coming and was prepared.

"Objection!" Knowles shot up. "Calls for hearsay, Your Honor."

"Your Honor, the defense argues that the statement made by the deceased to his daughter should be admissible under the California hearsay rule, specifically under the dying declaration exception California Evidence Code Section 1242. This exception allows for the admission of a statement made by a declarant while believing their death was imminent, concerning the cause or circumstances of what they believed to be their impending death."

Sabre locked eyes with the judge as if to transfer the weight of her argument through sheer force of will. "Mr. Gearhart made the statement to his daughter while he was in fear for his life, suggesting he believed his death was imminent. The content of the statement directly pertains to the crime element he witnessed, which is intrinsically linked to the circumstances leading to his death." She paused for a moment, ensuring her words sank in. "The context in which the statement was made—a father confiding in his daughter while fearing for his life—inherently carries an element of trustworthiness. Furthermore, excluding such a critical piece of evidence would undermine the pursuit of justice. Admitting this statement serves the greater good of uncovering the truth."

The DDA started to stand again, but Sabre went on. "Furthermore, the statement was against Mr. Gearhart's own interest. It contained his admission of involvement in a crime, which is inherently against his penal interest. By confessing his participation in the crime, he exposed himself to potential criminal liability, indicating the statement's veracity. It aligns with the evidence we have and corroborates Maverick's claims. For these reasons, the defense respectfully requests that the court admit the deceased's statement as an exception to the hearsay rule."

"Your response, Mr. Knowles?" The judge glanced at the opposing counsel.

The prosecutor stood. "Your Honor, the State contends that the statement does not satisfy the necessary criteria for exceptions. There is insufficient evidence to prove that the deceased genuinely believed his death was imminent at the time he made the statement. The fear for one's life does not necessarily equate to a belief in imminent death, which is a critical distinction for the dying declaration exception. The circumstances surrounding the statement are vague and lack specificity. Without clear context or corroboration, the reliability of the statement is questionable. The daughter's recounting of the statement might be influenced by her interpretation or memory, reducing its trustworthiness. The statement was made in a highly emotional context, which could lead to misinterpretation or bias. While the statement may appear to be against the deceased's interest, there is insufficient corroborating evidence to verify its accuracy. The passage of 30 years adds to the difficulty of substantiating the declarant's involvement and the truth of the statement. Also, the context in which the statement was made is unclear and potentially ambiguous. Therefore, the prosecution respectfully requests that the court exclude the deceased's statement from evidence."

The judge seemed to weigh the arguments.

"Your Honor," Knowles started again, "the reliability of such statements is highly questionable—"

"Mr. Knowles," Sabre cut in. "We're not dealing with mere hearsay but a man's final acknowledgment of a truth he perceived as life-threatening. It's a truth that my client has a right to present in his defense."

The judge raised his hand, palm out. "Okay, I've heard enough."

Sabre waited, poised for whatever ruling might come next, ready to leap into action.

"Objection overruled," Feldman said. "Ms. Brown, you may proceed with your witness, but you need to establish that Mr. Gearhart was in fact in fear for his life and/or his involvement in a crime that connects to this case."

"Thank you, Your Honor."

Sabre faced her witness. "Shelby, what did your father say that made you think he was in fear for his life?"

"He told me someone was after him, and he was afraid he wouldn't ever see me again."

"Did he explain why he thought that?"

"He said he had been hiding out for a while because he knew too much about the Elise Harrington case."

"Did you know what he was referring to?"

"Yes. I was about ten years old when it happened. She lived across the street from us. She was coming home late at night and she was kidnapped or murdered. No one ever saw her again, and they never solved her disappearance. I remember it well because the neighborhood kids were all afraid after that."

"You said your father 'knew too much.' Did he tell you how he knew about the case?"

Shelby took a deep breath. "He said he didn't want me to think less of him, but that he had helped the man put Elise in the car after he gave her some chloroform."

Sabre was surprised by that testimony, but concealed it and moved on. "Was the woman dead?"

"No. He said he could feel her breathing when he moved her."

"Did he know the man he helped?"

"Yes, it was –"

"Objection, relevance," Knowles shouted. "We don't need to try another case here. We just need to know how that relates to the present case."

"Sustained," the judge said.

"Ms. Williams, how does that case relate to the crime Maverick reported?"

"My father said he saw a reenactment of that old crime the same night Maverick did, and the same car was involved, a 1940 black and burgundy Rolls Royce Phantom limo."

A few whispers from the attendees behind her.

"Thank you, Ms. Williams." Sabre paused. "Did your father tell you why he believed his life was in danger?"

"Yes. He said he noticed a strange car parked near his place and felt like he was being followed. He was sure someone had found out where he was hiding."

"Did he express any specific fears related to his involvement in the crime?"

Shelby nodded, twisting her hands together. "He was terrified that the people who were involved in the crime back then were coming after him to silence him."

"How did your father describe his situation to you?"

"He said he was living in constant fear and didn't think he had much time left. He was convinced they would kill him to prevent him from talking."

"Ms. Williams, how did your father's demeanor and words during this conversation affect you?"

"It made me realize just how serious and real his fears were." She swallowed hard. "I'd never known him to be that scared, and he knew his time was almost up. He said, 'Shelby, if anything happens to me, it's because I know too much.' And that same day, he was killed."

"Now, coming back to this current case, did your father say he witnessed any of the things Maverick saw?"

"Objection. Leading."

"I'll reword, Your Honor," Sabre said. "Did your father tell you anything about the night Maverick claims to have seen a crime in his yard?"

"He said he saw the same car that was used in the Harrington crime thirty years ago."

"Objection, stating facts not in evidence." Knowles looked rattled. "It hasn't been established that a crime was actually committed in the Harrington case. No evidence was found at the scene, and no conviction was ever rendered."

"Sustained," Judge Feldman said.

"I'll reword the question," Sabre said. "Ms. Williams, you said your father told you he was involved in a crime thirty years ago, correct?"

"Yes."

"And that crime, how was it connected to this case?"

"My father said he saw the same 1940 Rolls Royce around the corner at both scenes."

"Did he say who that car belonged to?"

"Patrick Callahan."

"What else did your father see the second time, in the current case?"

"Objection," Knowles bellowed.

"I'll reword," Sabre had coached Shelby about this issue, then she'd done it herself.

"What else did your father *tell you* he saw?"

Knowles was on his feet. "Objection. Hearsay."

"Overruled," the judge said. "Under the dying declaration exception."

"He said he saw a man and a woman get out of the Rolls Royce in the pouring rain. The man placed something on the hood of his car. Then the two of them walked over to the wall and the man appeared to hit the woman over the head. She fell to the ground. He dragged her away, but then she got up and they got back in the car and drove off."

"Thank you, Ms. Williams," Sabre said softly. She turned back to her table and took a seat.

Knowles stood to cross examine the witness, but the judge raised his hand. "Let's break for lunch. Return at 1:30 sharp."

Chapter 50

Monday afternoon

"I believe you were about to cross-examine the witness, Mr. Knowles," Judge Feldman said.

The prosecutor stood. "I'm ready, Your Honor." He made several attempts at discrediting Shelby Williams, but gave up when he didn't make any progress.

"Let's move on," the judge declared.

Sabre called Chuck Anderson to testify that the surveillance footage belonged to him. Chain of custody was established, and the videos authenticated.

"Your Honor, we'd like to submit Exhibit B, the surveillance footage from Chuck Anderson's yard. My next witness will testify to its contents."

"Proceed."

Sabre called her next witness. Red-headed Karl Edwards, approached the stand. His gait was confident, his eyes sharp behind dark-rimmed glasses.

"Mr. Edwards," Sabre began, "could you please state your qualifications for the court?"

"Of course. I hold a PhD in Digital Forensics from Stanford University and have ten years of experience analyzing video surveillance for law enforcement agencies."

"What did you find upon reviewing this footage?" Sabre directed the court's attention to the large screen where grainy images flickered to life.

"Based on the timestamp and my analysis of the metadata," Karl explained, "the footage aligns with the time frame of Maverick's reporting. There is a car at the corner of the frame."

After some back and forth, Karl brought up the second video he analyzed and testified that there was a car in the same spot. He also pointed out the flash of light and what looked like "ghostly figures."

"Are you saying this supports Maverick's account of seeing something that might have been construed as a crime?"

"It's very possible. I can't tell what the figures were doing because of the angle, but it could be the way he reported it."

"Thank you, Mr. Edwards. No further questions."

"Cross, Mr. Knowles?"

The prosecutor stood. "You stated there were 'ghostly figures' in the video. Are you suggesting Maverick saw ghosts?"

"Not at all. What I believe he saw was some kind of video show projected on the wall."

Knowles nodded, undeterred. "Let's talk about the footage itself. You stated it supports Maverick's account of the events. However, isn't it true that the figures in the video are indistinguishable? You're not even certain they were people, correct?"

"I believe they were a projection of people."

The DDA made a few more runs at Edwards' credibility, but nothing that damaged their case.

The courtroom was quiet as Gary Venable took the stand, his presence solid and reassuring. The man had a rugged honesty about him, his eyes clear and direct.

"Mr. Venable," Sabre addressed him warmly, "you've been Maverick's foster father for how long?"

"Going on three years now," Gary said.

"And in that time, have you ever known Maverick to make up stories?"

"Never," Gary stated without hesitation. "The boy's been through a lot, but he's got a strong moral compass. If Maverick says he saw something, then he saw it."

"Even when his friends doubted him, when it would've been easier to retract his statement, he stuck to his story, correct?"

"Absolutely. Maverick doesn't back down from the truth."

"Thank you, Mr. Venable. No further questions."

As Sabre sat down, the prosecutor rose, his eyes narrowing at Gary.

"Mr. Venable," Knowles began, "you have taken many troubled teens into your home, correct?"

"That's right," Gary replied.

"Indeed, fostering children like Maverick can present challenges. You wouldn't want to see any harm come to them or their reputations, would you?" Knowles asked.

"Of course not," Gary shot back, "but that doesn't mean I'd lie for them."

"Isn't it true that Maverick recently lied about having a young woman in his room?"

"That's true, but it's not the same thing. He doesn't make up elaborate stories."

"Until now."

"Objection," Sabre said.

"Sustained. Please refrain from commentary, Mr. Knowles."

"I apologize, Your Honor." Knowles turned as if to sit down, then paused dramatically. "Just one more thing, Mr. Venable." The DDA turned back suddenly. "Isn't it true that you receive substantial funding based on the number of children in your care?"

Gary's face reddened with indignation. "I would hardly say substantial. Besides, this isn't about money. It's about justice."

"Isn't it true, Mr. Venable, that as a foster parent, you might feel compelled to defend Maverick regardless of the truth? To see him in a more favorable light than others might?"

Gary's jaw set firm. "I stand for what's right, not for what's easy."

"No further questions."

Gary was released. He stepped down from the witness stand. "Stay strong, Mav," he whispered, squeezing Maverick's shoulder as he passed by.

"Your Honor, the defense calls Mr. Henry Lawson to the stand," Sabre announced, her voice reverberating slightly in the high-ceilinged room.

Henry Lawson, a man in his late forties with a meticulous beard and glasses perched on his nose, took the stand. He wore a smart blue blazer that contrasted with his salt-and-pepper hair.

Once sworn in, Sabre approached him. "Mr. Lawson, could you please tell the court about your profession?"

Henry adjusted his glasses. "Certainly. I am a forensic telecommunications analyst. I specialize in analyzing and interpreting data from telecommunications systems to assist in legal cases."

Sabre nodded. "Mr. Lawson, were you asked to examine certain telecommunications data related to this case?"

"Yes, I was," Henry confirmed.

"And what did your examination reveal regarding the defendant, Maverick's phone records?"

"I found that Maverick received multiple phone calls that correspond with the times he claims to have witnessed crimes from his window."

"Can you tell who these calls came from?"

"Not who, because the calls were made from a computerized number, which means they were likely generated by a computer or an automated system, not a regular mobile phone."

"Could you clarify for the court what the significance of these computer-generated calls might be in the context of this case?"

Henry leaned forward, his hands clasped before him. "Certainly. The pattern of calls suggests a high likelihood that they were deliberately timed. It appears these calls could have been used to prompt Mr. Maverick to look out his window precisely when these alleged crimes were taking place."

Sabre continued. "Mr. Lawson, in your expert opinion, is there a technical possibility that someone orchestrated these events to manipulate what Maverick witnessed?"

"It is not only possible, but likely," Henry stated firmly. "The precision of the timing of the calls in relation to the events suggests a coordinated effort to control Maverick's observations."

Sabre then faced the judge. "Your Honor, I have no further questions for Mr. Lawson."

"Cross, Mr. Knowles?"

"Mr. Lawson, thank you for your testimony," Knowles began. "You mentioned that these phone calls were made from a computerized number. Could you explain to the court exactly how you determine a number is computerized?"

Henry nodded, his expression neutral. "Certainly. A computerized number typically does not follow the standard numbering format used by telecommunications providers. They often originate from VoIP services—Voice over Internet Protocol—or are generated by software designed for automated tasks."

"So, you are saying these numbers are from a VoIP service. Isn't it true that many businesses and even individuals use VoIP services for legitimate reasons, including cost savings?"

"That is correct," Henry admitted, shifting slightly in his seat.

"And isn't it also true that identifying a call as coming from a VoIP service doesn't necessarily indicate anything nefarious or manipulative about the nature of the call?"

"That's correct," Henry replied. "However, in the context of this case—"

Knowles cut him off. "Yes, we'll get to the context shortly. For now, let's focus on the calls themselves. You said these calls were timed with the crimes the defendant witnessed. How precise was this timing?"

"The calls were placed within minutes of the reported times of each crime," Henry answered.

Knowles glanced at his notes, then back at Henry. "Minutes, you say. So, there was a gap. It wasn't to the second or even the same minute?"

"There is some question as to the exact timing on at least one of the reported incidents," Henry conceded.

Knowles paced a few steps, then turned sharply. "Mr. Lawson, you also suggested that these calls were likely used to prompt the defendant to look out his window. Are you suggesting the defendant was conditioned to respond to these calls by looking out his window?"

Henry hesitated, choosing his words carefully. "No, there is no evidence of conditioning. I am merely suggesting a possible explanation based on the timing."

"A possible explanation," Knowles repeated, emphasizing the word *possible*. "But you cannot say with certainty that these calls were intended to manipulate the defendant, can you?"

"I cannot say with absolute certainty, no," Henry admitted.

"One last question, Mr. Lawson. Did you find any evidence of who might be behind these computerized calls or any direct connection to the alleged crimes themselves?"

"No direct evidence linking the calls to an individual or the crimes," Henry confirmed.

"Thank you, Mr. Lawson. That's all the questions I have."

"Re-direct, Ms. Brown?"

"Just a couple of questions, Your Honor," Sabre said as she stood up.

"Mr. Lawson, do the phone records show any other computerized calls to Maverick in the last six months?"

"No. Only the three calls. He received one each night just before the crime took place outside his window."

"No further questions." Sabre sat down.

"Who is your next witness, Ms. Brown?"

"Ian Callahan."

The judge looked at his watch. "It's getting late. Do you think this witness will take long?"

"Most likely, and I expect there will be extensive cross examination."

"Then we'll recess for the day. We'll start with Mr. Callahan first thing tomorrow morning. Court is adjourned."

Chapter 51

Monday evening

The clink of heavy glass against the worn wooden counter punctuated the murmur of conversations at O'Malley's Tavern. JP nodded at the bartender before scanning the dimly lit room for his rendezvous. At a corner of the bar, Vinny DuBois waited.

"McCloud," Vinny said.

JP settled into the booth. "Thanks for coming."

"Couldn't say no to a beer. What's going on?"

"Thomas Callahan's son is testifying tomorrow in Maverick's case."

"Maverick, the kid who sees murdering ghosts." Vinny recalled the details. "So, what does this have to do with me?"

"Here's the thing." JP paused to order beers from a server, then looked back at DuBois. "Ian Callahan will testify that he reenacted the Elise Harrington assault. He's a gaming expert who creates lifelike videos. He filmed the reenactment and played the videos off the wall to make them look realistic, especially in the rain."

"That's wild. And sure explains a few things for Maverick." DuBois looked around for the server. "You think he knows what happened in the Harrington case?"

"He knew enough to reenact the crime."

"How old is this guy?"

"Can't be more than thirty."

"So, he's not old enough to have been involved, or even remember anything from back then."

"No. But he's lived with these people for a long time, and he may have heard or seen things he wasn't supposed to."

The waitress set down their beers, and JP paid for them. "And get this. He used his grandfather's old car, the same one that was used in the original crime."

"So, you think one of the Callahans kidnapped or killed Elise?"

"Most likely Thomas," JP said. "I'm guessing he found out Elise and Harper were in love. Maybe even discovered Elise was pregnant, assumed it was Harper's kid, and lost control."

"Or, maybe Daddy Dearest was protecting his son, or the Callahan name. That's pretty important to him."

"From what I've heard, they're both meaner than a sack full of rattlesnakes, so who knows?"

"True enough," DuBois said. "I talked to Shelby and she said her father helped kidnap Elise Harrington, but she wouldn't tell me who the perpetrator was."

"We had the same problem. She either doesn't know or she's still very afraid of someone."

"Truthfully, I don't think her father told her. She's been open about everything else."

"I think you're right," JP said. "I hope you can make it there tomorrow. Maybe Ian won't reveal anything we don't already know, but I thought you might want in the loop. I know it's important to your father to have the old case solved, and I'm pretty sure you don't want me getting in the middle of it."

"You got that right. I'll be in court tomorrow."

"If something happens and you can't make it, I'll update you. I'll be there as Sabre's investigator."

They raised their bottles in silent agreement.

~~~
~~~

JP stepped into the study where Sabre was still poring over her case files.

"Still at it, huh?" JP said.

"Ian's testimony could pivot the whole case." Sabre rubbed her tired eyes. "I just hope he comes through for us."

JP leaned against the chair behind her. "You think he'll actually show?"

"Hard to say." She finally glanced up at him. "Ian obviously has his own agenda. I just wish I knew what it was, so I knew how to prepare. I'm breaking the first rule you learn in law school."

"What's that?"

"Never ask a question you don't know the answer to."

"But you can't win without his testimony."

"Probably not, but we got good information into the record today. We have testimony that a car was there."

"But it was vague," JP said.

"And we established there was something that looked like figures outside his window."

"The ghost defense."

"And his foster father attested to his honesty."

"But he lied about having a girl in his room, and to the police when he said he made the crime up."

"You're right," Sabre said. "We need Ian's testimony. Besides, we have a judge who's connected to the Callahans."

"Has he shown any bias?"

"Quite the contrary, but that might be to overcompensate. What will count is his ruling." Sabre sighed. "I just hope I can ask the right questions."

JP planted a reassuring grip on her shoulder. "You've cracked tougher nuts than this Callahan kid."

"Thanks." Sabre took a deep breath, picked up her bottle of water, and turned off the desk lamp.

Her phone buzzed in her pocket. She pulled it out, tapping the screen to load a text message from Ian Callahan. Frowning, she read the words, trying to interpret their meaning and potential impact on the case.

Ian: *Be sure to ask about my background and why I did it. Also, allow my father to be in court if you want me to show up.*

"Look at this." Sabre held out the phone.

JP read the text. "Think he's looking for absolution or setting us up?"

"Hard to say."

Chapter 52

Tuesday morning

When Judge Feldman called for preliminary matters, Sabre cleared the way for Detective DuBois to be present in the courtroom as long as he wasn't called as a witness. She didn't mention Thomas Callahan. Sabre didn't expect him to show up, but if he did, she would deal with it.

The case was called, murmurs in the courtroom ceased, and Sabre stood. "The defense calls Mr. Ian Callahan to the stand."

Ian remained seated, but he glanced back at the courtroom doors. They opened and Thomas Callahan strode through in a perfectly tailored suit. The bailiff confronted Thomas, but didn't ask him to leave.

"Hello, Mr. Callahan," Judge Feldman said. "I know your son is about to take the stand, but juvenile court proceedings are confidential."

"The State has no objection, Your Honor," the prosecutor said.

"The concern is for the defendant," the judge explained. "Ms. Brown, your client has a right to exclude anyone who is not an interested party. What is his position?"

"We have no objection at this point, Your Honor."

Ian stood, walked confidently to the stand, and took the oath.

"Please state your name for the record," the clerk instructed.

"Ian Callahan."

The doors at the back creaked open. All heads turned as Detective DuBois eased inside. The bailiff approached him and they exchanged a few words, then the bailiff nodded at the judge. DuBois sat in the back without a word.

"Let the record show that Detective Vincent DuBois is present in the courtroom," the judge said.

"Mr. Callahan." Sabre turned her attention back to Ian. "What is your occupation?"

"I create video games. I'm an expert in my field and have received several awards for my realism. I can take a simple scene and make it look real."

"Do you know the defendant, Maverick McLaughlin?"

"Not personally."

"How do you know him, if not personally?"

"I know where he lives, and I've contacted him on three occasions."

"How did you contact him?" Sabre asked.

"I called him on his cell phone twice and told him to look out the window, then hung up. The third time, I called and just hung up when he answered."

"When did you make those calls?"

Ian gave the dates and exact time for the three calls, which matched Maverick's crime reports.

"Why did you call him?"

"I wanted him to look out his window and see the assaults."

"How did you know they were happening?"

"I was the one orchestrating them."

Thomas jumped from his seat, eyes bulging, and thundered, "Ian! Don't say another word! Talk to a lawyer before you incriminate yourself."

The judge hammered the gavel down. "Order! Order in the court!"

Sabre remained composed. "Your Honor." Sabre turned toward the bench, "I ask that Thomas Callahan be reminded of the decorum expected in this courtroom."

The judge leveled a stern gaze at him. "Sir, one more outburst and you'll be removed. Do you understand?"

Thomas sank into his seat, his chest heaving with restrained fury.

"Please continue," the judge instructed.

Sabre looked at Ian. "Please tell us how they were orchestrated?"

Ian Callahan swallowed hard. "Actually, the first night was staged with real people. I set up the scene like the Harrington crime from thirty years ago." His jaw clenched.

"And the next two times?" Sabre prompted.

"The other nights were enhanced videos," he confessed. "I projected them onto the wall."

"Did you do all this by yourself?"

"Objection, relevance," Mr. Knowles said.

"I'll rephrase, Your Honor," Sabre said. "Was Maverick involved in this charade in any way?"

"No. As I said, I don't even know the kid. And I'm sorry for any harm I've caused him."

"Thank you for that," Sabre said. "You stated that you set up the scenes like the Harrington crime. How do you know about that case?"

"I've done a lot of research because I know my family was very close with Elise Harrington. My father was once engaged to her."

"What purpose did you mean to serve?"

"I wanted someone to reopen the cold case and find out who killed Elise Harrington."

"You think she's dead?"

"I know they never found a body, but she disappeared."

"But why did you go to such unusual lengths?"

"I've tried many times to get the cops or the district attorney to open this case and find out who did it. No one would listen to me, so I decided to try another way using something I know how to do."

"Why did you want the case opened?"

"Objection. Relevance." Knowles was on his feet again.

"About time," Thomas muttered.

"That's enough, Mr. Callahan," Feldman cautioned. "Overruled." He turned to the witness. "You may answer the question."

"I know that thirty years ago, several members of my family were prime suspects in Elise Harrington's disappearance. Both Thomas and Patrick Callahan were questioned."

"So, you were trying to clear their names?"

"No. I was trying to get justice for Elise."

"Knowles!" Thomas called out. "Stop this circus!"

The prosecutor stood and turned around. "I don't work for you." Then he pivoted back to the judge. "However, this is way off base. I object, Your Honor, on relevance grounds."

Sabre knew she had gone too far, as did the judge. "Sustained. Please change your line of questioning, Ms. Brown."

"Thank you, Your Honor." She paused. "Mr. Callahan, was your video good enough to convince someone watching that it was real?"

"It was *that* good. Especially with the rain coming down."

"Is that why you only did this on rainy nights?"

"Partly. It was storming the night Elise disappeared. I made it as true to life as I could. I have a copy of the video if you want to see it."

"Thank you, Mr. Callahan, but if we need it, we'll let you know."

"I think Elise was my mother," Ian abruptly announced.

The DDA jumped up. "Objection! No question pending."

"Sustained," the judge said.

"Your Honor," Knowles said. "I request a recess. I'd like to speak to Ms. Brown, perhaps even have a look at those videos."

"That seems like a good idea, Counselor. We'll break for lunch. I'll see you back here at two o'clock."

After the judge walked out, Thomas rushed to his son. "We need to talk!" Thomas commanded.

"I don't have anything to say to you right now." Ian crossed his arms.

Thomas reached for Ian, but his son side-stepped to avoid him. DuBois was suddenly in front of Ian, while the bailiff confronted Thomas. "You need to leave this courtroom right now."

"Listen, punk, you don't tell me what to do."

"I do in this courtroom. You can leave, or I can take you to a holding cell." As he spoke, two other sheriffs burst through the doors.

Thomas raised his hands. "I'm leaving."

Chapter 53

Tuesday late morning

Sabre, JP, DuBois, and Ian remained in the courtroom while Maverick went to lunch with his foster parents.

"You did a good job, Ian," Sabre said.

"You sure did," DuBois added. "Can we talk? Somewhere private."

"Sure," Ian replied. "But I'd like Sabre to join us if that's okay."

"Of course."

"Mike," Sabre said to the bailiff. "Can we go out the back door to a conference room? We don't want to encounter Thomas Callahan."

"No problem," Mike said.

They slipped out the back door where Mike escorted them to an empty conference room. A minute later, they took seats at a table in a small windowless room. DuBois extracted a notepad and pen from his coat pocket, and Sabre turned to Ian. "I need to make it clear that I'm not your attorney. Anything you say here is not protected by privilege."

Ian nodded. "Understood." "Good," Sabre replied. "Then let's see what else you have in your bag of tricks."

DuBois' voice was measured, his tone firm. "Ian, I gotta hand it to you. That was some testimony today." He tapped the notepad with the back of his pen. "Not every day we get a curveball like that in court."

"Thanks," Ian said, managing a half-smile.

Ian turned to the detective. "What's this about? Is it the reenactment thing? Are you going to arrest me?"

"No. We'll deal with that later. It's the Harrington case that's got my attention." DuBois' eyes were alight with energy.

"Right." Ian exhaled, as if releasing a pressure valve. "After everything that happened, I had questions. About who I am, you know?" He fidgeted with his fingers on the tabletop.

"Go on," urged DuBois.

"Some of my friends were doing the Ancestry.com DNA testing, and it seemed harmless enough. Spit in a test tube and mail it off ..." Ian's voice trailed off momentarily. "But I discovered I had another uncle besides Harper. Since my mom, the woman who I thought was my mother, was an only child, I just figured Grandpa had a kid out there that he kept secret, or didn't even know about."

"Did you confront anyone?"

"Not then. I did a little more research on Ancestry.com and discovered that Harper was in their database, but it gave us a sibling match instead of an uncle/nephew match. That made no sense to me, so I confronted Uncle Harper. He said there must be some mistake and encouraged me to let it go. He said whatever I found out would probably hurt more than help."

"But you didn't let it go?" DuBois asked.

"No. I decided to check my father's DNA. So, I took some hair from his brush to a lab and had it analyzed. It turned out that he was my brother as well, making Patrick my father." Ian took a breath. "Then I went to see Ted Harrington, the uncle I had just learned about."

The information was stunning, and Sabre had a hard time keeping quiet. But she let DuBois handle the questioning.

"Elaborate for me," the detective said. "What did you learn from Ted?"

"Besides that, his sister, Elise, was my mother?" Ian drew in a deep breath. "He had his own theory about what happened to her. He believed Thomas killed her."

"Your father?"

"Technically, he's my brother, but yes. Ted said their father told him Elise was in love with someone else."

"Did he know who?"

"No." Ian shrugged. "But he was convinced that jealousy was the motive."

"Do you believe him?"

Ian swallowed hard. "I think Ted genuinely believes it was Thomas. Maybe it was. The family always avoided talking about Elise. It's like they were hiding something. I just don't know for sure what it is. Would I be surprised if it turned out to be Thomas who killed her? No. He's not a nice person."

"How old are you?" DuBois asked.

"I'll be thirty in April."

"So, if your mother is Elise," Sabre said. "She was alive for at least seven months after she disappeared."

Ian nodded. "I know."

"Do you have any idea what happened to her after that?" DuBois asked.

"No."

"Did her brother have any contact with her?"

"Not since the night she disappeared."

"Did you learn anything else?" DuBois asked.

"Uncle Ted said there was a woman Elise confided in, that if she had contacted anyone, it would be her."

"Did he give you a name?"

"He couldn't remember it."

DuBois' eyes clouded with concern. "Now that your father, I mean Thomas, knows what you've done, are you afraid?"

"A little. No. Actually a lot. That's why I wanted to do this in public."

"Be careful," DuBois said. "We don't know how deep this goes—or who might be watching. At least one person connected with this case has already been killed."

"I will," Ian said.

"In fact, stick with me until we finish here today. I'll see that you're safe."

"I've always felt out of place in my family, but I never knew why." Moisture glistened in the corners of his eyes. "Finding out about Elise explained so much. I had to know more, to find her justice."

They all got up to leave, then Ian said, "Oh, one other thing."

DuBois gave him a quizzical look.

"I also found a half-sister. I don't know if she's my mom's kid or another of Patrick's, but she's three years younger than me."

"Have you talked to her?"

"I've tried. I sent her messages on Ancestry, but she hasn't responded."

Chapter 54

Tuesday afternoon

The mahogany door closed, sealing Sabre inside Knowles' austere private office. They faced each other across an expansive desk, its surface strewn with legal briefs and case files.

"We want nothing less than a dismissal." Sabre used her sternest tone. "With Ian's confession, and Gearhart's testimony about seeing the reenactment, there's no basis for the charges against Maverick."

"Confession or not," Knowles retorted. "We don't know that Maverick actually believed the videos were real."

"Fine. I'll put him on the stand and he can testify to it. Will that make you happy?"

"Maybe."

Sabre stood. "Come on, Knowles, dismiss the charges, or I'll see you in court."

"Fine." Knowles finally said, breaking the silence. "See you inside."

They walked back to the courtroom together and told the bailiff they were ready. Sabre took a seat at the table with Maverick. JP sat in the back with DuBois and Ian, who was still under oath and ready for cross-examination.

The judge entered, and the bailiff called the room to order.

"Be seated," the judge intoned, and the room settled into silence.

The prosecutor stood. "Your Honor, in light of Ian Callahan's testimony, the State wishes to dismiss the charges against Maverick McLaughlin." He cleared his throat.

Sabre's heartbeat quickened, but her face remained an impassive mask. She stood. "Your Honor, I respectfully request that the dismissal be with prejudice. Maverick McLaughlin has endured enough hardship due to these unfounded allegations."

The judge nodded. "Given the circumstances presented and the clear absence of intent, I'm granting the defense's request for dismissal with prejudice. This court will not be party to inflicting additional harm on a young man who has already suffered considerably."

"Thank you, Your Honor," Sabre said.

The judge looked directly at Maverick. "Young man, your foster father had nothing but good things to say about you. I hope you continue to make him proud. He appears to love you very much." Feldman brought down his gavel. "You're free to go. Court is dismissed."

"Justice served," Sabre whispered under her breath. She stood, smoothed her skirt, and turned toward Maverick.

"Let's get out of here," she said with a supportive smile.

Maverick looked up at her, his deep brown eyes reflecting a mix of disbelief and gratitude. "Is it really over?"

"It's over."

Together, they walked out into the corridor where they were greeted by Mr. and Mrs. Venable. "Thank you, Sabre," Edie said. "You've given us back our son."

"Let's go celebrate," Gary suggested. "Care to join us, Sabre?"

"Thank you, but I still have a lot to do today."

Sabre turned to see DuBois, Ian, and JP sitting on a hall bench. "What are you three plotting?"

"Just shootin' the bull," JP said.

"Vinny, can I talk to you a minute?" Sabre asked.

"Sure." He got up, and they took a few steps out of earshot. Sabre said, "I didn't want to say this in front of Ian, but I know that Elise was in love with Harper Callahan."

"Holy crap!" DuBois said. "So, she was engaged to Thomas, in love with Harper, and sleeping with Patrick? I guess she liked those Irish boys."

"We don't really know what her relationship was with Patrick. For all we know, he might have raped her."

A moment of quiet.

Then Sabre added, "And I think the woman Elise confided in is Mrs. Jenkins. She was her neighbor and the mother of Elise's best friend. JP has all her information."

They walked back to join JP and Ian. Sabre said, "I think you two should figure out what comes next."

DuBois said, "I need to visit Mrs. Jenkins."

"Who's that?" Ian asked.

"The woman Ted said was close to your mother."

"She probably won't tell you anything," JP said. "She's a hard nut to crack."

"Then come with me, JP," DuBois said. "I'm sure she won't be able to resist your charm."

"I bet if we take Ian along, she'll tell us a lot more."

"Let's go," Ian said.

Chapter 55

Tuesday late afternoon

JP and Ian climbed out of his truck in front of the home in Rancho Bernardo where Mrs. Jenkins was staying with her son. DuBois pulled up and joined them on the flagstone path.

"Remember, we're not sure what she knows or how she'll react," JP said as they walked to the door.

"Got it," DuBois replied.

Ian didn't speak. His jaw was set, eyes fixed on the house.

JP rapped sharply—a sound that echoed loudly in the quiet neighborhood. Moments later, the door opened. Mrs. Jenkins was wearing the same cardigan and looked a little nervous.

Then her eyes landed on Ian and her hand flew to her mouth. "Ian?" she gasped. "My lord, come in."

JP glanced at Ian, but he looked surprised too. *How did she know who he was?*

"Thank you, ma'am," JP said. He turned and gestured. "This is Detective Vinny DuBois."

"Mrs. Jenkins," DuBois said with a nod. "We appreciate you seeing us."

"Of course." She closed the door behind them, a storm of emotions playing across her features. "Please, let's sit in the living room," she suggested.

Mrs. Jenkins directed them toward a plush sofa and matching armchairs. "I'll put on some tea."

"Thank you," JP said. "Is your son here?"

"No. He's at work, and my daughter-in-law went to pick up the kids. She should be back shortly."

They waited silently in the warm room filled with the faint scent of lavender and the ticking of a grandfather clock. Soon Mrs. Jenkins came back with a tea tray and set it on the coffee table. Everybody ignored it. They were here for answers.

"Elise used to love visiting me after my daughter passed," Mrs. Jenkins' voice cracked. "We would talk for hours, her laughter filling the space." She glanced from one man to the other, until she settled on Ian. "You're here about Elise, right?"

"Yes, ma'am," JP said.

"I always knew I'd meet you some day, Ian."

"How did you recognize me?"

"I've been watching you grow up from afar since you went to live with the Callahans. I followed your sports when you were young, and any major events in your life. I keep up with the socialite happenings in case I can catch a glimpse of you."

"But how did you know about me? That I was even born, or where I was?"

"Elise let me know."

"Is she still alive?" The excitement in his voice was evident.

"I don't know. She stopped communication many years ago." Mrs. Jenkins sighed, sinking back into her armchair. "Elise was such a bright child. So full of life and mischief." Her eyes misted over. "She had this wild, curly hair and these big, expressive eyes that seemed to see right through to your soul."

Everyone sat in silence, listening raptly.

"When she was taken ..." The teacup in Mrs. Jenkins' hand clinked against the saucer as her hands trembled. "It was as though the light went out in my life. She disappeared so suddenly, vanished without a trace." A tear escaped, tracing a path down her cheek. "I lived in fear every day, not knowing if she was cold, hungry, or ... worse."

"Did Elise ever talk about feeling unsafe before she disappeared?" DuBois inquired.

"Never. That's what made it all so shocking. We thought we knew our neighborhood, our community." Mrs. Jenkins gulped back her emotions. "But I guess we never truly know what dangers lurk around the corner, do we?"

DuBois spoke softly. "Do you know what happened to Elise that night?"

Mrs. Jenkins' mouth opened, then closed. Her eyes darted to the floor, and for a moment, JP thought she might not answer.

Then with a heavy sigh she looked up. "Elise told me in one of her letters that Patrick found out about her and..." She stopped and looked at Ian. "Are you sure you want to hear this?"

"Yes! I'm trying to make sense of my world, and I'm tired of being lied to. I would appreciate the truth, good or bad."

Mrs. Jenkins nodded. "I'm assuming you already know Elise is your mother?"

"Yes. I figured that out when I discovered I had an uncle that wasn't related to the Callahans. I also know Patrick is my father."

That seemed to catch Mrs. Jenkins by surprise. "Then this part will be easy. Elise and Harper fell madly in love. They wanted to be together, but they were afraid to tell Thomas for fear of what he might do. I thought for a long time that Thomas found out and confronted her."

"What actually happened?" JP asked.

"Elise told me that Patrick somehow knew about Harper. She denied it, but Patrick was drunk and angry." Mrs. Jenkins looked at Ian and shook her head. "I hate to tell you this. You don't deserve it."

"Please," Ian said. "I need to know."

Mrs. Jenkins went on, but she didn't look Ian in the eyes. "Patrick raped her. He said that since she liked the Callahan men so much, she should experience the most powerful one." Mrs. Jenkins shuddered. "She never told anyone but me, and she swore me to secrecy."

"When was that?" DuBois asked.

"About two months before he had her kidnapped."

"So, Patrick didn't do the kidnapping himself?"

"No. It was his henchman, that big Swede, Lars something."

"Lars Iverson." Ian said, "his right-hand man all these years."

Mrs. Jenkins sighed. "He tried to grab her, but she struggled to get away, so he chloroformed and knocked her out. She came to at Patrick's. She thought they were going to kill her after he questioned her about her baby. When she suggested the child might be his, he decided to spare her. He wanted to know who fathered her child. Elise didn't know then. She wanted it to be Harper's, but since they never consummated their relationship, he was out. She was pretty sure it wasn't Thomas' because she stopped having sex with him as much as she could. He didn't seem to mind, since he was seeing someone else."

"Why didn't she just leave him?" Ian asked.

"She was too afraid. He was very powerful and vengeful. She was a pretty ornament on his arm and he used her for social events."

"And what did Patrick do when he found out the child was his?" DuBois prompted, his pen ready.

"When it turned out the baby was his, Patrick made a deal." Mrs. Jenkins looked at Ian and again apologized for what she had to say. "He told Elise he would spare her life in exchange for the baby. He took everything from her, even her freedom, but Elise hoped at least her child would be spared. He held her captive until the baby was born. She really expected him to kill her afterward, but he didn't."

DuBois scribbled in his notebook.

"Elise agreed to that?" JP understood the desperation that drove a mother to such lengths.

Tears brimmed in Mrs. Jenkins eyes. "It was the only way she could keep her baby safe. Patrick was a monster, but Elise was a mother first and foremost."

There it was—the ugly truth laid bare. Elise Harrington, victim of a cruel bargain that had cost her more than anyone could have imagined.

"But Patrick didn't keep me for himself," Ian said. "He gave me to Thomas. Why?"

Mrs. Jenkins closed her eyes for moment, then her voice trembled with emotion. Thomas didn't know you weren't his. He didn't know about Harper or the rape, so he never suspected a thing. He did know that Patrick had her in seclusion, but he probably didn't have any of the details."

Ian shook his head.

"Patrick, that cunning snake, made sure Thomas would raise you as his own flesh and blood. Thomas loved you from the moment he laid eyes on you. I know he wasn't the ideal father, but he did love you."

Ian's breath came in short, sharp bursts. "All this time, you knew?"

A single tear rolled down the old woman's cheek. "I wanted to tell you, God knows I did, but Elise begged me not to. She feared for your safety, for what Patrick might do if he ever found out that you knew the truth."

"Somehow, I don't feel very safe."

"Elise thought it was the only way to protect you," Mrs. Jenkins said. "She sacrificed everything for you—her life, her freedom, her chance to be your mother."

"Because of him, Patrick Callahan." Ian spat out the name as if it left a bitter taste in his mouth.

"Do you have any tangible proof?" DuBois asked. "Anything that can substantiate what you're telling us?"

A hush filled the room as Mrs. Jenkins reached beneath the coffee table and retrieved a small bundle of letters, the corners darkened by time.

"Elise was careful," she said, her voice laced with a melancholy strength. "She wrote to me only when it was absolutely necessary—for fear of being discovered. She also didn't want to risk my safety."

DuBois pulled on latex gloves and took the pack of letters. He unfolded the first one carefully, ensuring its fragile history remained intact.

"Dear Mrs. Jenkins," he read aloud. "I pray this letter finds you well, though I know my disappearance has caused you much pain. The truth is more twisted than the rumors. Patrick orchestrated my abduction. Not out of some misguided jealousy, but as a calculated measure to control the situation."

As Ian paced, DuBois continued.

"Patrick found out about Harper and me, yet he didn't dispose of me as I thought he might. Instead, he kept me isolated, waiting for the baby to be born so we could learn the paternity. It was a cruel game of chess, and I was a pawn caught between life and death."

DuBois paused to scan the page. "It goes on to implicate Lars."

DuBois put the letter back into the envelope.

"Let's see what's in the second one," Ian insisted.

DuBois read, "I have given birth to a beautiful baby boy. But my heart is heavy, because Patrick has taken him from me."

Ian's breath hitched, a sound so pained it echoed through the room. Mrs. Jenkins reached out to comfort him.

DuBois skimmed ahead, then turned to Mrs. Jenkins. "Elise implored you to protect yourself and never let Patrick learn that you knew his secret."

DuBois picked up the third letter and read aloud,"This may be the last time I write to you. It's too risky now—"

"Risky?" Ian said. "Did she live in constant fear?"

DuBois met his gaze. "According to this, Elise was determined to disappear."

"You never heard from her after that?" Ian asked.

Mrs. Jenkins shook her head. "No, but I always hoped ..."

DuBois carefully refolded the letters. "I'll need to take these, Mrs. Jenkins."

"It's okay. I know them by heart."

"Are you safe here?" JP asked. "When I was at your house, you received a phone call that seemed to make you uncomfortable. Have you been threatened?"

She smiled. "That was my son warning me not to talk to strangers. I think I'm fine. They don't seem to know I even exist. The only one who knew our connection was Harper and he'd never hurt anyone."

As they prepared to leave, Ian stood. "Thank you," he said to Mrs. Jenkins. "For loving and supporting my mother."

"I pray, that what I've shared today will help bring justice for my Elise." She looked at DuBois, "Please don't let them get away with it."

"You have my word, Mrs. Jenkins," DuBois said.

She reached out a trembling hand to Ian. "May you find peace in the truth."

"Be careful," Mrs. Jenkins called after them.

"Let's go," DuBois said. "We've got work to do."

The trio stepped out of the house, just as her son returned from work.

"Is everything okay?" he asked.

"It's all good," JP said.

Her son dashed inside, and the three men walked to the car.

"Can you make me copies of those letters?" JP asked.

"Sure, McCloud," DuBois replied, glancing at the envelopes under his arm. "But I need you to back off the investigation. It's official police business now."

"I'm good with that, but I'm going to try to find out if Elise is still alive. I have a source you may not have."

DuBois raised an eyebrow. "I don't even want to know what that is. I'll get you the copies." DuBois turned to address Ian. "You too, Ian. You need to let us handle this."

"I'll try," he said.

"You have to do more than that, or you'll get in my way."

"I will," he acquiesced. "But can you keep me informed?"

"I'll do that, but I'm a little concerned about your safety right now. Do you have somewhere you can go while we sort this out?"

"Yeah. I think I'll go visit my Uncle Ted Harrington. Besides, I have a sister to find."

Chapter 56

Tuesday evening

JP pulled into the court parking lot where Ian had left his car. JP turned to him and cautioned, "I don't want you to get your hopes up. But if your mother is alive, we have a good chance of finding her."

"Then why haven't the Callahans found her?"

"Maybe they had no reason to look. And they don't have my secret weapon."

Ian nodded. "I can't thank you enough, JP. I'm in your debt."

"Save it," JP said with a dismissive wave. "But there's one thing you gotta promise me."

"Anything," Ian replied.

"Elise has been off the grid for a long time. She may want to stay hidden." JP put a hand on Ian's shoulder. "Before we bring her back into this circus, we need her permission. You good with that?"

"Of course." Ian agreed without hesitation. "Her safety, her choice. I just want to know if she's alive. And if she wants to see me, I'm there."

"Then I'll get started. Meanwhile, you need to get out of Dodge."

"I'm headed straight to my Uncle Ted's house. I'm not comfortable going home."

"Good plan. But until we get a solid lead, I need you to hold off on reaching out to your half-sister, for our sake and hers."

"Of course."

"Now, tell me what you know about Elise's daughter."

"Her name's Brittany Upton. She'll be twenty-seven on the thirteenth of next month," Ian said. "That's all I know."

"That's probably all we need." JP jotted down the information. "Text me Ted's address and phone number in case I need it."

Ian reached for the door handle. "Let's hope your resources can unearth more than mine did."

JP grinned. "My source could find a whisper in a whirlwind."

~~~

At home, JP updated Sabre, then called Lana. "I could use your help again."

"Whatever you need."

He summarized what Elise Harrington had been through and explained what he needed.

"What do you have for me to start my search? I assume she's not using her real name."

"I have her daughter's name and birthdate." JP paused to text her the info. "My client dug that up on Ancestry.com. I also have her brother's name and address, but we're pretty certain she hasn't had any contact with him in thirty years."

"Send me that as well. It might help connect the dots."
~~~

Chapter 57

Wednesday, early morning

Lana went straight to work, glad to be able to repay some of the debt she owed JP and Sabre for all they'd done for her. She navigated through Ancestry.com with practiced ease, but found nothing more than she already had. She studied the sparse family tree branching from Brittany Upton's scant profile. Her father was listed as Philip Lewis, mother as Yvonne Lewis, maiden name *Smith*. She copied and pasted the information into a file.

Switching gears, Lana opened a new browser. Time to cross-reference the daughter's information with other databases, starting with public records—births, marriages, property-tax addresses.

Somewhere in the digital tapestry, Elise Harrington's fate was waiting to be uncovered.

With a couple of deft strokes, she bypassed a firewall, and a voter registration entry popped up: *Philip Lewis.* There was no entry for Elise Harrington or for Yvonne Lewis. *No surprise there.*

"Kingman, Arizona," she whispered. Her pulse quickened. If they were still married, she'd likely found Elise's husband. She searched death and divorce records for Yvonne Lewis but found none.

Pulling up multiple databases, Lana initiated a cross-reference check. Property records, utility bills, even an innocuous magazine subscription—all confirming the Kingman address.

Next, Lana scoured social media and found a community group in Kingman. In a photo of a charity event, she spotted a woman with the same high cheekbones and piercing gaze as the pictures of Elise Harrington in old newspaper files.

Jackpot! Image recognition software quickly compared the photos, and the match was undeniable.

Lana waited until daylight, then called JP with the news. "I've got an address."

"She's alive?" He sounded so hopeful.

"I don't know for certain, but I have an address for her husband that's as current as last month's electric bill." Lana texted him the address as she talked.

"Thanks, Lana. You just made a young man very happy," JP replied.

"That's my goal in life." She laughed and hung up.

JP hung up and called Ian. "I've got some news."

"Already?"

"Elise was married and had one child. We found an address …"

"She's alive?" He cut in. A sharp intake of breath was audible over the line.

"We haven't confirmed that yet, but we haven't found any indication that she's not."

"She's … geez, JP. That's incredible. Where is she?"

"I can't give you that just yet," he said firmly. "We have to make sure it's handled right—for her safety and yours. That was the agreement, right?"

"Right," Ian replied, though the disappointment was clear in his voice. "What's your next move?"

"I'm going to go to the address I have and see if I can meet with her personally," JP declared. "Gotta ensure she's protected and willing to come forward before we blow this thing wide open."

"Thank you, JP. I don't know how to—"

"Save it, kid." JP cut him off. "Just doing my job. Are you at your uncle's?"

"Safe and sound."

"Have you told him anything?"

"I told him I have hired an investigator to look into Elise's disappearance. I don't want to get his hopes up if she's already passed. I don't want him to go through the grieving process twice."

"That's very considerate of you."

JP ended the call, and prepared for his trip to Arizona.

Chapter 58

Wednesday morning

After a quick breakfast, JP climbed into his truck, and got on the road, eager to see if he really did have good news for Ian. No point in calling him until he had all the facts.

The six-hour drive was uneventful, miles of asphalt unfurling like a relentless gray river. Eventually, Kingman emerged, an oasis of civilization in the desert landscape. JP found Elise's address nestled in a quiet, unassuming neighborhood. He parked his truck along the curb and checked the revolver holstered under his jacket. He wasn't expecting trouble, but experience had taught him to prepare for it anyway. With a deep breath, he stepped out of the truck and approached the front door of the house.

The gray-haired man who answered the door filled the frame. "May I help you?"

"Hello, sir. My name is JP Torn, and I'm here to see Yvonne Lewis."

He stiffened and squared his shoulder, an instinctive defensiveness. "About what?"

"I'm a private investigator, hired by Ian Callahan. I think she'll want to hear this."

A voice from within cut through the tension. "Who is it, Philip?" Elise emerged from the hallway, her gaze landing on JP.

"Ma'am." JP nodded respectfully. "I'm here on behalf of Ian Callahan."

Shock swept over Elise, and her hand flew to her throat. "My son?"

"Yes, ma'am." JP watched as hope and fear waged war across her features.

"Philip, please." Elise's voice quivered. "Let him in. I need to hear what he has to say."

"How do you know he's working for Ian? Maybe it's just a ruse."

"Then they've already found me, so we may as well find out."

Philip seemed to wrestle with the decision, then, stepped aside reluctantly. "But I'm staying right here."

"I'd do the same," JP said.

They sat in the living room, Philip close to Elise's side.

Elise wrapped her arms around herself as if warding off a chill. "How can I be sure you really are who you claim to be?"

"Ma'am," JP said, pulling a leather wallet from his coat and displaying his PI license, "I've got no reason to deceive you. My only interest is in getting to the bottom of this situation—for Ian's sake and for yours as well."

"How did you find me?" Elise asked.

"Ian discovered he had a half-sister in the Ancestry.com database."

A flicker of disbelief crossed her features. "I had no idea Brittany had done that. We have to get that off."

"I take it, your daughter doesn't know anything about your past?"

"She doesn't."

JP looked at Philip, who showed no sign of surprise. "But you do?"

"We have no secrets," he said.

"Tell me about my son," Elise said.

JP explained how Ian had discovered that Harper was his brother, so he had Thomas' DNA analyzed and realized Patrick was his father.

"Oh no! I hate that he found out that way."

JP told her about the ruckus Ian had caused to draw attention to her cold case. Elise smiled at her son's tenacity and cried when JP showed her the current photo he'd taken of him.

"We know what Patrick did to you, all of it. But you might be relieved to know he had a stroke a few years ago, and is physically incapacitated."

"I have no remorse for that man," Elise said.

"I understand," JP said.

"Does Ian know how he was conceived?" Elise asked.

"I'm afraid so, but it only bothered him because of the pain it brought you. He's a pretty special young man."

Elise smiled.

"And Thomas? I know he raised him. Was he good to my son?"

"As good as Thomas could be. He's not a very nice person, as I'm sure you know. But I don't think he knows that Ian isn't his biological son."

"What do you want from us?" Her husband interjected.

"Ian wants to connect with you, but that's your choice." JP paused. "But you should know a homicide detective is working on a related case, and Lars Iverson is his prime suspect."

Elise clutched the edge of the couch and blinked rapidly.

"We know he's the one who kidnapped you, and recently, he killed another man to cover up the evidence connected to your case."

Elise gasped.

"The police are onto him, and they're close to making an arrest."

"What can I do?" Elise asked.

"You have several choices," JP said. "I can leave here and you can resume your life as it was. Ian has agreed that if you don't want to see him for whatever reason, he'll let it go." Elise frowned. "You can allow me to give Ian your information and you can work it out with him and I'll be done. Or, you can contact Detective DuBois and agree to testify if he decides to charge Lars with kidnapping."

"Would they do that? The rape case, I mean," Philip asked.

"It's not very likely they could make that case after so long," JP said. "Even with the proof of pregnancy, they'd have a hard time proving it wasn't consensual."

"Good, because as much as I'd like to see that man go to prison," Elise said. "I don't want to go through a rape trial. Besides, it sounds like he's already in his own prison. That must be hell for him to not be able to control everything around him."

"That sounds like justice to me," Philip said.

"The only way they could make the kidnapping charge is if you were to testify," JP said. "And even that would be difficult."

"Is that what you're after?" Philip asked.

"No." JP shook his head. "Whether you testify at Lars' trial makes no difference to me. But if they can put Lars in prison, you can stop looking over your shoulder."

"I can't imagine what that would be like. The threats went on for years, and I thought they'd never stop." Tears welled in her eyes.

"One more thing," JP said. "Ian also found your brother Ted."

"Oh, my. How is he?"

"I don't really know, but Ian is with him now."

"Does Ted know I'm alive?"

"No. Ian doesn't even know yet. But he won't share anything with your brother until you approve."

"What a thoughtful young man he is."

"He resembles his brother, Harper."

Elise smiled. "He was certainly the best Callahan of the bunch." Suddenly she looked uneasy. "If you're telling the truth, then Lars can find me as well. The walls I've built for decades could crumble at any moment."

"I understand your concerns. But no one else has my resource. And my pursuit is singular. I'm here for Ian, nothing more."

"I'll testify," Elise suddenly decided. "Lars can't get away with this. I need him out of my life."

JP stood and handed her his card. "In the meantime, do you want to see Ian?"

For a moment, Elise seemed to fold inward, her shoulders shaking with quiet sobs. "I've dreamed of this day," she said, tears streaming down her cheeks. "But I can't—not until I'm sure Lars can't come after us."

"Understood," JP replied. "Can I tell Ian you're alive?"

"Please do. And tell him I never stopped loving him and we'll be together soon." She swallowed. "And promise me you'll keep Ian safe until then."

"I'll do my best," JP assured her.

"And meanwhile, I think I know someone who can get Brittany's DNA test off of Ancestry.com." When Philip started to question him, he said, "Don't ask. But it's the same person who helped me find you."

"Take care, Elise," JP said, tipping his Stetson as he opened the door. A gust of wind caught the brim as he stepped out causing JP to hold on tight.

Chapter 59

Two weeks later

The bell over the door jangled as JP and Ron pushed their way into the cramped confines of Jo's Diner. The scent of freshly ground coffee beans mingled with the buttery aroma of pastries.

"McCloud," DuBois called out through the murmur of hushed conversations. He was hunched over a table in the back, a steaming mug in hand.

"You go talk to him," Ron said. "I'm going to sit here and visit with Jenna." He nodded toward the barista behind the counter.

"You're welcome to join us for breakfast," JP said.

"I'm good. I've already eaten, but I could use a good cup of coffee."

JP walked off and took a seat across from DuBois.

"I thought you'd like to know what's happening on the Harrington case," DuBois said. "And you owe me a breakfast for helping you out on this."

"You couldn't have solved this without me."

"Whatever. Let's order. I'm starved." DuBois signaled to the waitress, who came over and took their order.

"Here's where we're at." DuBois leaned forward. "Those two arsonists who scorched my dad's shed sang like birds."

"What did they say?"

"They both pointed fingers at Lars Iverson. According to them, Lars handed them the matches and a directive to send a message. They also claimed he was behind Gearhart's murder, even had evidence to prove it."

JP was relieved, but had to ask, "Is Patrick covering for him?"

"He can't. Lars claimed he was at the house with Patrick at the time of Gearhart's murder, but it just so happened that Patrick called out and Thomas had to assist him—because Lars wasn't around."

"Why was Lars so careless?"

"Because he's not that bright. Everything he did was planned and ordered by Patrick. Lars didn't know how to call the shots and not get caught."

The waitress brought their food, and for a few minutes they ate in silence, then JP asked, "Do you think Thomas Callahan had anything to do with the crimes?"

"It doesn't seem so. He was an entitled, egotistical kid who was more interested in his conquests than what was going on around him. He married shortly after Elise's disappearance, which didn't look good for him, but that was orchestrated by his father. Thomas told us he knew his father had *sent* Elise away to have *his* baby, and that his father would bring the baby back for Thomas to raise. That's why Thomas had to get married. He always did what Patrick told him to do."

JP shook his head. "What about his wife? She knew it wasn't her kid."

"Apparently, Patrick paid her well to hang around for a couple of years, then leave with a nice bank account. She was an aspiring actress, who seemed to enjoy the part. She even appeared in public for a few months with props to make her look pregnant."

"Then one day, she just left?"

"As far as we know, but we're still investigating that," DuBois said between bites. "So far, we haven't been able to find her. We got that information from Thomas."

DuBois' phone rang. JP finished his breakfast while the detective stepped away and handled the call. When he returned, DuBois said, "Lars took the deal."

"What was the offer?"

"They dropped the kidnapping and arson charges, and took the death penalty off the table, leaving a likely sentence of thirty years for Gearhart's murder."

"Why would the death penalty matter? We haven't executed anyone in California since 2006."

"I don't know, but it still scares some of these guys. Besides, this man has worked for the Callahans for forty years, and now he's lost his job and his home. He has a public defender because he has no money."

"He must've been paid pretty good from Patrick in the day," JP said. "What happened to all his money?"

"He was paid well when he worked for Patrick and well-compensated for his role the last years as his caretaker, or whatever he was, but he was a big gambler and is totally broke. I personally think he wants us to stop looking, because he has too many other skeletons he'd rather keep hidden."

"More bodies?" JP asked.

"Seems likely," DuBois replied, his eyes darkening. "He took the deal too quickly. There's more to this than he's letting on. He has an intense loyalty to Patrick, and insisted Patrick had nothing to do with any crimes he might've committed." DuBois shook his head. "But I didn't believe that for a second."

"I'm just glad he took the deal," JP said, "so Elise doesn't have to testify."

"I called her as soon as I talked to the DDA, and she's very relieved."

"She's been through enough hell as it is." JP stood and reached for the bill, but DuBois grabbed it first. JP thanked him, picked up his coffee cup, and headed to the counter where Ron was sitting.

Once seated, he told Ron what he had just learned, then called Elise. "It's JP Torn. DuBois told me about the plea deal. You okay with that?"

"Yes, I'm thrilled. I just want this to be over."

"Does that mean I can give Ian your contact information? He calls me every day to get an update."

"Please do."

JP grinned, then delivered the good news to Ian.

"So, are Elise and Ian going to connect?" Ron asked.

"They're both very excited to meet," JP said.

Just then Jenna walked up carrying a coffee pot. "Do you need more coffee?" she asked JP.

"Just top it off, please."

As she poured his coffee, she kept looking up at him. Finally, she asked, "Aren't you Conner's uncle?"

"Yes, ma'am. Do I know you?"

"I'm Aiden's mother, Jenna Armstrong."

From the Author

Dear Reader,

Thank you for reading my book. I hope you enjoyed reading it as much as I did writing it. Would you like a FREE copy of a novella about JP when he was young? If so, scan the QR code below and it will take you where you want to go. Or, if you prefer, please go to www.teresaburrell.com and sign up for my mailing list. You'll automatically receive a code to retrieve the story.

SCAN ME

Teresa

Also by Teresa Burrell

THE ADVOCATE SERIES

THE ADVOCATE (Book 1)
THE ADVOCATE'S BETRAYAL (Book 2)
THE ADVOCATE'S CONVICTION (Book 3)
THE ADVOCATE'S DILEMMA (Book 4)
THE ADVOCATE'S EX PARTE (Book5)
THE ADVOCATE'S FELONY (Book 6)
THE ADVOCATE'S GEOCACHE (Book 7)
THE ADVOCATE'S HOMICIDES (Book 8)
THE ADVOCATE'S ILLUSION (Book 9)
THE ADVOCATE'S JUSTICE (Book 10)
THE ADVOCATE'S KILLER (Book 11)
THE ADVOCATE'S LABYRINTH (Book 12)
THE ADVOCATE'S MEMORY (Book 13)
THE ADVOCATE'S NIGHTMARE (Book 14)
THE ADVOCATE'S OATH (Book 15)
THE ADVOCATE'S PHANTOM (Book 16)

THE TUPER MYSTERY SERIES

THE ADVOCATE'S FELONY

(Book 6 of The Advocate Series)
MASON'S MISSING (Book 1)
FINDING FRANKIE (Book 2)
RECOVERING RITA (Book 3)
LIBERATING LANA (Book 4)

CO-AUTHORED STANDALONE

NO CONSENT
(Co-authored with L.J. Sellers)

Printed in Great Britain
by Amazon

49084162R00162